COUNTRY BORN

COUNTRY BORN

LINDA LAEL MILLER

WHEELER PUBLISHING
A part of Gale, a Cengage Company

GALE
A Cengage Company

Copyright © 2022 by Hometown Girl Makes Good, Inc.
Painted Pony Creek Series #3.
Wheeler Publishing, a part of Gale, a Cengage Company.

LIBRARY OF CONGRESS CIP DATA ON FILE.
CATALOGUING IN PUBLICATION FOR THIS BOOK
IS AVAILABLE FROM THE LIBRARY OF CONGRESS.

ISBN-13: 978-1-4328-9648-5 (hardcover alk. paper)

Published in 2022 by arrangement with Harlequin Enterprises ULC.

Printed in Mexico
Print Number: 01   Print Year: 2022

For Steve and Deb Wiley.
I think the world of you.

Dear Reader,

As I write this, we're enjoying a crisp and sunny autumn day. My dogs, Tule (pronounced Toolie) and Mowgli (think *The Jungle Book*), are snoring contentedly away near my desk.

Fall is hands down my favorite season. There is, it seems to me, a sort of festive buzz in the air — pumpkins are on sale everywhere and soon they will be replaced by fragrant Christmas trees and stunningly beautiful poinsettias. I think this feeling I always have is in part a throwback to my childhood in Northport, Washington.

Autumn meant we were back in school, and I *loved* school. It meant Halloween was coming — my mother sewed wonderful costumes for us at her old Singer — and beyond trick-or-treating was Thanksgiving. Then, oh happy day, Christmas.

We didn't have much money, but somehow, my folks managed to make every holiday magical. Stir in a little love, and you're good to go, right?

If you're reading this, either you've run across this brand-new, never-before-seen story, *Country Born,* the final book in the Country trilogy, in your favorite store, or you've already purchased it. Thanks for that, by the way.

In this story, I'll introduce you to J.P. Mc-Call, one of the sexiest heroes I've ever invented, and the smart, beautiful and accomplished Sara Worth. Sara is a published writer and the mother of teenagers.

I sympathize, and maybe you will, too.

Alas, my teenager is all grown up now. And I'm so proud of her.

All that said, I hope you're being careful and staying well.

These are challenging times, for sure, but

we're all in this together, and we need to remember that. We'll pull through this, as a nation and as a planet, as long as we calm down and cooperate.

Don't forget — whether you were raised in a town like Painted Pony Creek, Montana, or in a big city, you are country tough.

With love,
Linda Lael Miller

CHAPTER ONE

Sara's call had come through at 6:00 a.m. sharp, jolting J.P. McCall a little, even though he was a lifelong rancher and thus an early riser.

Sara was, after all, the sister of one of his two closest friends, Eli Garrett, the current sheriff of Wild Horse County, Montana, a man with a dangerous job, and it didn't help that she opened with a breathless, "This is an emergency, J.P."

"What is it?" he'd asked, hoarse with alarm. "What's going on?"

In moments like that, his PTSD, a relic of his tour of duty in Afghanistan, always spiked.

Fortunately, such moments were relatively rare. He still had the occasional nightmare, and sometimes, a loud unexpected noise triggered a dizzying rush of adrenaline, pure fight-or-flight.

When that happened, he went off by

himself and breathed his way back to the real world.

"I've completely forgotten how it feels to ride a horse!" she blurted anxiously.

If J.P. hadn't thought as highly of Sara Worth as he did, he probably would have cut her off at the knees — and attractive knees they were — for scaring him half to death.

Sara, who wrote under the pen name Luke Cantrell, was the successful author of two Western thrillers, featuring a Clint Eastwood–type hero named Elliott Starr, with another book currently in the works, according to Eli.

Clearly, she did thorough research.

"Seriously, Sara? *That's* your emergency?" He'd sounded irritated, but in actuality he was swamped with relief. The county under Eli's jurisdiction was a peaceable place, for the most part, with a relatively low crime rate, considering its size, but it definitely had its share of losers and troublemakers.

Just last winter, Eli was taken by surprise in his own backyard, savagely attacked and very nearly killed.

Eli was a friend J.P. couldn't lose, like Cord Hollister, the third member of the rowdy triad. The three of them had been tight since kindergarten, and the bond between them ran deep, like the roots of an ancient tree tangled with bedrock.

They were more than friends; they were blood brothers.

There was a silence. A very awkward one.

J.P. had looked down at his retired service dog, Trooper, standing beside him in the tall dew-dampened grass between the barn and the house, instantly alert, ready for trouble.

"It's all right, boy," he'd told the dog. "At ease."

For several seconds after that, no one spoke.

Then, sounding chagrined, Sara had murmured, "Oops. I guess my enthusiasm for accuracy got away from me. I'm sorry if I worried you, J.P."

She knew about his combat injuries, of course, and the subsequent case of PTSD that, though mostly under control, still sneaked up on him at times.

As a child, Sara had been a tomboy, and she'd sometimes hung around with Eli and, by extension, J.P. and Cord. She'd garnered a lot of information along the way, having sat around campfires with her brother's friends, fished in Painted Pony creek with them, raced barefoot down rocky country roads with them, often winning.

13

For a while, after his honorable discharge from the military, he'd even had a crush on her. Might even have pursued a relationship with her, if she hadn't fallen for an outsider named Zachary Worth and eventually married him.

"I'm revising my manuscript," Sara had explained in a burst when J.P. didn't immediately respond to her apology. "Technically, it was due last week, and I just realized that the scenes where the characters are on horseback don't ring true *at all*. I know it sounds crazy, since I've already written two books in the same series, but there it is. It just doesn't feel right."

"Okay," he'd muttered, stretching out the word. He could let this go.

He just had to breathe.

And then breathe some more.

He *had* wondered why she'd come to him with the problem, instead of Cord, for instance. Cord was literally world-renowned for his methods of training both horses and riders. And then there was Emma Grant, Cord's wife Shallie's best friend, who ran a therapeutic riding academy and could therefore provide whatever instruction Sara needed.

"I know what you're thinking," Sara had rattled on. "I could have gotten a few quick

14

lessons from Cord, or from Emma. Trouble is, the Hollisters are away, visiting Shallie's mom in Florida, and Emma has back-to-back classes booked, which leaves her with zero free time."

"All right," J.P. had finally capitulated. "Come on out to the ranch and we'll saddle up and ride."

Now, an hour later, here she was, standing in front of J.P.'s barn, clad in jeans, an old sweatshirt and boots that looked a little too new. Her dark hair, plaited into a single braid that reached almost to her slender waist, gleamed in the sunlight, and her silver-gray eyes were bright with eager determination.

With considerable help from J.P., she'd saddled Misty, a bay mare so tame that J.P.'s citified nieces, Becky and Robyn, rode her bareback whenever they visited the ranch.

His favorite gelding, Shiloh, was tacked up as well and ready to ride. Nickering and sidestepping with impatience.

"I insist on paying for your time, J.P.," Sara said, setting her jaw. "Don't even bother to argue the point — this is research and, as such, it's tax-deductible."

J.P. managed not to roll his eyes. "I'm not exactly short on money, Sara," he pointed out, with the slightest twitch of a grin tugging at one corner of his mouth.

He'd received a modest settlement from the government after being badly injured in Afghanistan, back in the day, and during the long months he'd spent recovering, he'd studied the stock market in depth and found that he had an uncanny knack for picking winners. Between that and his one-third stake in the family ranch, which he managed well, he was a wealthy man.

She was about to mount Misty, one booted foot already in the stirrup, both hands gripping the saddle horn, when she turned her head to look back at him over one shoulder. She smiled and something shifted inside J.P., sweet and poignant, soft as the brush of a moth's wing.

"Don't try to talk me out of it," she warned cheerfully. "I know you're bull-headed, J.P. McCall, but I'm a Garrett, remember. We're notoriously single-minded, as I'm sure you've noticed."

J.P. gave a rumbling chuckle, but he was still shaken. He wasn't a fanciful man, and this new element, whatever it was, left him off-balance — inwardly, anyway.

"We can argue all day," he pointed out, surprised that he sounded like his ordinary Montana-rancher self, "or we can ride."

"Let's get on with the research," Sara

urged, grinning. Then she hoisted herself off the ground, left foot in the stirrup, right leg ready to swing over Misty's broad back.

J.P. did a little research of his own, watching her shapely blue-jeaned backside as she swung, somewhat laboriously, up into the saddle.

She settled herself, sunlight rimming her like a golden aura, and, looking up at her, J.P. was nearly blinded.

The phenomenon wasn't entirely physical, and that confounded him further.

It was ridiculous, reacting like this, he decided, annoyed with himself.

Sara was Eli's sister, his *big* sister.

She had two kids, courtesy of her no-good, long-gone husband.

And, though she must have had opportunities, she'd shown no interest — as far as J.P. knew, anyway — in finding another husband or even a boyfriend.

She seemed content to raise her son and daughter, write her books and take part in community projects with her friends.

But wasn't she ever lonely, in a crowd or by herself, at odd hours of the night?

J.P. certainly was, though he was more than reluctant to admit as much. Those bleak bouts, like the infrequent but fiery, bloody flashbacks he sometimes endured, were among the many things he liked to forget.

With no other blood kin — her and Eli's folks had died when Sara was in middle school, and a few years later their guardian and aunt, Abigail Garrett, had passed away as well — Sara had focused on her children.

She'd had some kind of falling-out with her former father-in-law, a very wealthy man who owned vast stretches of land around Painted Pony Creek but rarely spent time in his secluded castle of a mansion, and apparently severed any and all ties with her ex-husband's family.

Naturally, Eli had helped out as best he could, but he'd been busy in those days, finishing up at the police academy down in Phoenix and then starting his career as a deputy sheriff.

Sara had remained in Painted Pony Creek, missing out on college, but educating herself in a variety of creative ways. Until recently, she'd worked in a day-care facility, having stuck with the job in the early days when Eric and Hayley were little so she could be near them.

Always a voracious reader, Sara had eventually begun to write books of her own, pounding away at a keyboard before and after work, keeping her own counsel.

J.P., as close as he was to Eli, hadn't known about that part of her life until a few months ago, when her second novel had made a big splash in the marketplace. Even now, very few people knew that Luke Cantrell, purveyor of gritty historical thrillers, was really Sara Garrett Worth.

She'd landed an impressive multi-book contract after these successes — J.P. had no idea how much money she made, and it wouldn't have occurred to him to ask — but she still kept a low profile professionally, preferring to live quietly in Painted Pony Creek. Through Eli, J.P. knew she'd managed her money wisely, setting up trust funds for her kids, paying off her mortgage and making a few improvements to her brick ranch house in town.

Apparently, unlike many of the newly prosperous, Sara didn't seem interested in the usual trappings of wealth — world travel, costly jewelry, designer clothes, fancy houses and cars. Not that there was anything wrong with those things; people had the right to spend what they'd earned however they chose.

She was different, that's all.

Sara lived in the same house she'd bought after Zachary left her, using part of the inheritance she and Eli had shared following the death of their parents to make a substantial down payment. J.P. knew this about Sara, not because Eli had confided in him but because, in small communities like the Creek, people picked up on things like that, as if by osmosis.

It occurred to J.P., in those moments of daylight reflection, that he and Sara had a few things in common, at least when it came to how they spent — and didn't spend — their money.

Now, looking up at Sara, he realized that he'd known her better than he thought he had, though he'd never bothered to look too far beyond the obvious: sister of one of his two best friends, divorcée, mother of two and now bestselling author.

Why hadn't he taken more notice of her?

Well, he'd sure as hell taken notice of her *now.*

The question was, where did he go from here?

Should he follow his gut instinct and try to get to know Sara as a *person* rather than just a background character in his life story? Or should he leave her alone, spare her the drawbacks of getting involved with a man like him? A man with scars, inside and out.

"J.P.?" Sara asked, gazing down at him from within the halo gleaming around her.

"Are you all right?"

"I'm fine," he lied somewhat gruffly.

With that, he turned to his gelding, swung up into the saddle and gathered the reins.

He gave Sara a sidelong look. "Let's go, Luke," he teased.

Now that he was mounted on Shiloh, he felt like himself again, firmly planted inside his body instead of slightly out of alignment with it.

Sara laughed. "Don't forget," she said, "I'm actually a green-horn. A total fraud when it comes to boots-in-the-stirrups type stuff."

With a motion of his hand, J.P. saluted her. "I wouldn't go that far," he replied easily. Sara might not have a lot of confidence in herself as a rider, but she wasn't a raw beginner, either. He knew she'd ridden with Shallie on occasion and, like him, she'd helped out over at Emma Grant's stables, working with kids.

He let Sara lead the way, and she soon eased Misty into a gentle trot across the expanse of the rolling pastureland.

J.P. kept up, as did Trooper, who, though not as agile as he'd once been, seemed to be enjoying the fresh air, the rich green smell of good Montana grass and the earthy scent of fertile land. The famous big sky was a cloudless dome overhead, edged, in the distance, by timbered mountains.

This was home, this wide-open space.

This was the place he longed for whenever he was away, the place that had healed him, body and soul, after endless, painful months in a military hospital back East. He drew it in deep, like a soul-breath.

As the minutes passed, Sara seemed to relax in the saddle, loosening her grip on the reins, taking in her surroundings instead of focusing on the space between Misty's twitching ears.

They didn't speak; it didn't seem necessary out here, where the sky and the breeze and the whispering grass spoke in a language all their own.

When they reached Painted Pony creek, the broad stream for which the town was named, they let the horses drink.

Meanwhile, Trooper dashed up and down the muddy bank, chasing a handful of butterflies, as happy as any dog could wish to be.

Watching him, J.P. smiled. He loved that mutt, and he didn't care who knew it.

"I appreciate this, J.P.," Sara said quietly, leaning forward a little, causing the saddle leather to creak, and patting Misty's long sweaty neck.

"It's no big deal," J.P. answered. Though, God help him, it *was* a big deal.

She drew a deep breath, seemed to relish it. "Sometimes I wish I'd raised Eric and Hayley in the country, instead of in town," she said.

He wanted to hear more. "Why?"

Sara raised her shoulders in a shrug-like motion, lowered them again. "I don't know, really, except that all this open space offers a special kind of freedom — no sidewalks, no paved parking lots, no traffic lights or crosswalks or supermarkets —"

"I guess it's coming back to you," J.P. observed.

She looked at him. "Growing up in the country?"

"That, and what it feels like to ride a horse," he said with a smile.

Sara and Eli's folks hadn't owned a big spread, like the Hollisters and the McCalls and a number of other families around Painted Pony Creek, but they'd raised their family outside of town, just the same. Before and after the loss of their parents, Sara and her brother had lived much as J.P. and Cord had, as kids, doing chores, swimming in the creek, riding and camping out, running barefoot through long hot summers.

She stared pensively at the creek then,

23

watching it tumble and swirl past, on its way to join half a dozen larger streams, then rivers.

"There are a lot of things I wish I'd done differently," she said. "With the kids, I mean."

"Like what?"

Sara shook her head, and it seemed she was looking inward now. "Hayley will be fine — she's so even-tempered and practical — but I worry about Eric."

J.P. recalled the trouble Eric had gotten into a couple of years before, when he'd hooked up with a bunch of budding criminals, released some livestock, among other offenses, and wound up in trouble with the law. The kid had done some community service after he was caught and, as far as J.P. knew, straightened out. The boy looked up to his uncle, Eli, and that, along with Sara's tough love, had probably been his saving grace.

He might have ended up like his pal Freddie Lansing, though.

J.P. shuddered slightly, remembering the day he and Eli and Melba Summers, a deputy at the time, had found the Lansing kid dead, hanging from a rafter in an old barn right there on the McCall ranch.

Since then, J.P. had had the place bulldozed, the weathered boards and beams and shingles hauled away to be burned.

"Is there any particular reason to worry about Eric?" he asked carefully. It was none of his business, and he didn't want to cross any personal boundaries, but if Sara wanted someone to confide in, he was willing to listen.

Sara smiled, looking slightly wistful. "No, he's behaving well enough," she said. Then, with a rueful chuckle, she added, "For a teenager."

The horses had drunk their fill by then, and they were tossing their heads, ready to be on the move again. The land was their natural habitat, after all; maybe they had some kind of genetic memory, some recollection of ancient days before the West was settled, when they'd run free and wild.

Or maybe the mustangs, still wild and multiplying with every passing year, served to remind them of how life had been, once upon a time. Genetic memory of the equine variety.

"I guess I'm ready to head for home," Sara said. "I don't want to take up too much of your time, and I need to get back to my manuscript."

Privately, J.P. reflected that it hadn't taken the woman long to achieve her purpose, but

25

he didn't comment. Back at the house, after he'd unsaddled the gelding and the mare and turned them out to graze with the rest of his horses, he'd probably go online, check the current status of the market, maybe make a few adjustments to his portfolio. Then he'd climb into his truck and make the fifteen-minute drive to his folks' corner of the ranch and the log A-frame they'd retired to, once J.P. took over the nuts and bolts of the family cattle operation.

The senior McCalls, John and Sylvia, were healthy, active and thoroughly independent, but J.P. liked to check on them every so often, just the same. His older sisters, Clare and Josie, lived in California and Virginia respectively, and they expected regular reports on the state of the parental units, via text or social media. They didn't entirely trust the pair to speak up if they needed help or simply wanted some company.

Sara brought J.P. back to the present moment with a soft, "Is it enough for you, this ranch, I mean? Maybe I'm overstepping here, but don't you get lonely?"

J.P. was surprised by the questions but, oddly, not offended. Now that Eli and Cord were both happily married, and starting families, lots of people probably wondered when he would follow suit. God knew his parents and sisters weren't shy about asking, though he always responded, with varying degrees of annoyance, that they ought to mind their own business.

"Everybody gets lonely sometimes," he replied after a few moments of silence.

The barn was in sight now, and the horses were picking up speed, ready to join the small herd grazing on tall sweet grass.

"I shouldn't have asked," Sara said quickly, obviously uncomfortable.

J.P. smiled, but sparely. "It's okay, Sara," he replied.

The truth was he *did* get lonely, especially at night, and he wanted a wife and family, too.

It was just that he wasn't willing to settle, when it came to love.

He dated a lot, mostly women from other towns, but marriage was something else. He wanted what his mom and dad had together, what Cord had with Shallie, and Eli had with Brynne — a true bond, so deep and so sacred that it seemed predestined, cosmic in scope.

So far, he hadn't met the right woman. In fact, he sometimes wondered if she was out there at all.

Or, assuming she was, if he'd be the right man for *her*.

He'd almost been a father once, though.

Nearly three years ago, on the proverbial dark and stormy night, he'd been engaged in a poker game with Eli and Cord, in the back room of Sully's Bar and Grill, when the door had burst inward and a skinny drowned rat of a girl had appeared out of nowhere.

She'd looked so much like Reba Shannon, the wild child who had nearly wrecked the trio of friends for good seventeen years before, that J.P. had thought, for a fraction of a second, that he was seeing an actual ghost.

Her name was Carly, she'd just hitchhiked halfway across the country, and she'd landed in their lives like a hand grenade with the pin pulled and announced, once the shock of her arrival had subsided a little, that one of the three of them — he, Eli or Cord — was her biological dad.

That long-ago summer of Carly's conception, when he and both his friends had fallen for Reba, each one believing, with the hormonal hubris of a seventeen-year-old boy, that they were her one and only, had almost faded from their combined memories by the time the girl showed up.

Said girl had grown up and come looking,

not so much for a father, but for explanations.

A series of events, some fortunate and some not, had ensued, and when the fat lady sang, so to speak, it turned out that Cord had been the one to sire this spirited little spitfire.

Like Eli's, J.P.'s reaction to the news had been mixed — he'd been relieved, naturally. But he'd also been disappointed.

Rock-solid man that he was, Cord had stepped up, taken responsibility, worked at getting to know his daughter. He'd married his wife, Shallie, and the three of them had created a family.

Now they had another child, Cord and Shallie, and they were beyond happy together.

J.P. didn't envy his friends. He was glad for them, but he wanted what they had, for sure. A wife and kids of his own. A family.

"Where did you go just now, J.P. McCall?" Sara asked as the two of them dismounted. "You seem awfully distracted this morning."

It wasn't a criticism, only a comment. He knew that by her expression and her tone of voice.

He grinned, took Misty's reins from Sara and led both animals into the cool hay-scented shade of the barn, where he pro-

29

ceeded to remove their saddles and bridles.

Sara, obviously a little saddle sore, limped alongside him, ready to help.

Instead of offering a belated answer to Sara's inquiry, J.P. countered with, "What about you, Sara? You've been divorced for a long time. Your kids are growing up. Don't *you* ever get lonely?"

Sara leaned down to scratch behind Trooper's floppy ears. The dog was leaning into her right leg, goofy with sudden adoration.

J.P. could relate.

Sara gave a rueful laugh. Shook her head. "The kids have taken up so much of my time and energy," she replied, "that I haven't had a *chance* to get lonely."

He hung up the bridles, placed the saddles and blankets where they belonged. "Eric must be about to start college," he said.

Sara ran her palms down the thighs of her trim jeans. Sighed. "He's a senior this year. Again." She paused, winced. "It had to do with that bad patch he went through. He let his grades slip so badly that he didn't qualify to graduate with the rest of his class."

J.P. remembered the *bad patch.*

And he could identify. He'd had a few of those himself, times when he'd checked out, both physically and emotionally, after the roadside explosion in Afghanistan that wounded him and killed half a dozen of his friends. His recovery — a grim and deliberate process of coming back to himself — had been long, painful and difficult on every level.

Not that he'd put the struggle entirely behind him.

It was, he supposed, a big part of the reason he'd avoided emotional intimacy with the many women he'd wined and dined since his recovery. He was afraid that, if he ever let his shadow-side show, he'd scare them away.

Or, worse, that they'd stick around, trying to *save* him.

"I know a little about Eric's troubles," he said at some length as they walked, side by side, out into the sunlight.

Misty and Shiloh followed amiably along behind them, eager to reach the pasture.

J.P. moved to open the gate, and both horses hurried through the opening, snorting and kicking up their hind legs as soon as he'd detached the lead ropes from their harnesses.

He chuckled at this display of equine delight, pulled the gate closed and made sure the latch caught, draping the lead ropes over one shoulder.

Sara looked pained, attempted a mild stretch and flinched visibly.

"You'll be sore for a few days," J.P. observed unnecessarily.

"I need to get more exercise," Sara confessed. "I spend way too much time at my computer."

"Maybe you ought to ride more often. It's good for the soul."

She smiled. "I agree, but I'm not sure there's enough ibuprofen in the world to get me through the tenderfoot stage."

J.P. thought of offering Sara a couple of Advil and/or a cup of coffee, but she'd already said she needed to get back to work on her novel, and he didn't want to come off as — well — needy.

"You'll be all right," he assured her. *Damn, McCall,* he told himself silently, *you're an eloquent son of a gun.*

"I don't have much of a choice," Sara pointed out lightly, without a trace of self-pity. "None of us do, really."

She was headed toward her car, parked beside his truck, and J.P. walked alongside her. It was the polite thing to do, but this was more than good manners, and he knew it.

This was reluctance to part.

He was about to bite the bullet and ask

Sara to come back soon, for another longer ride, when she opened her car door, reached inside and pulled out her purse.

It was plain, though trimmed with fringe.

J.P. held up both his hands. "Don't," he said.

Sara frowned. "But —"

"But nothing, Sara. I don't want money." He paused, feeling stupid and awkward. "You're my best friend's sister."

She tilted her head back, smiled at him, and he marveled at how beautiful she was. He'd always known that, hadn't he? So why hadn't it sunk in?

"Okay, but I demand a compromise."

"Such as?"

Her smile broadened, brightened. "You have to let me buy you dinner. We can go to Bailey's or Sully's — anywhere you choose."

Suddenly, he was fourteen again. All knees and elbows and Adam's apple.

"Umm —"

She looked worried. "Unless you're seeing someone. It's just a friendly dinner, but I wouldn't want to cause trouble."

"I'm not seeing anyone," he said, a little more quickly than he would have liked. Sara wasn't suggesting a date, he reminded himself, just a casual meal to repay him for a favor.

Sara's smile returned, nearly setting J.P. back on the scuffed heels of his boots. "All right, then. When?"

"Tonight?" J.P. said, and it felt like a risk.

Which was ridiculous.

It wasn't as if he were about to jump out of a low-flying plane without a chute, but it sure *felt* like that.

"Tonight will be great. Is Bailey's okay?"

"Bailey's is fine. Shall I pick you up, or do you want to meet me there?"

Sara beamed at him.

J.P. tried to catch his breath.

"Let's meet there. Seven o'clock," Sara said.

J.P. gulped, searched for his voice, found it. "See you at seven," he said.

"Excellent," Sara chimed. And then she rose onto the balls of her feet and kissed him lightly on his stubbly cheek.

Before he could respond in any way — except, of course, for the flipping sensation somewhere in his midsection — Sara was behind the wheel of her car.

He watched, rooted to the ground, as she fastened her seat belt, started the engine, shifted out of Park and drove away.

He was still standing there when she honked the horn in farewell.

He didn't move until Trooper bumped

against him, looking for attention — and possibly some extra kibble. Snapping him out of immobility.

J.P. chuckled and mussed the dog's ears.

After putting the lead ropes away in the barn, they went inside the house, the spacious but unassuming ranch house J.P. had grown up in. It was his now, since both his sisters were busy professionals, settled in homes of their own, and his folks preferred their compact A-frame.

He washed his hands at the kitchen sink, gave Trooper a dog biscuit and glanced at his laptop, open and booted up on the round oak table that, like much of the furniture, had belonged to J.P.'s great-grandparents.

Usually, the computer drew him, no matter what the time of the day or night, but today was different.

Today, his mind was reeling — with thoughts of Sara. Memories of her warm smile, her shining eyes, her throaty laugh.

CHAPTER TWO

"You have an actual date?" Sara's sixteen-year-old daughter, Hayley, asked, blue eyes wide, blond ponytail bouncing with emphasis as Sara set two places at the kitchen table, one for each of her children.

"No," Sara muttered in response. "I'm meeting a friend for dinner, that's all."

"You're pretty dressed up," Hayley remarked rather slyly. "Who is this — friend?"

"None of your business, kiddo," Sara replied patiently.

"You're meeting a *guy,*" the kid insisted. "Admit it, Mom. You have a *date.*"

"That's enough," Sara warned, exasperated. "Tell your brother it's time to eat, please."

Instead of heading for the living room, where Eric was probably engrossed in his phone, Hayley threw back her head and shouted, "Eric! Supper's ready and *Mom has a date with some guy!*"

Sara sighed, distracted and a little nervous. Neither she nor J.P. had used the word *date* when they agreed to meet at Bailey's at 7:00 p.m. and share a meal.

"Hayley," she said, feigning a glare.

Hayley shrugged in that irritatingly dismissive way of teenagers, turned on one sneakered heel and pushed open the door leading to the living room, leaping back when Eric appeared in the space, looking concerned. "Seriously? You're going on a date?" he asked, taking in her black jeans, shell top and short turquoise jacket. "Is that a smart thing to do?"

"Oh, for heaven's sake," Sara protested. "I'm meeting *a friend* for an ordinary dinner. It's no big deal."

Eric frowned. Unlike Hayley, he resembled her, rather than her ex-husband, and his gray eyes were troubled. "Whatever you say," he said.

"Wash up and eat your supper," Sara said, unwilling to discuss her plans for the evening any further, at least with these two. "And I expect the dishwasher to be loaded and the kitchen tidied by the time I get home."

"It's Eric's turn," Hayley pointed out. "He can take time out from texting Carly to do his chores." The relationship between Eric and Carly Hollister, Cord and Shallie's daughter, was an on-and-off kind of thing and, frankly, it worried Sara a little. Eric was younger than Carly by a little over a year, less mature emotionally, too, and when September rolled around, Carly would be off to college in LA, while Eric stayed behind to repeat his senior year and, hopefully, graduate this time around.

Life and young love being what they were, he'd be left behind in more ways than one, and while Sara knew that was the way things worked, she dreaded her son's reaction.

Flustered because she was due at Bailey's in less than ten minutes and already fending off a low-grade panic attack, Sara made a mental note to ask Eli to have a talk with Eric, try to prepare him for the inevitable changes headed his way.

"I don't care whose turn it is," she retorted, frowning at Eric, then Hayley. "I'm looking for results here, not arguments."

Grumbling ensued, but Sara paid no attention.

"Call or text if you need me," she said, over one shoulder, as she headed for the door that opened into the garage, car keys in hand, purse tucked under one arm.

Behind her, the grumbling shifted to mild bickering.

Situation: normal.

Inside her car, Sara pushed the button that would open the garage door, started the engine, backed out onto her driveway, buzzed the door down again and drove away from her brick house.

Because she didn't want to think about whether or not the kids were right, and she was about to go out on a date with J.P. McCall, Sara considered her clunky car. It ran well, and it was paid for, but it *was* the automotive equivalent of mom jeans.

Maybe she ought to spring for something a little more sporty — a roadster, perhaps, like the one her sister-in-law and close friend Brynne drove. Or, more properly, *had* driven. Since starting her business and the birth of her and Eli's twin sons, toddlers now, Brynne got around town in a minivan most of the time, though she still owned the roadster and used it whenever the babies were with Eli or their grandparents.

Sara could certainly afford a new car, but she couldn't see herself in anything flashy — or in a minivan. Eric and Hayley were far beyond the car-seat stage, obviously, and while that was a relief in a lot of ways, it was also a secret sorrow.

She'd loved being the mother of small children, despite the problems of being a single parent. But she definitely didn't miss the financial struggles, the sleepless nights and bone-deep fatigue, the constant vigilance required to keep her little ones safe and well.

Sara *still* loved being a mother, though. If anything, it was even harder now that Eric and Hayley were almost grown, and thus more independent. Not to mention more dramatic and often either sullen or surly.

To be fair, Hayley had been an easy child, and she was essentially good-natured, too. Sara missed the little-girl version of her daughter, tiny and sweet, pirouetting around the living room in her ballet shoes and a sparkly tutu, crowing, *Look at me, Mommy! Look at me!*

Eric, on the other hand, had been a challenge from the moment puberty kicked in, a moody kid, sensitive to slights, real or imagined, and often bitter over not having a father.

God knew Eli had stepped up, but in the final analysis, he was Eric's uncle, not his dad. And now that he had children of his own, Eli had less time for Eric.

Sara loved her son, but in the privacy of her own head, she could admit that she wished he were easier to deal with.

Eric had never been a sunny child, like

Hayley; he'd been quiet, studious and shy. Most likely, he'd been bullied early on, though to this day he wouldn't say one way or the other.

Today, both her kids were in that bewildering space where they were neither children nor adults, but struggling, sometimes fiercely, to leave their childhoods — and, it sometimes seemed, her as well — behind for good.

She arrived at Bailey's, a popular restaurant and bar widely acknowledged as a community gathering place, with nothing resolved, either where her children were concerned or with the date-or-just-a-friendly-dinner dilemma.

The place was hopping tonight and, for the first time, it occurred to Sara that the other diners, probably all locals and therefore people she knew, might draw some conclusions of their own when they saw her and J.P. seated at the same table and obviously, well, *together.*

"Sara Worth," she said aloud as she tucked her compact car into a parking space, "you're making way too much of this. J.P. McCall might be hot — okay, he's *molten* — but you've known him forever. He's your brother's friend and he probably thinks of you as an older sister."

An older sister, Sara thought glumly. *Yikes.*

She wasn't *that* much older than J.P. — only two years.

The attempt to reassure herself fell flat. Their actual ages, hers and J.P.'s, didn't matter, but that didn't mean J.P. thought of her as what she was — a healthy, successful and reasonably attractive woman.

He'd gone riding with her that morning, yes. And he'd agreed to meet her for dinner. But he probably considered this little get-together a simple favor.

Heat surged up Sara's neck to pound in her cheeks.

Was she making a fool of herself?

Should she text J.P., offer some excuse and go home?

A tap sounded at the driver's-side window and Sara turned to see J.P. standing beside her car.

He looked *way* too good in a newish pair of jeans and a crisp white shirt, open at the throat. His sand-colored hair shone, even in the dim light of Bailey's parking lot, and his easy smile struck Sara squarely in the midsection.

She rolled down her window, ready to claim she had a headache — a chicken-shit excuse if she'd ever heard one — and stared into that familiar, devastatingly handsome face.

How had she watched J.P. McCall grow from a scrawny ranch kid to a man without noticing — until today — just how good-looking he really was?

"Are you coming inside?" he asked, his smile relaxing into a slight tilt at one corner of his mouth. "Brynne is holding a table for us."

Sara found her voice, but barely. "Umm — sure. Yes."

He reached for the handle, pulled open the door.

Sara started to get out of the car, was stopped by her seat belt and blushed again. Head down, she fumbled to unfasten it.

J.P. either didn't notice the awkward movement or pretended he hadn't.

Sara drew a deep breath and admonished herself — silently, of course — to get a god-damned grip.

He was standing just far enough away to allow Sara a place to stand, and he extended a hand to help her.

It was a chivalrous thing to do, but a sense of chagrin flashed through Sara, as though she were an old lady he was helping to cross the street.

Sara pushed the car door shut and locked

it using her key fob.

She was behaving like an idiot, she knew that, but she couldn't seem to break the pattern.

"You look beautiful," J.P. said very quietly. Was that a pity-compliment offered only because she was so clearly, stupidly nervous?

"Thank you," she said, forcing herself to relax a little.

A *very* little.

His hand rested lightly against the small of her back as they crossed the parking lot to the sidewalk and headed for the restaurant's front door.

Bailey's was noisy and brightly lit that night, as always, and friends and neighbors waved and called out the occasional "howdy" as J.P. steered Sara, very gently, toward a side table, where Brynne was waiting, menus in hand, a big smile on her face.

Brynne, a stunningly beautiful blonde any day of the week, absolutely glowed with happiness and well-being. Married life suited her.

Occasionally, she helped out at Bailey's, probably because her parents, though lively, were definitely getting older.

Sara loved her sister-in-law dearly — they'd been friends long before she and Eli got together — but in that moment, she

44

wished Brynne wasn't making such a big fuss.

She greeted Sara with a kiss on the cheek and invited J.P. and Sara to sit with a grand gesture of one hand.

J.P., slightly flushed along his jawline, Sara suddenly noticed, cleared his throat and drew back a chair for her.

Sara sank into it, feeling winded, as though she'd just run a marathon — or a gauntlet.

J.P. took a seat opposite Sara, and when their gazes met, he winked.

Something about the gesture eased the tension, and Sara relaxed. This was a dinner with a friend, not a date, and that was okay.

It was fine.

Really.

"Coffee?" Brynne asked. "Or wine?"

J.P. asked for beer, and Sara echoed the request.

Somebody popped some coins in the jukebox and, a few moments later, Brad Paisley launched into "Alcohol."

Brynne walked away, and Sara and J.P. perused their menus.

"I'm buying," Sara reminded J.P. without looking up from her menu.

She felt, rather than saw, his grin. It was warm like an afternoon breeze in high summer.

"Okay," he agreed affably.

Sara risked a glance and saw that his hazel eyes were alight with amusement. "I mean it," she bumbled on. "Get steak, if that's what you want."

"Sara," he said. His voice was gruff and his eyes were still laughing, though not in a derisive way.

"What?" she croaked.

"Relax," he replied. "I don't bite."

Well, that's a pity, Sara thought with a sweet, secret shiver. Her wild side — she definitely had one — was trying to come out.

She wasn't having it.

She tried to sound businesslike. "I'm fine," she said briskly. And then she stuck her foot squarely in her mouth. "This isn't a date, after all."

J.P. raised one eyebrow, and that twitch was there again at the corner of his mouth. "Isn't it?" he asked.

Sara blushed, skirted his gaze. She was at a complete loss for words, which was probably for the best, given that she'd already made an idiot of herself.

Brynne saved her from having to respond by bringing two tall mugs of foamy, bubbling beer to the table.

"Made up your minds?" she chimed.

Sara swallowed. "Yes," she muttered. "I'll have the meat loaf special, please, with a dinner salad to start."

Brynne scribbled the order onto her paper pad and turned her dazzling smile to J.P. "How about you, cowboy?" she asked.

J.P. smiled back, closed the menu with a resolute snap. "T-bone," he replied. "Medium rare, fries on the side and hold the salad."

"Got it," Brynne said, accepting the offered menu and taking Sara's, too.

And then she hustled away.

"Mike and Alice must be taking the night off," J.P. observed when the silence had stretched well into the next song in the jukebox queue.

Johnny Cash, "I Walk the Line."

Folks around the Creek liked the classics.

"They're probably upstairs, looking after the twins," Sara said, relieved that the conversation had taken a turn toward the ordinary. Brynne's folks were devoted grandparents and the apartment was handy to the restaurant; until her marriage to Eli, Brynne had lived up there.

Now the place served as a sort of rest area and, when needed, quarters for out-of-town guests.

J.P. grasped the handle of his mug, lifted

47

it in a toast. "To remembering how it feels to ride a horse," he said.

Sara tapped her mug against his in acknowledgment and took such a big gulp of the brew that she nearly choked on it.

J.P. watched her, his head tilted slightly to one side. "Did you finish with the manuscript?"

Poor guy. He was trying so hard to make things easier.

That, or he was simply enjoying her discomfort.

He'd teased her plenty, when they were kids, usually in concert with Eli and Cord.

"Sort of," Sara answered with a deep grateful sigh. "I'll have revisions to do, after my editor reads the book. Once those are done, I'll take a few weeks off to recover — then start the next project. My publisher already accepted the proposal."

"What do you do when you're recovering?" he asked moderately.

Sara felt much calmer by then, but the pit of her stomach was still fluttering. She made a shrug-like motion with her shoulders, hoping to come off as casual and unflustered, and replied, "I read a lot. Not research books, but novels — I like mysteries." She enjoyed romances, too, the sexier the better, but she wasn't about to say so at this juncture — J.P. didn't need to know that her love life was entirely vicarious. "I try to make up for all the exercise I missed sitting in front of my computer by swimming laps at the community center and taking a few yoga classes."

"Sounds good," J.P. said.

"What do you do?" Sara heard herself ask. "To relax, I mean?"

He smiled. "Mainly, I ride. I like to read, too."

That caught Sara's interest. "Really?"

"Yeah, really," he answered with a touch of kindly irony. "I've been doing that since first grade."

Sara made a face. Barely noticed when Brynne set her salad down in front of her. "What kinds of books do you like?"

"Yours," he replied. "Among others."

He read her books?

Sara was surprised, though she probably shouldn't have been. She was good at what she did, and *lots* of people read her novels, if she did say so herself.

Which she didn't.

"What else?" she asked to keep from leaping right in and asking what he'd liked best about her books, and what he thought could be improved upon.

"Grisham, King, Barclay, Koontz, Co-

49

ben," he said. His voice trailed off, leaving Sara with the distinct impression that the list was considerably longer.

"No female authors?" she countered, though diplomatically.

"Like I said, you."

Sara blushed again, but less fiercely this time, took up her fork and picked at her salad. "And others?"

"And others," he confirmed.

"I don't suppose you'd be willing to read the manuscript I just finished?" she asked without meaning to at all. The job of first reader usually fell to Eli since, like her series character, he was both a man and a law enforcement officer, but he was busy these days with his job and growing family.

Too late she realized she was asking a great deal of a casual friend.

She nearly face-palmed.

But J.P. seemed pleased. "I'd like that," he said.

Sara took a few moments to take that in. "For real?"

He said nothing, just looked at her. And waited.

"You'll be honest?" she asked. "Tell me if something doesn't ring true?"

"I'll be honest," he assured her.

"Thanks."

"Sara?"

"What?"

"This *is* a date, isn't it?"

"I don't know," she answered. "Is it?"

J.P. chuckled. "I think so," he said.

She didn't comment.

Their food arrived and, for several blessed minutes, they were both occupied with the mechanics of eating.

Sara was amazed to find that she wasn't just hungry — she was ravenous. She'd had a light breakfast — toast and half a banana — before heading out to the McCall place that morning, come straight home after the ride with J.P., taken a quick shower and changed clothes, then lost herself in polishing certain scenes in her novel.

She'd forgotten all about lunch. Hadn't even bothered with a snack.

"This is so good," she said, referring to the meat loaf special she'd ordered. It came with mashed potatoes, tomato gravy and green beans. "How's your steak?"

J.P. chewed thoughtfully, swallowed and answered in his own good time. "Never a bad meal here at Bailey's," he replied. Another pause followed while he took another bite of steak and washed it down with a few sips of beer.

Sara was privately comparing her emotional state to a minor whirlwind — even before she'd taken up writing fiction, she'd thought in pictures — when J.P. asked a question that nearly caused her to choke.

"When was the last time you went out with a man, Sara?"

She forced herself to meet his eyes and found amiable curiosity there rather than the challenge she'd half expected.

"I've been pretty busy," she replied. "You know, with the kids and my career and everything."

"Hmm," he said.

"What does that mean?" Sara asked. For some reason, his response prickled.

Before J.P. could reply, though, she countered, "When was the last time *you* went out on a date?"

He looked away, very briefly, then looked back, holding her gaze. "Saturday night," he answered.

Today was Wednesday.

Obviously, unlike her, the man had a life.

She felt herself shrink a little, wishing she hadn't asked that particular question. The food remaining on her plate, so delicious only moments before, had lost all appeal.

J.P. surprised her — again.

He reached across the table, took her hand.

His skin was warm, strong and a little rough from hard work.

J.P. McCall was more than a stock-market wizard. He was a rancher.

He rode fence lines, herded cattle, bucked bales of hay.

And his touch shot gentle fire through Sara's veins.

It was then that she first admitted to herself that she wanted more of this man's touch. A *lot* more.

"Hey," he said. "I shouldn't have asked you about your private life. It's none of my business."

Sara couldn't speak. The fire had fanned out from her hand to blaze in the rest of her body and, damn it, in her face.

"I keep getting this wrong," J.P. said, still holding her hand.

For some reason, she imagined slow dancing with J.P., in a semi-darkened room, with a smoky playlist pulsing low in the background.

She'd missed so much, playing it safe.

"You're not getting anything wrong," Sara protested too quickly. "It's me. This is all so awkward."

"It doesn't have to be," he suggested.

"Oh, but it does," Sara said, keeping her voice down, suddenly aware that she and

J.P. were still drawing sidelong glances from the other patrons of the restaurant. "I can't remember the last time I felt like such an idiot."

Somehow, J.P. had finished most of his meal, while Sara had merely nibbled.

"You're anything but an idiot, Sara. You're just — well — a little out of practice when it comes to making small talk." A pause. "Or maybe I was right before, and I'm getting this wrong."

She laughed then. Actually *laughed.*

And it was a tremendous relief.

"You? J.P. McCall, the most sought-after bachelor in Wild Horse County, now that Eli and Cord are off the market?"

Instead of the cocky grin Sara might have expected, J.P. responded with a frown. "That's what you think? That I have to fight women off with a stick?"

It *was* what she thought, as a matter of fact.

J.P. was not only handsome, he was unabashedly masculine, smart, physically active, suave when he wanted to be. He didn't smoke, drink to excess or get into bar brawls. He'd turned a minor government settlement into a fortune, and he ran his family's cattle ranch like the pro he was.

54

And if all that wasn't enough, he liked to read.

In a day when so many men — and not a few women — seemed to prefer living virtually, through social media, that was saying something.

There was nothing virtual about J.P. McCall.

He was *real,* fully present and engaged with life, be it good, bad or indifferent.

"Yes," Sara answered belatedly. "I *do* think you have to *fight women off with a stick.* I've known you for a very long time, J.P. My brother is one of your closest friends. You were a girl magnet as a kid, and you're a *woman* magnet now."

J.P. sat back in his chair, let out a whoosh of breath in exclamation, but there was a twinkle in his eyes for all that.

"A *woman magnet*?" he repeated. "I should be flattered."

"But?"

"But I'm not. Flattered, that is."

"Sorry," Sara said, somewhat meekly, wishing she'd confined the conversation to other topics.

Though what those topics might have been, she couldn't have said.

"Are you finished?" he asked after several moments of awkward silence.

Sara blinked, confused. Embarrassed. Was he peeved by the things she'd said?

"Eating," he clarified, having read her mind, it would seem.

"Yes," she managed.

"Me, too," J.P. said. "Let's settle up the bill and get out of here."

"And go where?" Sara asked. Taking no chances that J.P. might grab the check, she'd called the restaurant earlier, given Brynne her payment details, along with instructions to tack on a 20 percent tip.

"You're sure you don't want dessert?" Sara pressed when J.P. didn't answer her last question.

That made him grin, and the message was so clear that Sara blushed *again.*

Inwardly, where all her organs seemed to be colliding with each other like bumper cars at the state fair, she relished the implication.

"It's too soon for that," she said, and then wished she hadn't commented at all. She wasn't the type to jump into bed with a man after one horseback ride and supper at Bailey's, but she'd probably sounded prim as an old-time schoolmarm just now.

His next words confounded her further.

"I'll wait," he said. And then he pushed back his chair and stood up.

Sara scanned the room, found Brynne and summoned up a smile of farewell.

Brynne made the call-me gesture with one hand, and then J.P. was drawing back Sara's chair.

The moment they were outside, in the cool night air, Sara snapped out of whatever spell she'd been under.

"I'd better get home," she said, starting toward her car. "The kids —"

J.P. took her arm, his grasp both gentle and firm.

He turned her around to face him there in the shadowy gravel parking lot beside the restaurant, curved his right index finger under her chin and lifted.

She felt the hard, healthy heat of his body close to hers and very nearly melted on the spot.

So much for snapping out of it, whatever *it* was.

"Fair warning," he said quietly. "I'm about to kiss you, Sara. If you've got any objections, you'd better say so right now."

She blinked.

Swallowed.

And said not a word.

Slowly, J.P. lowered his head, touched his lips to hers, just a light brush of skin to skin at first.

Despite herself, Sara gave a little whimper. Stiffened her melting knees.

And then he was kissing her for real, deeply and with just the right amount of pressure. Their tongues touched, then tangled, and Sara slipped her arms around J.P.'s neck, partly to keep herself from sliding to the ground in a puddle and partly because she wanted to pull him closer, make him part of her.

When the kiss ended, Sara was breathless and, she noted with both relief and womanly triumph, so was J.P.

"Holy shit," he said, almost gasping.

"Very romantic," Sara teased, though she was thinking pretty much the same thing.

"I felt like that once before," J.P. said presently, his arms around Sara, hers still circling his neck.

"Really?" Sara asked mischievously.

"Yeah," J.P. replied. "I was eight. Eli and Cord dared me to —" He hesitated.

"Go on," Sara urged.

He gave a short raspy laugh. "They dared me to piss on a fence. It was electric."

"And you did it?"

"Of course I did it. I had to prove I was a manly man."

She laughed. "Those little devils!" she said.

"I fell for it," J.P. said. "I accept my share of the blame."

It felt so good, standing there in the warm darkness, pressed against J.P.

He smelled of sun-dried cotton, starched and ironed the old-fashioned way, a hint of some leathery cologne and clean skin.

"Did you succeed? Prove you were a manly man?"

"No," he said. "I screamed like a banshee, and after I got up off the ground, I chased those two halfway across the county, yelling some pretty colorful threats. They got away — they had a head start, after all, since they didn't have to button up their jeans — and I went home and snitched on them to my dad."

Sara couldn't stop smiling, though she was mildly horrified to think of the foolish, dangerous pranks little boys pull on each other.

She waited.

"I thought he'd call Cord's granddad and your folks and get them in big trouble."

"He didn't do that?"

"No. He was sitting at the kitchen table, drinking coffee and reading a newspaper. After I told my story, he lowered the paper, looked at me and said, *Well, I guess you won't be doing a dumbass thing like that again, now will you?"*

"That was it?" Sara stifled a giggle, trying to recall J.P. as an eight-year-old, skinny and sporting a summer buzz cut.

"Mostly."

"Mostly?"

"He told me not to tell my mother."

"Good advice, most likely," Sara agreed.

"Definitely good advice. She would have freaked out. Rushed me to the ER for a fresh round of humiliation — not intentionally, of course, but because she was expecting my heart to stop beating or something — and then grounded me for half the summer."

"A narrow escape," Sara said. She paused, thoughtful. "So, let me see if I've got this right. You just kissed me, and it reminded you of urinating on an electric fence."

He laughed. "I'm a smooth talker. You said so yourself."

Somewhere nearby, a car door opened.

J.P. and Sara separated automatically, though with some reluctance.

They were back in the real world.

"You really have to go home?" J.P. asked eventually.

Sara nodded. "The kids," she reminded him, and her tone sounded a little wistful, at least to her.

60

"Okay," J.P. said, pleasantly resigned. "Then I want to see you again, Sara."

"That's good," Sara answered, "because I want to see you again, too, J.P. McCall. What do you suggest?"

"Another horseback ride," he said. "A longer one this time. Maybe a picnic. In the meantime, you could email me your manuscript. I'm eager to read it."

All of it sounded good, though Sara wondered if she could trust herself, picnicking alone with this man, out there in the wide-open spaces.

"I'll send you the book when I've finished the revisions," she said. "As for another horseback ride, well, I'm pretty sore from this morning. It's been a long time."

"Only one way to get past that," J.P. reminded her. "Get back in the saddle."

Back in the saddle.

Maybe that *was* the best thing to do, both literally and figuratively. Take a few chances. Give romance a try.

Lord, she was so tired of being lonely.

Sara's cheeks burned anew, and she was glad of the relative darkness. She was also tongue-tied, painfully so.

J.P. seemed to sense that. He kissed her forehead, stepped around her and waited to open the car door for her.

61

She got out her keys and pressed the proper button on the fob.

The lock snapped in response, and J.P. reached for the handle.

While she eased into the seat — the ibuprofen she'd taken earlier in the day had long since worn off, and now her thighs, knees and backside were aching again — J.P. got out his phone and texted her his email address.

"I'll call tomorrow," he said as she fastened her seat belt.

She nodded. "I had fun tonight," she told him, rather shyly.

He grinned. "Really? I could have sworn you were scared to death the whole time. I half expected you to leap out of your chair and bolt at any second."

"I'm not used to — this."

"We'll take it slow," he promised and, for some reason, his words, and the way he said them, made her throat tighten and her eyes sting.

So this was what it was like to spend time with a man, another grown-up?

Oh, she'd been on a few dates over the years. Even tried a dating app or two.

But every experience had been either deadly boring or flat-out disastrous.

"Okay," she said.

Lame.

J.P. smiled again, shut the car door and waited until she'd started the engine.

Then he turned and walked away toward his truck.

Sara was still holding her phone — she'd checked to make sure J.P.'s text had come through — when a new message landed with a beep.

The sender was Hayley, and the text was alarming.

Mom, come home quick. This guy is here — and I think he's our dad!

Chapter Three

J.P. paused, about to get into his truck, when Sara's car sped past him, spitting gravel. Her tires squealed when she hit the paved street and ran the only traffic light in town to head for home.

He frowned. The kiss they'd shared was still reverberating through his system, and Sara had seemed to enjoy it as much as he had.

Sure, Sara had been extra nervous throughout the evening, but they'd had a good time together — hadn't they? And they'd made plans — horseback riding and a picnic at his place.

Had he said or done — or *not* said or done — something to upset her?

He hauled open the door of his truck and hoisted himself behind the wheel. Should he follow her? Ask her if everything was all right?

That was his inclination, but after a little

more thought, he decided against the idea. Sara might be out of practice when it came to first dates, but she wasn't the type to fly off the handle at some imagined slight.

She was a strong, independent woman — he liked that about her, liked it a *lot* — and she didn't need some yahoo checking up on her. If Sara needed help, she'd call Eli, her brother — and only if she couldn't handle whatever was going on herself.

Going against his considerable pride, and masculine tendency to butt in whenever he saw a woman facing any kind of struggle, J.P. started his truck and headed out of town, toward his ranch.

It seemed an especially lonely place, that rambling house, empty except for good ole Trooper, who would be awaiting his return with the kind of eagerness only dogs can manage.

For all that, he thought of Sara as he navigated the familiar roads leading the way home. And he worried about her.

When he pulled up in front of the house ten minutes later, he spotted Trooper through the living room, keeping his clumsy watch from his favorite lookout post, the back of the couch.

A Lab mix, Troop was too big to fit there comfortably, but that never seemed to bother him.

The thought struck J.P. that his faithful dog was getting up there in years, and that gave him a hard pang of sorrow, square in the center of his heart.

His throat tightened momentarily, and the backs of his eyes stung.

He shook his head, but the emotion stuck.

J.P. shut off his truck, got out, locked it and headed for the front door.

Trooper barked joyfully when J.P. entered the house, enjoying an ear ruffle and then rolling over for a belly rub.

"Missed you, too," he said gruffly, once the dog had been thoroughly greeted.

The interlude had provided a distraction from his thoughts about the animal getting older and the inevitable parting that lay somewhere down the road, but on another level he continued to fret about Sara.

What had happened between the plans they'd made and her driving out of Bailey's lot at NASCAR speed?

Obviously, she must have received a text or a phone call, but she might simply have remembered something she'd forgotten to do, something really important.

J.P. shoved a hand through his hair, sighed and made his way toward the old-fashioned kitchen. There, he flipped open his laptop, booted it up and went to the fridge for a beer.

Hooking one foot around the leg of a chair, he dragged the seat back from the table and sat down.

Instead of going online, however, as he'd intended, he pulled his phone from his shirt pocket.

Three messages, and none of them were from Sara.

He thumbed his way through, in order of arrival.

His mom had invited him to supper.

Too late for that. He'd text her back in a few, though he probably wouldn't mention that he'd already eaten at Bailey's, with Sara.

His mother would be a little too pleased that he'd gone out with a local woman, for once, instead of cruising Tinder for the kind of dates she probably thought, quite correctly, were all about one-night stands, not finding a wife.

It was early days with Sara, and he wasn't ready to answer hopeful questions from his sweet but sometimes nosy mom.

The second text was from his broker's admin, reminding him of a conference call on Zoom, scheduled for the next afternoon.

He confirmed his plan to attend by texting

back the requested Y.

Eli had sent the last message, less than ten minutes before.

Somebody's been messing with the mustangs again, running them with ATVs and the like. The Land Management people are up to their eyeballs in other kinds of trouble, so they've asked the county to step up. Any signs of trespassing on your land?

"Shit," J.P. rasped, scrolling to Eli's number and hitting Call.

"Garrett," Eli answered. He was probably driving and hadn't looked to see who was calling.

"It's J.P. What's going on with the wild horses?"

"I don't know much more than I said in the text," Eli answered. "The feds found half a dozen mustangs cowering in the back of a canyon not too far from your southern property line. They were winded and a couple of them were scratched up pretty badly from scrambling through the brush."

J.P. cursed. "Kids?" he asked, remembering the trouble Sara's boy, Eric, Freddie Lansing and a handful of others had stirred up a couple of years before. They'd turned

68

livestock loose, among other things, and some of those animals had been injured.

Eli sighed. "Probably," he said. "And, yeah, before you ask, I'm definitely going to question Eric. I'm on my way over to Sara's place right now."

J.P. said nothing about seeing Sara earlier in the evening. It would have been out of context and, basically, none of Eli's concern. "Is there any reason to think he's involved? Eric, I mean?"

Maybe, he thought, Sara had gotten word of the problem somehow, and raced home to confront her son.

"I hope he isn't, but I have to consider him for obvious reasons." A pause. "Even if he's not part of this latest cluster, he might know something."

"What can I do to help?"

"Cord will be back from Florida late tonight. I was thinking the three of us and maybe a couple of my deputies could saddle up early in the morning and sweep that rangeland of yours. See if we can find any-thing."

"Sounds good," J.P. replied. "I'm warning you, though, Eli — if we catch any thugs trying to run wild horses to death, you might have to arrest *me,* because I'm going to kick some ass."

Eli laughed, though he knew J.P. was at least 90 percent serious. "Maybe I ought to deputize you. Would that keep you from taking the law into your own hands?"

"Probably not," J.P. said. "How many horses will we need? I can trailer them up and meet you — where?"

"The mouth of Shadow Canyon. We'll fan out from there. But there's no need to bring horses — Cord has that covered."

"Cord's horses are fine, but they're mostly misfits," J.P. protested. "Mine are trained for roping and driving cattle out of thick brush and tight spots. They're used to fancy maneuvers."

"I need six horses, saddled and ready to ride, seven tomorrow morning at the latest. I don't care if they're yours or Cord's, so I'll let the two of you work that out. He's probably still on a plane, though, so you might not be able to reach him for a while."

Mentally, J.P. chose six of his best horses for the job, including Shiloh. "See you in the morning," he told Eli. "Good luck with Eric."

And look after Sara.

"Tomorrow at seven," Eli confirmed, and the call ended.

J.P. immediately dialed Cord.

As expected, he got his friend's voice mail.

70

"I'm providing the horses," he said, skipping over *hi, how are you* and all the rest and going straight to the point. It was the way he did things. The way all three of them did things. "See you tomorrow at Shadow Canyon."

That was that.

J.P. paced the kitchen floor, planning, wishing he could mount up right that second and head out to find the bastards who'd been tormenting mustangs, though he knew that would be a damn fool thing to do, given that they'd need daylight to spot any tracks or other evidence and, furthermore, Eli would be justifiably pissed.

He was the sheriff, after all, and the BLM — Bureau of Land Management, a federal agency — had contacted him, not J.P.

Going all vigilante wasn't going to help; he knew that. But that didn't mean he wasn't tempted.

He stopped, looked down at Trooper, who was staring up at him, waiting for some signal.

"Come on, old buddy," he told the dog. "Let's go out to the barn and make sure the tack is ready for tomorrow. Maybe we'll hitch up the trailer, too."

Trooper was game for any adventure, as usual.

Being out of doors soothed J.P., as it always did, and he was calmer by the time they reached the barn.

He opened the double doors and gave them a push, so they creaked on their ancient hinges. Then he cranked on the overhead lights.

The horses, their stalls lining both sides of the breezeway, blinked and nickered in surprise. He'd fed them before leaving for town to meet Sara earlier, but they made it clear they'd be up for another flake of hay, just the same.

J.P. smiled, walked down the line, pausing at each stall to stroke a nose or pat a neck. The dusty tang of horseflesh calmed him further, and he rolled his shoulders, dispelling some of the tension coiled there.

He stopped at Misty's stall, spent a couple of minutes talking to her. She was older than the other horses he owned, and a little overweight, and he wouldn't be taking her to the canyon tomorrow. She could manage a few hours of squiring a green-horn around the ranch, but she wasn't nimble enough for the task Eli had in mind.

As he made his nightly rounds, he thought about Sara.

She'd stood with him, here in the breeze-way, while he'd taken off Misty's and

Shiloh's tack, just that morning, and she'd left a vacuum behind when she'd gone.

He wondered again if she was all right.

Patted his shirt pocket, took out his phone, squinted at the screen.

No new messages.

He thumbed his way to her slot in his contact list. Drew a deep breath. Texted her the briefest of questions. You okay?

There was no response, and that didn't surprise him.

Whatever her reasons for rushing home from Bailey's — and away from him — she was definitely safe. By now, Eli was there, and if there was trouble, he'd have her back for sure. He was about to slip his phone back into his pocket and head for the house when it rang in his palm.

He squinted, saw his sister Josie's name.

And he frowned.

He and Josie weren't especially close, and they usually communicated by text or email, most often about their folks.

It was pretty late for a brother/sister chat.

"Josie?" he asked, concerned.

Josie lived in Virginia and worked for a lobbyist. Like her only brother, she was an early riser, which made it stranger still that she'd call this late at night.

"J.P.," Josie blurted. Her voice was odd —

was she crying? "Thank God you picked up."

A muscle tightened in the pit of J.P.'s stomach. His first thought was that something had happened to their mom or dad, but that didn't make sense. If either of the elder McCalls had a problem, the other would have called him, not Josie.

"What's going on?" he asked.

"I'm losing my mind, that's all!" Josie exclaimed. "I hate to ask, but I really need your help, J.P."

Did she need money? That didn't seem likely, since she and her husband, Ted, both pulled in high salaries. Ted was a successful lawyer, with political aspirations.

Not that J.P. would refuse to help out, if his sister needed a loan or something.

"With what?" he asked patiently.

"I'll talk to Mom and Dad soon, I promise, but right now I can't face telling them that Ted and I are thinking of separating — they don't need the hassle," Josie said.

None of this was making a lot of sense.

Josie and Ted were on the verge of breaking up?

"Josie, explain," J.P. ordered.

She sighed a sniffly sigh. "Ted and I are having problems," she said. "I think we'll be okay, but we're yelling a lot, if you know what I mean. I'm afraid Becky and Robyn will be traumatized or something. And Becky's been hanging around with this boy — he's not a bad kid, really, but he's a little wild and —"

Robyn and Becky were J.P.'s nieces, twelve and fourteen respectively, and he loved them, albeit in that awkward way of bachelor uncles.

"Josie," J.P. counseled quietly. "Take a breath."

She did.

There was a tremulous silence, and then she went on, rushing to get everything said. "I'm hoping they can come and stay on the ranch for a few weeks."

The kids visited the ranch most summers, and usually stayed at the A-frame with their grandparents. He usually wasn't consulted, let alone asked to run interference in a situation he didn't understand.

"Just call Mom in the morning, Josie," he said cautiously. "She'll understand, and she'll be glad to see the girls. So will Dad."

He spent time with his nieces whenever they visited, took them riding and to movies and the like, and they'd spent the night several times, bunking in their mom's old room, but they were, well, *girls.*

Josie sighed again. "I know," she said

75

sadly. "I just hate to worry them, that's all. I'm pretty sure Ted and I will make it, but here's the thing, J.P. Mom will grill me about what's going on, and I don't have the emotional wherewithal to discuss this with anyone besides Ted and our marriage counselor."

"Just tell her that, Josie," he reiterated.

"I can't. It's all I can do to tell *you*."

"If it's that bad," J.P. reasoned quietly, "then maybe you should come home, too. Take some time to clear your head, get a fresh perspective."

"I really can't," Josie insisted.

"So exactly what is it you want me to do?"

Josie was crying, and trying hard to hide the fact. "I know this sounds crazy, J.P., and I'm sorry. It's just that I'm figuring things out as I go along, and not doing such a great job of it. Please, just meet the girls when their plane lands — I'll text you the details once I've made arrangements — and bring them home to the ranch. If I'm still incommunicado by then, tell Mom and Dad we wanted the visit to be a surprise."

"You're right, Joze," J.P. replied, finally in motion, heading out of the barn, turning off the lights. "This is crazy. But there's obviously more to the story, and I don't get why you're not telling me what it is."

76

"Just trust me, please," Josie said, confirming his suspicions. "I will explain, but I can't do it right now — I just can't."

"All right," J.P. said with a sigh of resignation, crossing the dark yard, Trooper scampering along ahead of him. "But I'm not going to lie to the folks, Josie, and you shouldn't, either. They deserve better."

Josie thrust out a long shaky breath, and J.P. could picture her running a hand through her short blond hair. "Fair enough," she said.

"Keep me posted. I'm here to listen, if that's what you need."

She gave a little sob. "Okay," she replied. A long pause, then a tremulous, "J.P.?"

"What?"

"Thank you. You have no idea how much I appreciate this."

"You're welcome," he said, and he meant it, even though life seemed to be getting more complicated by the minute.

First, Sara.

Then the call from Eli, relaying the mustang situation.

And now this.

What had happened to his orderly and relatively quiet life?

Chapter Four

The SUV blocked the garage door, forcing Sara to park in the driveway. Not a major inconvenience, but the fact of it lifted her already-tight shoulders to the level of her earlobes, just the same.

She got out of her car, slammed the door hard and headed up the walkway.

The front door opened as she approached, spilling light onto the old-fashioned porch between slatted shadows.

Hayley stood awkwardly in the gap. "Mom's home," she called out to those inside, without looking away from Sara's face.

Before Sara got as far as the porch steps, another SUV swung into the driveway behind her car.

Eli.

Sara would have preferred to handle her narcissistic ex-husband on her own, without her brother *or* her children there to watch her morph into a she-wolf and tear out Zachary Worth's throat.

She'd kept her opinions about her ex to herself for years, at least around the kids, but now, faced with the reality of the man, she found she'd reached a breaking point.

She supposed it was a good thing Eli was there, especially with Eric and Hayley present, and besides, she might need backup.

Or a credible witness.

She stopped, stood still, breathing deeply and slowly.

Eli reached her side. Spoke gently. "Sara? What the hell is going on here?"

"Didn't you get the same memo I did?" Sara managed after a few more steadying breaths.

"Mom?" Hayley prompted, still posted in the doorway. Zachary's arrival must have come as quite a shock to her; she'd been just shy of two years old when her parents divorced.

"What memo would that be?" Eli inquired quietly, raising one hand in Hayley's direction, a gesture familiar to all of them.

Give us a minute.

"Zachary is inside," Sara said, and for all the deep breathing she'd done, her voice was shaky. "I thought that was why you came over — that someone must have clued you in."

Eli shook his head. Touched Sara's elbow. "I'm here about something else," he told her, with another glance at the house.

"What?"

"Something that can wait," he replied. His fingers tightened around Sara's elbow, just a little. "Let's find out what he wants."

Glumly, furiously, Sara nodded.

Together, they headed for the front door.

Hayley stepped back to make way for them, and Sara read both relief and anxiety in her daughter's face.

"Eric let him in," the girl fretted. "I told him not to, but he didn't listen."

Sara managed a smile, reached out to touch Hayley's cheek. "It's okay, honey," she said. "You texted me right away, and that's all anybody could reasonably expect."

"You're not mad?"

"I didn't say that," Sara replied evenly, aware of her son and his father standing at the periphery of her vision, in front of the empty fireplace. "I'm not angry with *you.* Your brother is another matter."

Eli gave Sara's elbow a light squeeze, then let go. "The kids and I will be in the kitchen," he told his sister. "If you need me, give me a shout."

Eric glared, set his jaw and folded his

arms. "I'm not going anywhere," he said.

"That's what you think," Eli answered mildly. Immovably.

At last, Sara fixed her gaze on Zachary, the man who'd fathered her children, betrayed her and left Eric and Hayley behind without a second thought.

Like the SUV blocking Sara's garage door, Zachary's suit was expensive, probably custom-made. He still had that head of curly blond hair, though it might be receding a little at the temples, and his cornflower blue eyes twinkled with — something — as he regarded Sara.

He was still handsome, and he was charming — if one didn't look past the carefully maintained veneer.

His gaze slid to Eli, who was still at Sara's side.

"Well," he said, breaking his silence, "Sheriff Eli Garrett. Looks as though you've come up in the world."

Eli said nothing. He disliked Zachary, as did most people who'd known the man for more than a day or two, but he wasn't the reactionary type.

Neither was Sara — most of the time.

Realizing Eli wasn't going to waste any words on him, Zachary gave a long-suffering sigh and draped one arm around Eric's taut shoulders. "Go with your uncle and your sister," he said. "Your mother and I need to talk."

"I want to stay here," Eric said, seething. The look of obstinate fury in his eyes broke Sara's heart. When, exactly, had she become the enemy? "Mom was out on a date tonight," he went on, his tone accusing.

"That's enough, Eric," Eli put in. His tone brooked no argument.

Eric flushed, stepped away from Zachary's side and stormed toward the kitchen, where Hayley was waiting, probably scared and undoubtedly confused.

And why wouldn't she be? Zachary had never visited, never called, never sent a birthday card or a Christmas gift.

He was a stranger to her.

And to Eric, though it seemed he'd rewritten his personal history, no doubt casting Zachary as the vanquished hero and Sara as the shrew who'd driven him away.

She felt her shoulders droop a little, and promptly straightened them.

This was no time to let down her guard.

"Sit," she told Zachary, gesturing toward one of the wing chairs in front of the fireplace.

Zachary shot his cuffs, tilted his head to one side. "Not before you do," he said. "It wouldn't be the gentlemanly thing to do."

Sara refrained, with great effort, from pointing out the irony of that statement. She merely nodded and perched herself on the edge of the floral-patterned love seat she'd purchased the day her first novel was released.

"How is it that you and Eric seem to be so familiar with each other?" she asked evenly.

Zachary spread his hands, smiled. "The miracle of social media," he said. "Eric tracked me down online some time ago, and we've been in touch — at least virtually — ever since." A smug pause. "He didn't tell you, obviously."

Of course. She should have thought of that.

She said nothing.

"I've missed you," Zachary said, lowering his voice to a croon.

Beyond the kitchen door, Eric and Eli were arguing.

Sara couldn't make out what they were saying, but she could imagine it well enough.

"Spare me the act," she said. "You don't care about anyone but yourself, and we both know it." She paused, drew and slowly released another breath. "Why are you here?"

Zachary looked hurt.

So much for not putting on a show.

"I'm here," he answered, apparently giving up on getting the expected reaction, "because I want to spend time with my children." He paused, looked down at his hands, which were loosely clasped between his knees. When he looked up, his blue eyes were a touch less impudent, and the smirk he'd worn until that moment slipped away into a mirage of sadness. "And because my father is dying."

Sara concentrated on her own hands, letting them rest calmly in her lap. It took everything she had not to wring them.

"I'm sorry about your father," she said, and she meant it.

She hadn't liked the man very much, but then, she hadn't known him well, either.

When she and Zachary had been married, he'd always been away somewhere.

Sara had met Richard Worth exactly once, when he'd come back to the Creek and summoned her to the palace, soon after Zachary's departure, ostensibly to apologize for his son's perfidy and offer her a generous stipend in return for the courtesy of being a mother to the grandchildren he'd never shown the slightest interest in getting to know.

Sara could have used that money — there was no denying that. She'd never gone to college, and there hadn't been a lot of job opportunities in the Creek — she'd been glad to be hired on as a helper at a local day-care center, where she made minimum wage for the first five years.

She'd known, of course, that Zachary would find a way to avoid paying child support.

So she should have said *yes* to Mr. Worth's offer, from a practical standpoint, that was.

And maybe she would have, if, after apologizing, he hadn't launched into a diatribe about cold ambitious women who drove their husbands away by taking jobs and thus humiliating the head of the household.

It was a cold, virulent and ugly speech, and Sara had listened in stunned silence, heat pulsing in her cheeks. When he'd finally stopped long enough to draw a breath, she'd looked him straight in the eye and told him to stick his money and his rampant chauvinism where the sun didn't shine.

He'd laughed and taunted her, said she'd come crawling back with her hand out.

Sara would have died first.

85

"He must be quite old by now," she added, realizing she'd drifted off and left the conversation hanging.

"Ninety-seven," Zachary said, feigning reverence for the venerable patriarch.

Things had quieted down in the kitchen, much to Sara's relief.

"Okay," Sara said, apropos of nothing.

"You've done a great job with the kids," Zachary announced.

"How generous of you to say so," she replied, perhaps a bit snappily.

Again, that expression of pseudo-injury. "And you're still bitter, obviously."

"I'm not, actually. I don't give you any space in my head, you see. There's no room for people like you."

"*People like me?* Have you forgotten, Sara, that I'm the father of your children?"

"Biologically, yes. You were basically a sperm donor. Thanks for that, by the way — and for not one damn thing besides."

Zachary's mouth took on the shape of a slow sexy smile.

Once, that smile had melted her knees.

Now it was just smarmy.

She suppressed a slight shudder. "Why now?" she ventured. "Why this sudden interest in Eric and Hayley, after all this time?"

Zachary pretended to pull a knife from his chest. "You think I didn't care about them? About you?"

"I *know* you didn't care," Sara retorted, careful to keep her voice low so the kids wouldn't hear. "Fathers who love their children stick around to raise them, or at least lend a hand once in a while. They visit and make phone calls, and remember birthdays and graduations and Christmases. You didn't do any of those things, and no excuse you can make will change my mind — you were downright negligent, and while Eric may be susceptible to your charms, I assure you, I am not."

"Whoa," Zachary responded, flinching theatrically. The man should have been an actor; he was a born performer. "I didn't expect a rousing welcome, but I guess I didn't realize just how much you hate me, either."

"I don't hate you," Sara corrected him. "I wouldn't waste my energy doing that."

"No second chances?"

Sara shook her head, kept her spine straight, but not rigid. "I've already given you more chances than I should have, and I see no reason to accommodate you now."

For the first time, Sara saw anger flare like blue fire in his eyes, and his jaw tightened almost imperceptibly. "You can't stop me from spending time with my children, Sara," he said. "I'm their father, and I have a legal right to see them."

"You're right," Sara admitted, trying hard not to let her despair show. "I can't."

"So we don't have a problem."

Sara considered her children. Hayley, she knew, would be shy around Zachary, reluctant to see him without her mother or another trusted adult present. Eric, on the other hand, was clearly vulnerable and, from the looks of things, ready to believe his long-lost dad had returned because he wanted to be a father.

No doubt Zachary had fostered that belief, while he and Eric were communicating behind her back.

She stifled a burst of anger, collected herself.

She would have to handle this very carefully; get herself, Hayley and Eric into family therapy, pronto. Eric was already seeing a counselor once a week, so he would probably balk at the idea of more *shrink time,* as he called it, but there was no other choice, as far as Sara could see.

As she'd suspected, Eric hadn't mentioned his brush with the law during their online chats.

She told Zachary all about it. Admitted she was afraid the boy might go off the rails again, if both she and Zachary didn't tread lightly.

They were, after all, in the middle of an emotional minefield, and a single misstep could send Eric hurtling in the wrong direction again, maybe for good this time.

Zachary listened thoughtfully, and when Sara had finished, he said, "All the more reason for us to cooperate with each other, Sara. Surely you can see that."

Sara wanted to cry, but she was damned if she would let this man see her shed a tear. "If you can help," she said, rather stiffly and with no small measure of doubt, "I'll be grateful." She met Zachary's gaze directly then, and held it. "If, on the other hand, you hurt him, I will make you pay. In spades."

Zachary gave a low humorless laugh. "You've turned hard," he said. "You're not the Sara I remember at all."

Sara ignored that. She was a single mother and, even with Eli's help, she'd had to fight for every inch of progress she'd made, building a solid life for herself and her children.

So, no. She wasn't the softheaded romantic she'd been when she and Zachary were together.

Thank God.

"Hear me, Zachary," she said. "Believe me when I say, if you give me cause, if you do anything — anything at all — to harm my children, you will see a side of me you've never imagined."

He arched one eyebrow, shifted slightly in his chair. "Threats, Sara? I wouldn't have thought you'd stoop to that."

"Not threats, Zachary," Sara answered. "Promises."

Zachary sighed. Got to his feet. "I guess we've reached an impasse — for tonight, anyway. Suppose I say goodbye to the kids and head for home?"

"Good idea," Sara agreed. "Where *is* home these days?"

"I'm back in the ancestral pile," Zachary said. "It's been closed up for years, as you probably know, so it's pretty damn spooky."

"Sucks to be you," Sara replied sweetly.

Zachary laughed. Glanced in the direction of the kitchen.

"Eric," Sara called. "Hayley. Come and say good-night to — our guest, please."

Eric reappeared first, looking chagrined, angry and a little pale.

Hayley followed reluctantly behind him.

"With your mother's permission," Zachary said, probably more for Eli's benefit

90

than Eric and Hayley's, "I'll be in touch tomorrow about our spending the day together."

Hayley shrank back a little, and Eli rested his hands gently on the girl's slender shoulders, silently reassuring her.

Eric frowned at Sara, visibly braced for a refusal and more than ready to object if one came.

"We'll discuss it in the morning," Sara said, holding her son's gaze firmly, but speaking as gently as she could. "Tonight, I think we all need to calm down and get a good night's sleep."

Zachary nodded, his face full of false diplomacy. "Good night, kids."

"Good night," Hayley said, in a near whisper, her eyes still wide with confusion.

"I'll walk you to your car," Eric told Zachary. His tone was belligerent, daring Sara to object.

"Guess I'll go along," Eli said.

Silently, Sara blessed her brother.

Eric cast a resentful glance in his uncle's direction, but he knew a protest would be futile.

To Sara, that was an encouraging sign.

"I'll call you tomorrow," Eli told Sara as he went out.

She nodded, mouthed the word *thanks*.

When the male contingent had gone, Sara crossed to Hayley, cupped the girl's cheeks in her hands.

"You okay, kiddo?" she asked.

"I guess so," Hayley said. Tears welled in her lovely eyes. Cornflower blue, like her father's.

"Pretty big shock, huh?" Sara dropped her hands to her sides. "Your dad appearing out of nowhere, I mean?"

"Yeah," Hayley agreed. "Do I have to spend a whole day with him? My — my *dad*?"

"Not if you don't want to," Sara said.

"He can't force me?"

"Nobody is going to force you to do anything, sweetheart. Not on my watch — *or* your uncle Eli's."

Hayley relaxed a little. "Where has he been all this time?" she wanted to know.

"Good question," Sara replied. "I have no idea, but I'll tell you this much — it *matters* where he's been, and what he's been doing. Your uncle can find out everything we need to know about Zachary's past, and if there's any reason to think he could possibly harm you or your brother in any way, I'll make sure he doesn't get near you."

"What do I call him?" Hayley fretted.

"Let's not worry about that tonight,

sweetheart. Why don't you get ready for bed? Settle in for the night? I'll look in on you in a little while."

"Can he make me call him *Dad*?"

"I've already told you, Hayley — you don't have to do anything you don't want to do, not where Zachary Worth is concerned, anyway." Sara leaned forward, planted a quick kiss on her daughter's forehead. "In the meantime, try not to worry, all right? You won't have to deal with this alone — and that's a promise."

Hayley sighed, swiped at a stray tear with the back of one hand and nodded. "Okay," she replied, in a near whisper. Then just before turning to head for her room, "Thanks, Mom. Love you."

"Love you, too," Sara replied.

Eric was still outside with his father, the two of them busily weaving their singular psychological threads of resentment and personal angst into a chain of opposition.

Divide and conquer. That was Zachary's motto. If he could drive a wedge between Sara and her son, he would do it, not out of any particular animosity — Zachary was far too shallow to sustain *any* emotion, healthy or otherwise, for very long — but simply because he could.

To him, it was a game. Something to

amuse him in the short term.

Sara waited out another surge of adrenaline, then marched herself to the kitchen, where she surveyed her wine collection, housed in its special refrigerator under the long counter.

After a few turbulent moments, she turned and walked away.

Grabbed a glass from a cupboard, went to the sink and poured herself a dose of cold water. Drank it down.

She was refilling the glass when she heard the front door open in the near distance. She sat down at her usual place at the table, water glass in hand, and sipped.

Outside, she heard engines start up.

Vehicles driving away.

Eric's palms struck the other side of the kitchen door hard — but not too hard.

His face was stormy when he stepped into the room.

Without speaking, he hauled back a chair, opposite Sara's, and flung himself onto the seat.

Sara bit back a smile. It was a lot of work, being a teenager, and she marveled that anyone — child or parent — survived the treacherous passing.

"I want to see him, Mom," he blurted out, after a long tempestuous silence. "I want to spend time with my dad."

His gaze met hers, full of challenge.

"Okay," Sara said.

Eric's gray eyes widened slightly. He hadn't been expecting capitulation, of course. *"Okay?"* he repeated. "That's all you have to say?"

Sara took a few restorative sips from her water glass, savoring the clarity of simple hydration. Then, in her own good time, she replied, "It's not one one-thousandth of what I have to say, Eric. Most of it can wait, though."

"What can't?" the boy asked, still testy, and now wary, too. "Wait, I mean?"

"This. You were out of line tonight, making that remark about me going out on a date. And I'm not even going to get into the fact that you've been in touch with your father for some time, without my knowledge, because right now, I don't believe I can be rational about it."

Eric flushed, set his jaw. But he didn't speak.

"I'm not married to your father, and I haven't been for many years. I don't have to explain my personal choices to him *or* to you, and I will thank you to remember that."

"Maybe, once you cool down," Eric said carefully, "you might see that Dad is a good guy, and want to get back together with him."

Sara felt a rush of frustration, and struggled not to show it. Tried to keep her tone moderate, calm. Reasonable.

"That isn't going to happen, Eric. Not ever."

"You won't cool down?" This, too, was a challenge, but not an angry one.

She considered telling a little white lie, saying she'd already gotten her temper under control. Then, as she had with the wine, she dismissed the idea as a bad one.

"I will," she said. "Soon."

"You must have loved Dad once," Eric said, wheedling now. The heat had subsided from his face, but his earlobes still pulsed deep pink.

"I thought I did," Sara clarified, flinching inwardly at the word *Dad*. "I was very young when I met your father. I was immature and sheltered and generally not ready for a grown-up relationship."

Eric frowned, evidently dissatisfied with her answer. "You won't even give this a chance?"

Sara suppressed a sigh. She was so tired.

And she felt strangely displaced, right there in her own familiar kitchen, seated at the table where she'd eaten at least a thousand meals, across from the man-child she'd conceived and carried to term, nurtured and raised, loved and fought with.

For the briefest fraction of a second, she was back on the McCall ranch, mounted on a stodgy mare, with J.P. beside her, astride his powerful gelding.

She felt the fresh kiss of the breeze, the warmth of the sun.

The jolt that had passed through her as she looked into the man's eyes.

Half a heartbeat, and she was back.

Eric was watching her, waiting for an answer.

Unfortunately, he wasn't going to get the one he wanted to hear.

"Even if your — if Zachary — wanted to rekindle an old flame — and I'm pretty sure he doesn't — I *don't*. There's no going back, Eric, and don't press me for reasons, because most of them are none of your business."

"Are you going to see him again? The guy you were out with tonight?"

Sara considered that. Smiled.

"I hope so," she said, recalling the parking-lot kiss. Tingling a little at the memory, which was visceral.

Eric's eyebrows met above the bridge of his nose as he scowled. *"Seriously?"*

The contempt in his voice and expression nettled Sara mightily. "Seriously," she affirmed, without hesitation.

"Who is he?" Eric demanded.

"That," Sara responded, "is no concern of yours."

"You know I'll find out!"

Sara arched an eyebrow. "So?"

Once again, Eric was fuming. "You think it's none of my business who you're going out with," he spit out, in a near hiss, "but it *is,* because you're my mother, and if you get all involved with some guy, I'll have to deal with him. And so will Hayley."

"I *do* think it's none of your business," she affirmed. "It was one dinner. I'm not sure there will ever *be* anything for you — or your sister — *to deal with.*"

"All these years, you've been — well — our mom. You worked at the day care and sometimes you spent time with your friends, or Eli's, but except for a few lunches and movie dates, you never brought a man into the equation. *Now,* just when Dad is back in town and we have a shot at being a family, the four of us, you're *seeing somebody?*"

"*We* are a family, Eric," Sara pointed out evenly. "You, Hayley and me. We have been all along, and we don't need your father — or anyone else — to complete the circle."

How long, she wondered silently, and with a degree of despair, had her son been yearning for his father to return and fulfill his misguided fantasies about the family of his dreams?

How sad had he been? How lonely?

And why hadn't she noticed?

Sure, Eric was very good at hiding his emotions, but surely there must have been signs. Signs she'd missed somehow.

Once again, her heart cracked. Painfully.

Maybe her friends had been right. Maybe she should have dated actively after the divorce, found a good man, a husband for her, a stepfather for Hayley and Eric.

Stepfathers got a bad rap sometimes, she reflected. She'd known a number of solid ones, though, grown-up, integrated guys who had married a woman with children and raised those children, loved them as if they'd been their own.

Because, in their hearts, they *had* been theirs. Biology be damned.

Instead of setting out to find one of these admittedly rare men, Sara had braced her spine, jutted out her chin and muscled her way forward, fierce, determined to be strong, independent, two parents in one.

She'd mostly succeeded, she thought, but that didn't mean she'd made the right choices, done what was really best for her children or for herself.

"I'm still your mom," she told Eric, after the long silence had settled, nearly tangible, between them. "But I'm more than a mom. I'm a *person,* Eric. Not some life-size cardboard character leaning against a wall, forgotten and gathering dust, whenever you and your sister are off doing your own thing."

Eric sighed. His shoulders were hunched. "If you say you have needs, Mom, I will *hurl.* Right here, right now."

Sara laughed, and some of the tension dispelled. "Okay," she said, with a twinkle in both her eyes and her tone, "I won't say it."

"As Hayley would say," Eric retorted, almost himself again, "eeewwww!"

"Go to bed," Sara said.

A hesitation. "You won't stand in my way? You'll let me see Dad whenever I want?"

"You're almost a man, Eric. You have to make your own choices. I'm just hoping you'll make the right ones."

He shoved back his chair, but didn't rise. Splayed his long graceful fingers and thrust them through his dark hair, rumpling it further. Sighed again, heavily.

"There's one more thing."

"Great," Sara replied. "Let's hear it."

"Uncle Eli came here to see me. Tonight, I mean. I might be in trouble again."

Sara, having lapsed into a certain wary complacency only moments before, was on red alert again. *"What?"*

When Eric met her eyes, his were glistening with tears he wouldn't allow himself to shed. "I didn't do anything wrong, Mom. I know I effed up before, but I'm a law-abiding citizen now, I swear."

"What did Eli say?" Sara ventured carefully.

A familiar litany thumped within her brain like a second heartbeat.

Not again, not again, not again.

"Somebody's been chasing wildlife on four-wheelers," Eric answered, staring past his mother's right shoulder as though seeing the scene unfold on the far wall of the kitchen. "Messing with mustangs and deer."

Sara closed her eyes briefly, the litany still drumming within her.

"When I got in trouble before — with Freddie Lansing and the other guys — we let loose a lot of livestock," he reminded her, quite unnecessarily. "Because this new — problem concerns animals, Eli had to question me. Make sure I wasn't involved."

"Were you?"

101

Eric's anger, never far beneath the surface, surged upward again to pulse in his face and roughen his voice. "*No,* Mom," he growled. "I've learned my lesson and, trust me, I'll never break the law again."

Sara believed her son, though she knew the decision was rooted in her heart, not her head. Although they'd never had pets — she wasn't sure why — she'd never imagined, let alone seen, Eric doing deliberate harm to anyone or anything.

"Why do you think you might be in trouble, then?" she asked reasonably. "Does Eli think you were involved?"

Eric's fingers were still in his hair, buried deep. Rubbing hard at his scalp. "I don't know," he replied. "You know how Eli is. He doesn't say what he's thinking. He said — he said he'd find out if I was part of this, and he'd arrest me, right along with the rest of the bunch. In other words, being his nephew won't get me out of anything."

"It didn't before," Sara recalled. It had nearly knocked Eli to his knees, emotionally, when he'd rounded up that band of troublemakers the first time, and found Eric among them, but he'd shown no favoritism toward his sister's son.

Eli was incapable of hypocrisy, and Sara respected him for that.

Practically everyone did.

"No," Eric said, shaking his head, untwining his fingers from his hair, smiling a sad, weary, rueful smile. "No special treatment. That's the rule."

"It's a good rule," Sara pointed out.

Eric sighed. "True."

It was a profound relief to hear her son agree with her. These days, that was pretty rare.

"He asked me if I'd heard anything," the boy went on. "Some of the guys bragging about it, stuff like that." He paused. "And before you ask, no. I don't know a damn thing about this, and I hope it stays that way."

"Me, too," Sara said.

Eric hauled himself to his feet, stretched. "Guess I'll hit the shower and then crash," he told her. "Maybe things will look better in the morning."

"Eric?"

He'd turned away from her, headed toward the door an instant before she spoke, and though he stopped, he didn't look back. "Yeah?"

"I'm not your enemy. I'm your mother, and I love you, and I want you to be happy."

Eric tilted his head back, listening. Said not a word.

"Maybe I come on a little strong sometimes, with the mama-bear thing, and I'll
work on that, I promise. But I'd do pretty
much anything to keep you from wandering
off the path, and that probably isn't going
to change."

He gave a short nod. Sighed again. "You
want me to keep Dad at arm's length," he
proffered, though he sounded resigned
rather than annoyed. "Forget all about him."

"Some part of me does want that, yes,"
Sara admitted softly, "but I realize I don't
have the right to dictate your emotions. I
won't interfere unless —"

"Unless what?"

"Unless I see you taking on certain behav-
iors your father is well-known for."

"Like?"

Sara was talking to her son's back, and
she couldn't gauge his reaction, but she supposed that didn't matter. "You'll find out
soon enough," she said sadly. "But if you
want the CliffsNotes, look up *narcissism*
and pay close attention to the symptoms."

"I know what a narcissist is, Mom," Eric
said, very quietly and without venom. "We
studied personality disorders in Psychology
back in sophomore year."

"Review the subject," Sara persisted, but
gently.

Eric thrust out another gusty, angst-ridden sigh, nodded once more and left the kitchen.

Sara sat at the table for a long time.

Presently, she noticed the weight of her cell phone in the pocket of her jeans, pulled it out and swiped the screen with a practiced motion of her thumb.

There was a text from J.P.

It was simple, straightforward and not in the least romantic, but it made her heart skitter, just the same.

You okay?

CHAPTER FIVE

The sun was well up the next morning when J.P. reached the mouth of Shadow Canyon, pulling a loaded horse trailer behind his truck, Trooper riding shotgun in the front passenger seat.

He'd driven slowly, jostling over cow paths posing as roads, stopping once to jump out of the truck, climb a low ridge and survey his main cattle herd, grazing peacefully in a shallow valley alongside Painted Pony creek. He saw no signs of immediate or recent distress, no tire tracks in the grass, but decided to ride out later for a better look.

He was the first to arrive at the meeting place he and Eli had agreed upon the night before, and that was all right with him. He liked being alone in a wide-open space, taking in the sounds and scents and sprawling blue expanse of the sky.

Trooper leaped out of the truck through the open driver's-side door, and J.P. let him wander, nose to the ground, getting his bearings.

The canyon, carved out of striated rock by a passing glacier — or several of them — many millions of years before, was a massive crevice, wide at the mouth and running more than a mile back into the belly of Black Moon Mountain, narrowing gradually to a point.

Little sunlight reached the depths, but for the first five hundred yards or so, there was grass, though sparse and stubbly. In a few places, springs bubbled up from somewhere deep underground, but they were shallow and often dried up.

The dark canyon — hence its name — was hardly hospitable, even for wild critters like deer and elk, bears and bobcats, coyotes and wolves, but it served as a refuge, for desperate animals, frightened into flight.

Unfortunately, it was also a trap.

J.P. wanted to investigate, and the land he was standing on was legally his own, but he knew that, this time, Eli was calling the shots.

He rounded the truck and trailer, rolled up the metal door and lowered the ramp, made sure it was locked in place, and climbed inside. J.P. wove his way between the horses to check them out, seeing that they'd survived the bumpy ride overland safely.

They were bred and trained for roping and herding cows, these horses, and used to being trailered from one place to another. But it was still a risky enterprise, and J.P. took every possible precaution, before, during and after any trip, short or long.

That day, they were hitched three abreast, with space at the rear of the trailer for turning them around to be led down the ramp to the ground, and J.P. snapped on lead ropes and guided the animals out of the trailer one by one.

Shiloh, his gelding, came last, and he lifted his nose to the wind first thing, pricked his ears forward, nickered and pranced a little.

A roiling plume of dust appeared in the distance, speeding along the winding dirt road that crossed the McCall ranch about three-quarters of the way, then swerved north onto Cord Hollister's place.

Hollister pulled up alongside J.P.'s truck in his own similar rig, shut off the engine and joined J.P., who had just saddled Shiloh and moved on to tack up a second gelding.

"How was Florida?" J.P. asked to start the conversation rolling. Cord wasn't one to volunteer information, trivial or otherwise.

Cord grinned. "Hot," he said.

"Still a man of few words, I see," J.P. observed wryly.

His friend chuckled and shook his head as he took a saddle and blanket from the back of J.P.'s truck and commenced to help out. "I could say the same thing about you, my friend," he said lightly.

By the time Eli and two of his deputies arrived, all six horses were ready to ride.

"Looks like we're short one member of the posse," J.P. observed.

Eli gave him a look. "No," he said, cocking a thumb in the direction of the dirt road behind him. "There will be six of us, according to plan."

J.P. looked in the direction Eli had pointed and saw a police cruiser barreling toward them.

"You're kidding me," he said.

"I'm serious as the proverbial heart attack," Eli replied.

The cruiser came to a lurching, dirt-flinging stop nearby.

The driver's-side door flew open and Melba Summers, Painted Pony Creek's chief of police, stepped out. She was in full uniform, waving one hand in front of her face as she walked toward the rest of them, trying to dispel some of the dust.

Melba Summers was a good cop. She'd

saved Eli's life, in fact, back before she'd resigned her job as a deputy to accept the new and better position the mayor had offered her.

She was strong, smart, beautiful and Black.

She was also heavily pregnant. As in, due to pop in just a month or two.

J.P. fought down an objection, knowing it would get him nowhere.

Eli smiled at Melba. He respected her, obviously, and moreover, he *liked* her, but like the other men gathered to ride rough under a hot sun, possibly for hours, he had his misgivings.

"Don't you dare patronize me, Eli Garrett!" Melba warned, looking stern. "I'm here to oversee this shindig, and don't give me an argument. I'm the freaking *chief of police,* and you are *not* going to sideline me just because I'm a pregnant woman!"

Eli put his hands out from his sides in a conciliatory gesture. "I wouldn't think of sidelining you, Chief," he said, with just the slightest hint of a grin taking shape around his mouth. "Certainly not because you're a woman, but I've got to admit, I thought you planned on riding horseback, and I certainly had my reservations about letting you bounce around in a hard saddle for half a day. Maybe longer. Damn, what if — well, what if you'd mounted up and knocked something loose?"

Melba raised an eyebrow. "Like a baby, you mean?"

"Yeah," Eli retorted. "Like a baby."

"Well, that isn't going to happen, because I mean to hold the fort right here, while you yahoos do all the riding. Furthermore, I'm not ready to deliver. My maternity leave doesn't begin for another two weeks."

"I hope you've informed the baby," Eli said.

"Do you want to hear my plan or not?"

Eli made an irritated beckoning gesture with one hand.

"You're out there," Melba said, "something happens. You need medics, for instance, or you find a body and you need the coroner, Doc Stone, and his sidekick, Sam Wu. So you radio Melba J. Summers, chief of police, and she — *I* — send for reinforcements."

"Fine," Eli replied, his voice clipped. Obviously, he was still uncomfortable with Melba's present delicate condition, but he knew when he was beaten.

She was a sight in her dusty blue uniform and billed hat, with her badge glinting at its front. Her service belt must have been buckled through the last available hole, and the front of it disappeared beneath her wide round belly.

"What are you looking at?" she demanded, sweeping the whole assembly up in a glare.

Nobody spoke.

They all turned away quickly, mounted their own horses, Eli included.

Naturally, he took the lead. "I'll ride into the canyon, see what I come across," he said. "The rest of you fan out, you pick the direction, and look for anything out of the ordinary — tracks, signs of a campfire, dead or injured animals. We'll stay in touch by radio." He paused. Looked at Cord and then J.P., who, of course, were not equipped for the form of communication just mentioned, and cell service was hit or miss that far out. "You two probably know every inch of this place and all the adjoining ranches, too. Split up and check all the potential hideouts. We'll meet back here in two hours. Is everybody clear?"

There were nods, muttered agreements and the like.

J.P. rode off alone, except for Trooper, thinking of all the places he and Cord and Eli had discovered, roaming the McCall and Hollister ranches as kids: caves, mine shafts, crumbling line shacks and cabins.

If a person — or a group — wanted to lie low out here, there were plenty of places to hide.

He decided to start at the farthest part — an ancient line shack maybe three miles distant — and work his way back from there. The shack wasn't far from his folks' A-frame, which made it a less likely choice as a robber's roost, but it had one thing in its favor: if Trooper got tuckered out, he could visit J.P.'s mom and dad until the search was over.

The day was beautiful, though it promised to be hot later in the day, and J.P. found himself enjoying the ride. He stopped alongside a wide spot in the creek to let his horse drink, Trooper lapping up cool water right next to Shiloh.

Sure enough, the dog's tongue was beginning to loll, and he'd slowed down a little, picking his way along over the rough ground as though his paws hurt.

The sight stabbed J.P. in the deepest part of his heart and, not for the first time, he wished dogs lived forever.

When Trooper's time came, J.P. would grieve sorely and for a long, long time.

As it turned out, there was no sign, at least outwardly, that any human being had been near the old line shack in a while.

J.P. rode the perimeter, just the same, then got down off Shiloh's back and peered inside the tumbledown structure.

Nothing.

He mounted up again and headed for his parents' place, about three-quarters of a mile west of the line shack.

The sliding glass doors on the side of the A-frame were wide open to the fresh air and blue sky when he got there, and J.P.'s mom, Sylvia, tall and slim and fair-haired, like her son, was busy in the yard, hanging laundry out to dry.

Like her husband, Sylvia liked to do a lot of things the old-fashioned way, when that was possible. She owned top-of-the-line appliances, including a clothes dryer, but when the weather was good, she preferred to dry shirts and socks and jeans — and especially sheets — in the sun.

Seeing J.P. approach, she finished pegging a white sheet to the line and then stooped to greet Trooper, who trotted toward her.

She laughed and bent to ruffle the dog's ears in happy welcome.

"Breakfast is over," she told J.P., smiling as she straightened again, "but the coffee's on and I could be persuaded to whip up a batch of pancakes or some waffles."

J.P. grinned, shook his head. "Thanks, but

I can't stay. Eli drummed up a posse and I'm on it." He glanced down at the tired dog. "Trooper could use a break, though. Mind if he stays awhile?"

Sylvia McCall laughed again, not from amusement but from sheer joy. She'd had her share of trials and tribulations, like everyone else, but despite all that, she was one of the happiest people J.P. knew.

She believed, and had told her children often enough, that happiness was a decision, a choice, not something that had to be bestowed by some benevolent outside force or chased down and wrestled into submission.

Like Abraham Lincoln, Sylvia thought most folks were about as happy as they made up their minds to be.

"Sure, he can stay." She shaded her tanned face with one hand, looked up at J.P. "Is this about the mustangs and the deer?"

"Yes," J.P. answered, standing in his stirrups for a few seconds to stretch his legs. He was still in his thirties, though forty was only a few years away. Was he getting old, like Trooper? "I don't suppose you or Dad have seen or heard anything unusual?"

Sylvia sighed. Lowered her hand, squinted because the sun was still in her eyes. "A few times, late at night, we thought we heard

115

motors. Not trucks or cars, but those off-road things that sound like a chain saw or a lawn mower being cranked up. Your dad wanted to go right out and investigate, but I told him, *John, your last name is McCall, not Wayne. You stay right here in this house!*"

J.P. smiled. "Where is Dad, anyway?"

"He went to town, mainly for chicken feed, but I daresay he'll stop off at Bailey's before he comes home to grab some lunch and gossip with the other old-timers. I expect him back around one o'clock."

J.P. nodded, remembering the Zoom meeting he had scheduled for the afternoon. "Have you heard from Josie?" he asked tentatively.

Sylvia shook her head. Her short curly hair bounced around her face, giving her a youthful look. "No," she said. "Is there a reason why I should have?"

He was between a rock and a hard place.

"Was that a question you can't answer?" his mother asked.

J.P. nodded again, and even that was a concession.

"Maybe I should call Josie," Sylvia mused.

"I'd wait, if I were you," J.P. replied. "Be ready for a visit from the girls, though. I'm pretty sure they'll be headed our way soon."

Sylvia's smile was wide. "Well, now, *that's*

good news."

J.P. was relieved. Maybe this mess, whatever it was, would work out without anybody getting their feathers ruffled.

Not that either John or Sylvia were all that easy to ruffle.

"I'd better go," J.P. said, before issuing a gentle command to Trooper.

The dog slunk toward the house, climbed the stairs to the deck and plunked himself down under the glass-topped wrought iron table for some shut-eye.

"We'll look after our grand-dog here," Sylvia said. "Trooper and I will see you later. And you be careful, J.P. If the troublemakers you and Eli are after are low enough to run deer and pester wild horses, they're probably a danger to people, too."

J.P. touched the brim of his hat. "Yes, ma'am," he said solemnly. He was armed with a .38 tucked into a saddle holster, but she didn't need to know that.

Sylvia waved him away. "Get out of here," she said with affection.

After another glance at Trooper, who looked comfortable, lying there on the warm floor of the deck, shaded by the tabletop, J.P. rode away.

He headed for the cabin next.

The roof was falling in, and the front door

lay like a ramp in front of the threshold, but this was nothing new.

J.P.'s great-great grandparents, Alva and Mansfield McCall, had parked their broken-down covered wagon here, early in the last century, staked their claim and built themselves a one-room cabin.

The original plot of land measured the standard one hundred and sixty acres. But over the coming years, Alva and Mansfield had slowly added to their holdings, raising crops and cattle, saving most of their money in the good times and riding out the bad ones with a kind of endurance that was all too rare in this day and age.

They'd produced seven children, three of whom had lived to adulthood.

Two sons and a daughter.

They had sweat to hold on to the ranch, as had several subsequent generations, including J.P.'s own father.

Now it was his.

No wife, no children.

Would the McCall legacy die with him?

Would Becky and Robyn, who would inherit if J.P. produced no heirs, pass the place down to their kids, if they had any, or would they simply sell out and forget all about the men and women and children who had worked and struggled, suffered and celebrated, lived and died on this land?

The thought saddened J.P. deeply, and the old and mostly secret desire for a family of his own flared fierce within him as he dismounted, left Shiloh to graze untethered and walked toward the wreck of a cabin.

Looking it over, he rubbed his chin, felt the beginning of a beard roughening his jawline, even though he'd shaved only a few hours before.

There wasn't much left of the little house, actually.

These days, it was a home for spiders, mice, rabbits and other such critters, but it hadn't been a *real* home for almost a century, and it would never be one again.

Books and movies romanticized the old West, painting it as a simpler time, but the lives of those early McCalls had been hard ones, for sure. As had those of all their neighbors.

The nearest doctor was probably miles away, and haphazardly trained.

Accidents happened, and sickness could strike suddenly, out of nowhere.

J.P. had read, in an old diary kept by one of Alva's daughters-in-law, about a neighboring family living a few miles away. They'd started the day as a unit, a father and mother and six sturdy children.

Diphtheria had sneaked in with no warning whatsoever, and by nightfall four of those six children, lively and full of plans at breakfast time, were dead.

The next day, the parents had dug four graves, with no help from anyone, due to the contagious nature of the disease, and laid two sons and two daughters to rest, with only each other for solace.

J.P. made a mental note to come back in a day or so and hack away the bushes. Pay his belated respects.

Presently, he hauled himself back into the saddle and nudged Shiloh into a trot.

He was burning daylight, and there were still those caves to scout out.

He wondered if Eli and the others had found anything and, more out of habit than anything else, pulled his phone from his shirt pocket.

Not surprisingly, he had no service.

He rode on and examined the first of several caves nestled into the low foothills surrounding Black Moon Mountain.

It was small, that cave, and there was no room for a full-grown adult to stand upright.

As kids, J.P., Eli and Cord had claimed that rocky hole in the hillside as a fort, certain it had once been part of a village. They'd scoured it for arrowheads, pot shards and Native hieroglyphics, all to no avail and spit-sworn to keep its existence a secret until death.

They'd been ready to start high school when Cord's grandfather informed them that generations of boys had staked their claim to that cave.

After that, they'd lost interest.

The second cave, high on the hillside and inaccessible even on horseback, was probably another dud — in terms of evidence, anyway. But J.P. dismounted and climbed up there anyhow, cursing as he went.

As he'd expected, there was nothing.

The third and final cave, also a few dozen yards up the side of the hill, could be reached by a narrow trail.

Here, J.P. hit figurative pay dirt.

The trail had been churned up recently, and using the flashlight feature on his phone, he made out the shadowy shapes of several off-road vehicles, hidden well back from the mouth of the cave.

Upon further investigation, he identified no less than four mud-caked, rust-speckled ATVs parked there. A motorcycle, cobbled together out of random spare parts, leaned against the cave wall.

None of the rigs sported license plates, but J.P. found the VINs after scraping away a few layers of dirt with the blade of his pocketknife.

"Hello," J.P. muttered, and after leaving the cave, he checked his phone again.

Oddly enough, he had service again, though he knew it would be sketchy.

He speed-dialed Eli.

Zip.

Maybe the sheriff was still in the canyon, where the signals from the nearest cell tower couldn't reach.

He scrabbled back down the trail to Shiloh, hauled himself into the saddle and set out for the meeting place at the base of Shadow Canyon.

Cord had already returned, and so had the two deputies.

Melba had gone back to town once the deputies arrived.

Charlie Canfield, one of these deputies, had found the remains of a campfire in his travels, and a few crumpled beer cans on the far side of the creek, but Cord and the other deputy had come up dry.

J.P. told them about the ATVs and battered motorcycle he'd found in the last of the three caves.

Charlie let out a long whistle. "The sheriff is going to find *that* interesting," he predicted. Like the rest of them, he was hot and dusty, and being unused to riding horseback, he was most likely saddle sore, too.

"Did anybody bring beer?" the other deputy asked.

Cord grinned, walked to his truck and pulled a cooler out of the back seat.

The four men were slaking their thirst when Eli rode out of the canyon, looking grim.

J.P. lowered his can of beer and approached. "You found something," he said, looking up at him.

Eli's face was rock-hard. "Half a dozen dead deer," he said. "Looks as though they were run until they collapsed."

"Shit," J.P. cursed, crumpling the beer can in one hand.

"J.P. found something," Cord put in.

"What?" Eli asked, his gaze on J.P.

J.P. handed his friend a cold one and resettled his hat. Then he told the sheriff about his discovery.

"Let's have a look," he said.

Of course, he knew where the cave in question could be found, and he decided to drive there in his official rig, a rugged SUV.

He turned to Cord and J.P. "Charlie and Ned and me will check out the cave. If you two wouldn't mind tending to the horses,

123

I'd be grateful." He paused. "Hell, I *am* grateful. Thanks, both of you, for everything you did."

"That's it?" Cord asked, annoyed. "We don't get to be in on the follow-up?"

"You're civilians," Eli pointed out. "And I've already pushed my luck by roping you into county business. We can meet sometime in the next few days, if you want, and I'll fill you in on the details."

Eli's tone was mild and his manner was easy, but that didn't mean he hadn't made up his mind about turning them loose. They knew their friend well; he would tell them what he wanted to, when he wanted to, and that was the end of it.

The three of them made plans to meet at Scully's for lunch the next day, and Eli and the deputies got into the SUV and drove off.

Cord and J.P. dutifully unsaddled the horses, gave them each a quick rubdown with rags, and then loaded the tired animals into the trailer, securing them carefully.

"Want me to follow you to your place and help you unload?" Cord asked.

J.P. smiled, slapped his friend on the shoulder. "I can manage," he said. "You go on home and rest up from that trip to Florida. You pretty much had to hit the ground running."

Cord returned the smile, sighed. "Thanks," he said. "I'll do that."

They parted then, driving away in their separate trucks.

J.P. picked up Trooper on his way home.

Like always, the dog's very presence soothed him. They'd crossed some dark mental valleys, the pair of them.

In the early days of his recovery, when the pain had been incessant and flashbacks had haunted him, asleep or awake, Trooper had kept him going.

Back at the house, J.P. headed straight for the shower, where he scrubbed off the sweat and trail dust and thought about dead deer and wild horses and ATVs hidden in caves.

He wanted to know a hell of a lot more than he knew now for certain. Maybe, as Eli would definitely point out if challenged, J.P. *wasn't* a lawman, but these crimes — if there *were* crimes — had been carried out on his land.

At least some of them, anyhow.

Didn't that give him a say in how things were handled?

Stuck somewhere between yes and no, he got out of the shower, dried off and put on clean jeans and a worn T-shirt, a relic of a long-ago rodeo up in Kalispell.

He padded barefoot back to the kitchen, built himself a sandwich, grabbed a bottle of water and sat down at the table.

He'd left his phone there, beside the laptop, and remembering that he'd messaged Sara the night before — had it really been just last night? — he decided to check for a reply.

His heart turned skittish when he saw that she'd responded to his uninspired, You okay?

I'm fine. Is that horseback ride and picnic you mentioned still an option?

It was a simple, ordinary text, and yet it made J.P. want to leap up, let out a whoop and punch the air with his fist.

He didn't want to startle the dog — or act like a damn fool — so he stayed in his chair, grinning widely as he typed his reply.

Name the day, he wrote, and we'll take it from there.

To his surprise, she responded immediately.

Saturday?

J.P. didn't hesitate. That was two days away.

126

Saturday will be great, he wrote back.

You provide the horses, Sara replied, and I'll bring the food. What time?

J.P. considered the question. He rolled out of bed at *sparrow-fart,* as his dad liked to say, so it would have been fine with him if she showed up before sunrise, but other people, especially if they lived in town, liked to sleep in on weekends.

Sara might be one of those people.

And he didn't want to seem too eager. That might creep her out.

So he wrote, How about 10 or 11 o'clock? I'll have the horses saddled and we'll have time to pick out a place for the picnic.

Sara answered with, Suppose we split the difference and I get there at about 10:30. Anything in particular you'd like to eat?

His response to that perfectly innocent question was a strident surge of heat and an instant erection. *Now that you mention it . . .* he thought, but didn't write.

He waited a few moments, collecting himself, and then responded.

Whatever you decide on will be fine with me, Sara. See you Saturday.

Her answer was a caricature emoji giving a thumbs-up.

127

He grinned at that, then set his phone aside, finished his sandwich and waited for his hard-on to subside.

When his makeshift meal was over, he decided to check out his sister's girlhood bedroom, a large space Clare and Josie had shared, though often not willingly.

Clare, the eldest, resembled Sylvia. She was tall, blonde and innately practical, and she'd been the studious type in high school, dating now and then but not seriously.

She'd been married briefly, after grad school, but it hadn't lasted.

Clare remained single, and she seemed to like it that way.

Josie, the middle child, was small, and she'd been one of the popular kids. Her grades were high, seemingly without effort, and things had come easily to her.

Being so different from each other, and two years apart in age, Clare and Josie butted heads plenty of times.

J.P., the youngest by almost seven years, had steered clear of what his folks referred to as the *Sister Wars* as much as he could. He loved his siblings, but the truth was he hadn't known them very well, given the age gap. Besides, they'd been *girls.*

Which meant they might as well have been aliens from the planet Pink.

By the time he'd entered middle school, they were both grown up and gone, visiting for a week or two in the summer, sometimes coming home for Christmas or Easter.

J.P. hadn't really missed them, though early on there had been plenty of times when he would have traded them for brothers in a heartbeat.

Cord and Eli had filled that role nicely, however.

Now he stood in the doorway of the room, remembering those thrilling days of yesteryear.

The wallpaper was pale pink, with tiny rosebuds printed on it, and the curtains over the long cushioned window seat were white lace.

There were two twin-size beds with matching frilly linens, and a few plush animals — a unicorn, a teddy bear, a good-sized elephant — were still in evidence, though a bit timeworn and threadbare.

All the furniture, nightstands, bureau, desk and chests of drawers were white, and the carpet — the only one left in the entire house — was a dusty shade of rose.

The place could use some tidying up, but in a weird way, it looked as though Clare and Josie had just stepped out and might return at any moment, find him there and yell at him to get out of their room.

He grinned at that.

And he almost, but not quite, missed them.

His once-a-week cleaning service would show up on Friday, so no worries about the place being ready for human habitation whenever the nieces actually arrived.

Thanks to the renovations he'd done a few years back, his old bedroom was now a guest space. These days, it boasted sleek modern furniture and a spacious adjoining bathroom with a fancy claw-foot tub and a shower large enough to accommodate a small orgy.

And it had never housed a single guest.

J.P. went on to the master suite, where he slept.

This part of the house had been renovated a few years after his parents had made the permanent move to their A-frame. With the exception of his sisters' shared quarters, he'd changed practically everything.

The house was big, with a huge living room, a combination man-cave/library and plenty of built-ins. For all that, when and if he found the right woman and started a family, he planned to add on.

The right woman.

The phrase snagged in his mind, and a

reckless thought arose from the tangle.

Maybe — just maybe — Sara was that woman.

But was he the right man for her?

He still had flashbacks, on occasion. Nightmares, too.

Should Sara — or any other woman, for that matter — have to deal with those things?

CHAPTER SIX

Eric's phone, always within easy reach, began to buzz and jiggle on the surface of the breakfast table.

Sara, who hadn't slept well, hoped the caller would turn out to be his girlfriend, Carly Hollister, or one of her son's other friends, but she knew even as Eric answered that she wasn't going to get her wish.

"Sure, Dad," Eric said, beaming. "That would be great. See you in half an hour."

A pause. "Right, I'll tell her. 'Bye."

Hayley, finished with her light meal of yogurt and granola and standing at the sink, had stiffened at the word *Dad,* though she didn't say anything.

With jerky movements, she rinsed her bowl and spoon and stowed them in the machine.

Sara watched her daughter out of the corner of her eye, while keeping Eric in her sights at the same time. It was a trick mothers learned early and well.

Eric spared his sister a distracted glance, and if he noticed her discomfort, he didn't acknowledge the fact. Instead, he met his mother's gaze and announced, "Dad's picking us up in half an hour. He'll give Hay and me a tour of the mansion and the new housekeeper will serve lunch. We're supposed to bring our swimming suits, because the pool is ready and waiting."

"I'm not going," Hayley said. "Mom said I don't have to."

Eric frowned. "Why not?" he asked. Hayley had his full attention now, and the mood in the kitchen bristled a little.

Hayley spread her hands. "I don't even *know* the man," she said. "He could be an axe murderer!"

The *axe murderer* part was an exaggeration, but Sara didn't offer a comment. Hayley was making a point, however dramatic her delivery, and she had a right to speak her mind.

Eric gave a bitter growl-like chuckle, shoved back his chair and stood, gathering up his empty plate, silverware and the glass he'd recently drained of orange juice. "That's stupid," he said with the kind of cutting disdain only teenagers can carry off. "He's your *father.* And how are you sup-

133

posed to get to know Dad if you won't spend any time with him?"

Hayley moved out of his way as he approached the dishwasher, though her mannerisms revealed recalcitrance, rather than any sort of intimidation. She could be emotional at times, but that had more to do with her age than her actual personality.

"Maybe I don't *want* to know him, Eric," she told her brother. "Did you ever think of that? He *abandoned* us, remember?"

Sara felt like a spectator at a fencing match. But, again, she didn't feel compelled to intercede. *Good point, kiddo,* she thought.

"Everybody makes mistakes," Eric responded with a shrugging motion of one shoulder. He was bending a little, placing his plate, glass and silverware in the dishwasher. "Give the guy a break, will you?"

Hayley folded her arms. "Why should I?" she countered. "What did he ever do for me — for any of us?" The girl's cheeks flashed pink. "He couldn't be bothered to even show up all these years, and now, all of a sudden, he's decided to play the loving father? If you don't think there's something suspicious about that, brother dear, then you're not too bright."

Sara, still seated at the table, took a sip of coffee, then set her mug down beside her own plate. She'd devoured her toast and jam, leaving only crumbs behind.

"Hayley," she said evenly. "Your brother is *very* bright, just like you."

Both children flung a glare in her direction.

"What do you mean *suspicious*?" Eric demanded, turning back to his sister. "You've been watching too many of those crime shows online."

Hayley *was* a fan of crime shows, gobbling up episodes of *60 Minutes,* both the American and Australian versions, and *Forensic Files.* Most of her friends watched makeup and style videos on YouTube, Instagram or TikTok instead, but they all wanted to be models and actors and, eventually, wives and mothers.

Hayley's goal was to earn a degree in Criminal Justice and one day succeed her uncle Eli as the sheriff of Wild Horse County.

Marriage and motherhood, thank God, were not on her radar yet.

After all, she was only sixteen.

"It makes more sense than playing stupid computer games all the time," Hayley replied. "And *here's* what I mean by *suspicious* — Daddy Dearest doesn't call, doesn't visit, doesn't do *anything* for more than a *decade,* but now here he is, out of the blue, acting like he gives a damn about either of us!"

Sara felt a pang at Hayley's words, not because she sympathized with Zachary, but because she had assumed that her daughter was content with having one parent. Indeed, she'd seemed happy to rely on Eli as a father figure, and he had met her expectations, showing up at all her birthday parties, sporting events, spelling bees and the like.

Eli had been the one to escort Hayley to the dad-and-daughter dinner at school the previous year, and she'd seemed so happy with the plan.

Now that she was getting an idea of how deeply Hayley's resentment and hurt over her father's absence ran, Sara wondered if she'd been too complacent where her daughter's emotional health was concerned.

Hayley had always been the *easy* child, while Eric had been, if not entirely difficult, certainly a challenge. For all that, Eli had been there for Eric, always — taken him fishing, taught him to ride — all the things a man does for a fatherless nephew.

Or a son.

Tears stung the backs of Sara's eyes. Had Hayley gotten the attention she needed from her, being the wheel that rarely squeaked?

She laid a hand to her own chest, fingers splayed.

She took a deep breath, released it and tuned back in to the conversation between her son and daughter.

"Maybe Dad ignored you, but he and I have been messaging for a while now. Three months, in fact. And maybe he was *afraid* to get in touch any sooner than he did," Eric pressed. "He says Mom poisoned us against him."

The very suggestion speared Sara in a very tender part of her heart. She'd worked hard not to bad-mouth Zachary to the kids, though it hadn't been easy.

She'd confided in Eli a few times over the years, though, and vented to several of her friends. Possibly, Eric had overheard, taken in her words, stashed them away in his mind, where they'd turned to stone.

"I did no such thing," Sara said firmly. She was a morning person, at her best and most confident in the earlier hours of the day.

That was why she wrote until noon, then spent the rest of her workday researching, revising or brainstorming new ideas.

She glanced at her phone, saw the time.

She was due at her computer in fifteen

137

minutes. Although her editor hadn't gotten back to her with revision notes yet, she was already combing through the manuscript, looking for contradictions, typos, loose ends.

Both children had ignored her protestation of innocence.

"Well, I don't want anything to do with him," Hayley was saying, her tone heated. "As far as I'm concerned, he's nobody."

"Then it's your loss, I guess," Eric retorted, seething. He favored Sara with another glare, this one accusing, and blasted his way out of the kitchen.

A silence fell.

Sara stared at her phone, comforting herself with the knowledge that Saturday morning she would pack up a picnic lunch and head out to the McCall ranch to spend a few hours with J.P.

He was part of the reason she hadn't been able to settle down and give in to her usual deep sleep the night before.

She was excited.

Intrigued.

Unfortunately, the *other* reason she'd tossed and turned was Zachary.

Like Hayley, she was suspicious. Why, after showing no interest in his children for such a long time, had Zachary suddenly returned to Painted Pony Creek?

"I'm going over to Amanda's for a while, if that's okay with you," Hayley said, interrupting her mother's thoughts. "She ordered some temporary tattoos on Amazon, and we want to try them out."

"Just be sure they're temporary," Sara replied.

Hayley, more relaxed now that Eric had left the room, laughed softly. "They're sort of a trial run," she admitted. "Amanda's thinking of getting a real one."

"Amanda can do what she wants. *You,* on the other hand, will be grounded until you turn forty if you sneak into some tattoo parlor and get inked on — any part of your body."

Hayley grinned, stopped by Sara's chair and bent to plant a kiss on the top of her head. "You know I wouldn't do that," she said. "You have to be eighteen, and none of the local shops would let me in the door anyway, with Eli Garrett for an uncle."

Sara smiled, squeezed her daughter's hand. "Can we talk sometime soon, honey?" she asked. "About your father?"

Hayley hesitated, and her grin fell away. "What is there to say? I think he's a waste of space, and I don't want anything to do with him. Case closed."

Case closed.

Hayley Worth, future sheriff.

"Did you miss him, Hayley? Did you wish you'd had a father, like most of your friends?"

Hayley shook her head. Laid one slender hand on Sara's shoulder and gave her a light squeeze. *"No,"* she said good-naturedly. "You've been a great mom, and Uncle Eli filled in all the father gaps. I'm good, so don't go plotting stories about me like I'm one of your characters, okay?"

Sara smiled again, patted her daughter's hand. "Okay," she confirmed.

As a writer, she *did* sometimes invent scenarios in her busy brain, starring her children, her brother, her closest friends.

The ones about Eli were the worst, since his job was dangerous.

She shook her head.

She was not going to worry about the kids, or what Zachary might be up to, or Eli getting injured or killed in the line of duty.

She would think about her current writing project until noon.

Then she planned on getting out her battered wicker picnic basket — stored in the garage — and cleaning it up. Come Saturday morning, she would fill it with goodies from the deli and bakery at the supermarket.

Just thinking about another horseback ride

140

with J.P., and a romantic picnic in some shady spot, probably near the creek, gave her a reckless little thrill.

She'd loved Zachary once, very deeply, and though her children had been her main concern ever since, she'd been hurt, too. Deeply disillusioned.

She still didn't truly trust herself to choose a good man.

And she'd been lonely.

She'd ignored that, repressed her personal desires, told herself she was a mother first and a woman second. She'd held the line, fought the good fight, put her children and their needs ahead of everything and everyone else.

Now Eric and Hayley were nearly grown up.

Before she knew it, they'd be away from home, attending college, then starting careers, getting married, having children of their own . . .

Sara put on the mental brakes.

No use getting too far ahead of herself.

Sufficient unto the day . . .

She stood up, rinsed her plate, utensils and coffee mug, put everything into the dishwasher, added soap and started the machine.

She heard a car pull up outside, watched

as Eric zoomed past her with a desultory wave of one hand and a muttered, " 'Bye, Mom."

"Have fun," she said, softly and too late.

Eric had already closed the front door behind him.

Sara was booting up her computer, ten minutes later, when Hayley appeared in the doorway of her home office.

"They're gone, right?" she asked.

"If you mean your father and your brother," Sara replied, "then, yes, they're gone."

Hayley's grin was back. She waggled her fingers at Sara and chirped, "See you later, Momster."

Sara turned in her swivel chair to look directly at her daughter. "We still need to have that talk at some point. About your dad, I mean." A pause. "And don't forget — no tattoos."

Hayley raised one palm, as though swearing an oath in a court of law. "No tattoos," she promised. "Except the kind that wash off, that is."

Apparently, she'd decided to ignore the prospect of a dad-discussion.

Sara chuckled and shook her head. The talk about Zachary could wait, though not for very long. "Have fun, Silly-bug. I'll see you later."

Hayley was already turning away.

"Hayley?" Sara called after her, her tone tentative.

Her daughter paused, turned around. "Yeah?" she asked, with gracious impatience. Hayley had her moments, like any teenage girl, but she was a good kid all around.

"I love you."

Hayley's pretty face softened. "Love you, too," she said.

And then she was gone.

The house felt beyond empty.

Sara decided she needed a little more caffeine in her system, and poured more coffee.

When she returned to her office, her phone was jiggling about on the surface of her desk.

Her first thought was that one of the kids needed her.

Her second was that J.P. was calling to say he'd changed his mind about the horseback ride and the picnic.

The reality — it was Brynne, her sister-in-law and close friend.

"You didn't call me," Brynne accused cheerfully when Sara had answered with a relieved *hello*. "You just left me hanging.

Wondering about you and J.P., sharing a table at Bailey's and looking for all the world like two people on a date."

Sara laughed softly. "Is that what we looked like?"

"Stop stalling," Brynne said. "You know damn well what I mean."

"I guess you could say it was a date," Sara allowed, very slowly.

Brynne gave a little cry of delight. "I *told* Eli there was something going on between the two of you, and he said to mind my own business. I told *him* I had no intention of doing any such thing."

Sara couldn't stop smiling. "Men," she commiserated.

"Right?" Brynne chimed. "Are you seeing him again? J.P., I mean?"

Sara hesitated. She wasn't sure what was happening between her and J.P., and she didn't want Brynne planning a wedding.

Now that she had started her combination art gallery, studio space and wedding venue business, Brynne might very well be thinking in terms of white lace and promises.

"Yes," she admitted at long last. "But it's early days, Brynne. I'm not sure where this is going — if it's going anywhere at all."

"You're perfect for each other!" Brynne said.

"I don't know about that," Sara said.

"I do," Brynne persisted. "I've known both of you forever, remember."

"Brynne —"

"Don't worry," her friend said quietly. "I won't say a thing. Except to Eli, of course, and you know how he is. The original strong, silent type."

Sara felt a surge of love for her friend. "How are the twins?"

"Growing at a truly frightening rate," Brynne answered. Then, more cautiously, she went on, "I hear Zachary is back in town."

Sara released a loud sigh and said, "Yes. He's playing the misunderstood-but-very-devoted father at the moment."

"That bastard," Brynne said.

"Exactly," Sara replied.

"Listen, I actually had another reason for calling, Sara."

"Yes? What would that be?"

"I was thinking you might want something different to do, between finishing the current book and starting a new one."

"Such as?"

"Helping me out with this monster of a wedding coming up over at the lodge."

The lodge was the name Brynne had given her rustic establishment, for the sake of convenience.

"What would I be doing?"

"Lots of things. Like I said, this is an event of gargantuan proportions. Three brides — triplets. Horses, people in medieval costumes — a cast of thousands, or at least it *seems* that way. The future mother-in-law is a terror, and the mother of the brides? A bona fide momzilla. The whole thing is going to be an absolute nightmare, and I haven't been able to hire *half* the extra staff I'm going to need."

"You're making a great case, Brynne," Sara said, amused. "The trouble is it's a case *against* my saying yes."

"Please," Brynne said, humorously plaintive. "I'll pay you handsomely, as they say in English novels."

Sara didn't have to consider the offer further; she'd made up her mind the moment Brynne first hinted that she needed help.

She hesitated anyway.

"Sara?" Brynne prompted.

"You know I'll help," Sara replied.

"Yes!" Brynne crowed.

"I've still got a couple weeks of work to do on the book," Sara warned.

"That's fine," Brynne replied. "I'm interviewing a wedding planner over lunch today.

He's super-qualified, but I've never actually met him. Why don't you join us? I could really use a fresh perspective."

"He?" Sara echoed, intrigued.

"Yes. His name is David Fielding, and if he looks anything like his profile photos, he's Cary Grant–handsome. He's worked all over the world, and his weddings have been featured in major magazines, on TV, you name it."

"And he wants to work in Painted Pony Creek, Montana?" Sara asked, with surprise rather than sarcasm. "That's interesting. How old is this man?"

"Midforties, I'd guess," Brynne replied, sounding distracted now. Little wonder, since she had twin babies, not walking yet but crawling for sure — usually in two different directions.

Sara adored her nephews.

"Well," Brynne went on when Sara didn't speak again. "Will you join us or not?"

"I'll join you," Sara confirmed. "Where and when?"

"One o'clock sharp, over at Sully's."

Sara raised an eyebrow. "Not Bailey's?"

"No," Brynne replied. "I don't want the regulars ogling this poor man."

"You don't think the clientele at Sully's will do the same?"

"It's quiet there in the afternoon. They do most of their business at night."

"If you say so," Sara agreed, unconvinced the place would be quiet at *any* hour of the day.

"Plus," Brynne admitted, "Eli will be there. He's been working long hours lately, and by the time he gets off duty at the end of a double shift, he's usually beat. If I get a chance to see him during the day — even if he's busy with something else — I take it."

"You both work too hard, if you ask me," Sara said. "Not that you *did* ask me."

Brynne sighed, but it was a contented sound. "We love what we do," she said.

Sara felt the faintest twinge of envy, not because Brynne and Eli enjoyed their jobs — she loved her own work — but because they had each other.

She changed the subject. "Do I need to dress up to meet the legendary David Fielding?"

Brynne laughed softly. "Absolutely not. This is *Sully's,* not the dining room at the Ritz-Carlton. Wear jeans if you want."

"Brynne Garrett," Sara replied, with mock sternness, "if I get there, clad in casual clothes, and find you wearing one of your designer suits, I will *not* be pleased."

"Trust me," came the cheerful response.

"I'm in jeans, sneakers and a white blouse, as we speak, and I don't intend to change clothes. David, on the other hand, might show up in a tuxedo."

Sara laughed. "A tuxedo at Sully's Bar and Grill? *That* would definitely cause a stir."

"See you there," Brynne said.

A brief update on the Garrett twins followed, and then the call ended.

Sara concentrated on her work until noon, as usual, then shut down her computer and left the office for her bedroom. She'd showered earlier, so she just swapped out her baggy sweatpants and ancient T-shirt for blue jeans, a red tank top and a lightweight navy blazer. As a final touch, she applied minimal makeup, brushed out and re-braided her hair, and misted herself with cologne.

It felt good, dressing up, looking her best.

Because she worked at home, she rarely took the time to spruce herself up, beyond the basics — to the point that Hayley and Eric sometimes chided her for it, especially if their friends were around.

Surveying herself in the full-length mirror on the back of her bedroom door, she was willing to admit — to herself, anyway — that she needed to up her game, put in a little more effort.

Maybe, she decided, she'd do a little shopping after the lunch with Brynne and her potential employee/business partner, whichever Mr. Fielding might become. The Creek boasted two fairly decent boutiques, catering more to tourists than to locals, but it wouldn't hurt to glam up a little.

The decision had nothing to do with J.P. McCall and their upcoming date, nothing at all. She certainly didn't need fancy clothes for a horseback ride and a country picnic, now did she?

At 1:00 p.m., she arrived at Sully's, parked her boring car in the gravel lot and headed for the main entrance.

Brynne and her interviewee had arrived early, and they were already seated. Eli stood behind his wife's chair, and Sara wondered why her brother didn't simply sit down — but only briefly.

Her attention landed on David Fielding, bounced away and landed again.

The man was breathtaking to look at, though not in a showy way.

He wore a beautifully tailored gray suit, rather than the tuxedo Brynne and Sara had joked about over the phone, but he stood out, all right, amid the few farmers, ranchers and truck drivers there for a burger and a few rounds of cold beer.

Noticing Sara before the others did, Fielding rose to his feet with an easy, graceful movement, smiled and extended one hand in greeting.

"You must be Sara," he said, and she might have been the only other person in the known universe, the way he looked at her. "May I call you Sara?"

Sara nearly stuttered her response. "Yes."

"Sara," Brynne said, sounding amused. "This is David Fielding, the man I told you about."

"Call me David," he interjected graciously.

"David," Sara repeated, still a little stunned.

Eli bent to plant a kiss on his wife's cheek and then, as an afterthought, kissed Sara's cheek as well. "I'd better go," he said as David pulled back Sara's chair. "J.P. and Cord are waiting in the back room."

J.P. was in the back room?

Should she boldly go where so many other women must have gone before, walk into the poker room and say hello?

Or should she make a run for it?

Sara sank into her chair, mildly dizzy. She flashed a you-didn't-mention-that glance at Brynne.

"Eli's bringing them up to speed on a case," Brynne explained.

151

There was a twinkle in Eli's eyes as he met Sara's gaze. Just how much did he know about her time with J.P. at Bailey's or the date planned for Saturday?

"I'll say howdy to them for you," he told her before turning his attention to David, who was seated again. "Nice meeting you," he said to the other man.

David nodded and Eli walked away, soon disappearing into Sully's infamous back room.

A waitress approached the table, passed out a trio of creased menus covered in vinyl. Her name tag read Julie, and she was popping her gum as she walked away.

Brynne looked mildly embarrassed. She was probably thinking she should have conducted this interview at her family's restaurant instead of the local cowboy/biker bar.

The Creek was thriving, for a rural Montana town, but it didn't boast any elegant dining establishments.

Everyone perused their menus in thoughtful silence.

Eventually, Brynne and Sara opted for Cobb salads, while David chose a classic club sandwich.

Julie returned, the picture of desultory disinterest, took their orders and returned quickly with a round of iced tea.

Sara, over the shock of David Fielding's good looks and continental sophistication, yearned momentarily for a sip of wine, just to settle her nerves. She hadn't expected to run into J.P., but then, maybe she *wouldn't* run into him.

Maybe he, Eli and Cord would remain hidden in the back room, their favorite place to play poker or pool, and she wouldn't have any reason to be nervous.

She took a few restorative sips of iced tea while Brynne and David chatted amicably about the weather in general and Sully's in particular. David seemed to find the place pleasantly rustic, rather than seedy, despite its sawdust-covered floor, rough-hewn beams, battered bar and gum-smacking waitress.

"I suppose you're wondering what brings me and my partner, Evan, to the Montana countryside," David said, as the heavy crockery platter holding his sandwich was placed in front of him.

Both Brynne and Sara caught the reference to a male partner, but neither of them cared. Such unions weren't especially common in places like Painted Pony Creek, but they weren't unheard of, either.

"It did cross our minds," Brynne said,

picking up her fork and looking down at her salad before meeting David's eyes again. "You have quite a résumé."

"Thank you," David replied smoothly. He took a bite from his sandwich, chewed politely, swallowed. A grin lit his handsome face. "Evan has always wanted to live in the country. Raise a garden, keep sheep, all that."

"And you?" Brynne prompted.

Sara remained silent, keeping one figurative eye on David and one on the door leading to the back room. This wasn't her interview, after all. She was here in an advisory capacity, nothing more.

David's shrug was elegant. "Evan and I have been together for nearly twenty years, and we've always lived in major cities. Now that both our daughters are in college, we've decided it's time to make a few changes. Slow down a bit, at least in terms of my ridiculously long hours and the constant social demands that go along with my work."

Brynne's own work was plenty demanding, given how crazy prospective brides, grooms, parents and future in-laws could be, and Sara wondered if David's plan to *slow down a bit* might be a problem.

Apparently, it wasn't. "Around here, there

won't be the kind of social demands you're probably used to. We do barbecues, barn dances and church potlucks, mostly."

David smiled. "Evan will be delighted," he said. "And so will our daughters, when they visit."

He spoke as though the job — or business partnership, if that was on the table — was a done deal.

Sara forked a piece of avocado and nibbled at it, saying nothing.

Maybe Brynne had gone ahead and hired David, without waiting for Sara's opinion, which would make sense, since Sara knew next to nothing about the wedding business. She and Zachary had eloped; her flowers had been from the supermarket and the dress she'd worn to her high school graduation had doubled as her gown.

"I'm hoping you're not planning to set up your own operation," Brynne said without rancor, "and compete with me. We get plenty of business — a lot of it from surrounding towns and some from farther away. The Creek is considered picturesque, you know — but I don't think the community could support two private venues."

"And *I'm* hoping you'll hire me," David countered pleasantly, "and give me a chance to show you what I can do. Once I've proved

155

myself, I'm planning to approach you about an official partnership."

Brynne sat back in her chair, clearly surprised, but she was smiling. "You're very direct," she said. "I like that in a person."

David inclined his head slightly. He had nice brown hair, expensively trimmed with sexy touches of gray at the temples, and his eyes, also brown, shone with gentle intelligence.

He reminded Sara of the actor Mark Harmon.

If David decided to settle in Painted Pony Creek, with his longtime partner, a lot of single women were going to be disappointed.

"I might as well tell you that Evan and I have already put in an offer on a farm, south of town," David said. "Don't worry, though. If you don't hire me, I won't compete. We've saved a decent amount of money, and Evan is a very successful web designer, so we'll be just fine financially."

After that, David and Brynne talked shop.

Since David had been in the wedding-planning business for nearly two decades, he had all kinds of experience. He told marvelous stories about the various nuptial disasters he'd dealt with, and very soon he had Brynne laughing, and Sara joined in, finally forgetting that J.P. McCall was around somewhere, if unseen.

"I'd like to show you around the venue, if you have time," Brynne said, addressing David, dabbing away tears of laughter with a paper napkin.

"I have time," he replied, glancing at his watch.

They'd all finished their food by then.

"Evan is welcome to join us if he wants," Brynne said.

David smiled. "Thank you," he said, "but he's probably busy pacing off a pasture or something. Suppose I meet you there, at the lodge, in half an hour?"

"Of course," Brynne agreed.

David excused himself and left Sully's by the main door.

Brynne and Sara immediately exchanged a glance.

"Hot," Brynne remarked.

"As a two-bit pistol," Sara agreed.

They were quiet for a few moments.

Finally, Sara broke the silence. "Are you going to hire him?"

"We still have to discuss salary," Brynne responded, "and with his expertise, he might be out of my price range, but yes. I'm going to offer him the job and hope like hell he accepts."

Julie swiveled by, ignoring them.

"Check, please," Brynne said pointedly. Then, leaning forward and lowering her voice a little, she asked, "So what did you think of him? Besides that he's hot, I mean?"

Sara smiled. "He'd probably be a real asset," she said. "Especially when it comes to dealing with difficult brides and their entourages. And he's certainly had a lot of experience, if those stories of his are any indication."

"My thoughts exactly," Brynne said, with resolution, as Julie handed over the check.

"So why did you really invite me, Brynne?" Sara pressed good-naturedly. "Because you knew J.P. would be here, meeting with Cord and Eli? Maybe you were hoping we'd run into each other, he and I?"

Brynne had the good grace to blush a little. She got out a credit card and handed it to the impatient Julie, along with the check. "No harm done," she said. "We *didn't* run into him, did we? He and Cord must have come in by the back way."

"Thus foiling your devious little plan to throw us together," Sara challenged.

Brynne opened her mouth, then closed it again.

The door to the back room creaked open.

Sara knew, without turning around, that Brynne's tactic had worked after all.

CHAPTER SEVEN

J.P. was thinking about Eli's update on yesterday's discoveries out on the ranch — not surprisingly, the ATVs and the motorbike he'd found in the cave were stolen — when he spotted Sara.

Although he'd known the woman for most of his life, and had thus encountered her many times, something had changed between them the other night, when he'd kissed her in Bailey's parking lot. Maybe even before that, when they'd gone riding and the sun had rimmed her in a full-body halo, like some cowgirl saint.

There was an actual impact, a slamming sensation that nearly took his breath away. His heart beat a little faster and his throat thickened and he hoped he didn't look as foolish and awkward as he felt.

What *was* this?

Cord nudged him from behind and he realized he'd come to a full stop.

Feeling his neck go warm, J.P. forced himself to break the spell and start moving again.

He smiled at Brynne, then at Sara. Said hello.

Sara's eyes were a little too bright and her face was flushed. He hoped she wasn't coming down with something.

"Hello, J.P.," she said. Then she added, with a nod, "Cord."

An invisible charge seemed to arc between himself and Sara.

"How did the interview go?" Eli asked Brynne, breaking the tension. He cast a sidelong — and slightly smug — glance in J.P.'s direction, probably to let him know the electricity hadn't gone unnoticed.

Brynne drew close to her husband, stood on tiptoe to kiss his cheek and stepped back. "David will be a real asset to the business, if I can rope him in. He's planned weddings for some pretty upscale people, so he might be too expensive."

Eli lifted one corner of his mouth in a grin as he held Brynne's gaze.

Talk about electricity.

"The man is willing to consider a job in a relatively remote Montana town, as opposed to working in New York, London or Paris. Most likely, he's well aware there will be trade-offs," Eli said reasonably.

"I hope so," Brynne said with a rueful little sigh.

"Don't worry," Eli replied, patting her shoulder reassuringly, before leaning in to give his wife a light kiss on the mouth. "I'll probably be home later than usual," he added with clear regret. "Some folks out for a trail ride found a mustang mare and her colt tangled in an old spool of rusted barbwire. They'll be all right — Cord's taken them to his place, and the vet's been out to tend their injuries — but since there hasn't been barbwire on either the McCalls' or the Hollisters' place in thirty years, we think it might have been set out on purpose, like some kind of trap. I need to take a good look around, and if I find anything, I'll want to follow up on it right away."

Brynne nodded, used to a lawman's hours. Her beautiful dark blue eyes shimmered with sadness. "I just don't understand. Accidents happen, but to think anyone could be so deliberately cruel —"

J.P. was listening to the conversation, but his mental focus was definitely on Sara. She looked as sorrowful as Brynne.

"Did this happen on your ranch?" she asked, turning her silvery eyes on J.P.

There was no accusation in her voice or

her expression, but J.P. felt defensive anyhow, at least for a moment.

"No," he said with a gruffness he hadn't intended. "Cord's."

Sara said nothing in reply.

Cord broke the conversational impasse with a jovial, "I'm out of here. Gonna saddle up as soon as I get home and head out looking for more barbwire and the like." He paused, slapped J.P. on the back, just a tad too hard. "Eli will be there, but we could use your help, too, neighbor," he added. "There's a lot of ground to cover."

"Sure," J.P. ground out, befuddled, his gaze still stuck on Sara.

Damn, but he felt like three kinds of idiot.

Cord had given him an out, though, and clumsy as it was, he said his farewells and followed his friend out of Sully's into the blazing afternoon sunlight.

J.P. blinked a couple of times, then put on his sunglasses.

His truck was parked beside Cord's, so they headed in the same direction.

Cord was grinning as he ambled along toward his rig. "So," he said affably, "the rumors are true."

J.P. stiffened. "*What* rumors?"

"Come on, man. It's all over town. You and Sara Worth have a thing goin' on."

"It's not a *thing*," J.P. replied, feeling oddly testy. He was usually pretty amiable, not subject to moods. "We went horseback riding — it was research for the book Sara's working on — and then she bought me dinner at Bailey's to say thanks."

"If that's all there is to it, why are you so damn prickly all of a sudden?"

J.P. huffed out a sigh. Adjusted his shades. "It's gotten under my hide, all this stuff going on with the mustangs and the other critters."

"I feel the same way," Cord said quietly. "But I still think the way you froze up in there just now had more to do with Sara than the outlaws we're helping Eli hunt down. You weren't expecting to see her, and when you did, you reacted as though somebody had just rammed you in the belly with the broad end of a baseball bat."

J.P. was quiet for several seconds, aware of Brynne, Sara and Eli at the periphery of his vision, leaving Sully's together, saying their goodbyes, going their separate ways.

"I'm not ready to talk about this yet," he said, at last.

"Fair enough," Cord replied kindly. "See you at my place in half an hour or so?"

"I'll be there," J.P. answered.

With that, Cord got into his truck and J.P.

got into his.

He'd had no particular plans for the afternoon. The cleaning people were hard at work, getting his house ready for visitors, and he'd be underfoot if he hung around. Same thing if he paid an unscheduled call on his folks.

Besides, if there were more coils of barb-wire or anything similar on the Hollister place, his or any other, he wanted to find them before another critter got hurt.

He had several hundred head of cattle to think about, not to mention the horses he turned out to graze most days, and so did Cord. Their other neighbors ran smaller operations, but they had livestock, too.

This thing with the ATVs and the barbwire was everybody's problem, not just Eli's. Both the Creek's small PD, competently headed up by Melba Summers, and, to a more limited degree, the feds were gearing up for more trouble.

J.P. watched as Eli pulled out of the parking lot first, followed by Brynne, driving that sweet roadster of hers, and then Sara, in her nondescript compact.

He smiled at the sight of that car, thinking how little it suited her. Seemed to him, Sara was more the sports-car type.

Sure, she had two kids, but they were both

teenagers now. They probably didn't love being hauled around in a mom-mobile.

He waited, waved Cord to go ahead.

Thought about kids.

His smile faded as he pulled out onto the highway behind his friend.

Maybe he was getting ahead of himself, but he wanted kids of his own, at least two, and preferably more.

Sara, though she was only two years older than he was, might be over raising children, now that hers were nearing adulthood.

Or she might hesitate to have more kids simply because she was in her late thirties.

For J.P., giving up his dream of being a father would be a deal-breaker.

On the other hand, if he loved a woman the way he wanted to love, with all his body, mind and soul, and she didn't want kids, would he be able to turn his back on her and walk away?

The question nagged at him all the way back to his place.

He realized he was jumping to a lot of conclusions; he and Sara hadn't discussed the matter of children, given that it was so early in their relationship.

If they even *had* a relationship.

And suppose the topic scared her off?

Back at the house, he parked the truck,

summoned Trooper from the house and whistled for Shiloh, grazing in the nearby pasture with the other horses.

The gelding came readily to the fence.

Still mulling over the dilemma — could he see himself with a woman who didn't want children? — he threw a halter over Shiloh's head, buckled it on and led him toward the barn. Saddled the animal by muscle memory, since his mind was miles away.

In town.

With Sara.

He came to no conclusion.

Trooper, who had greeted him joyously when he got out of the truck, lay in a patch of shade now, close to the barn, his tongue lolling.

And here was another quandary.

Trooper lived to hang out with people, especially J.P. himself. Leaving him behind, after calling him outside, and thereby getting his hopes up, wouldn't be kind, either.

J.P. sighed, pulled his phone from his shirt pocket.

Speed-dialed Cord and Shallie's landline.

"Hey," a perky feminine voice answered on the third ring. "Is it really you, Uncle J.P.?"

Carly.

J.P. smiled. "Hey yourself," he replied.

"Dad just pulled up. Do you want to talk to him?" He heard curiosity in her voice; most likely she was wondering why he hadn't called Cord's cell. These days, reaching somebody over a landline was a crapshoot.

Except, of course, if he happened to be calling his parents.

"Not at the moment," J.P. replied. "I'm on my way over there, so I'll see your dad again soon enough. I was actually hoping you'd let my dog hang out with yours for a few hours. Cord and I have some riding to do, and it might wear Trooper out, following us around."

Carly was, among her other stellar traits, an avowed animal lover. "Sure!" she replied with genuine enthusiasm. "That would be great. I haven't seen Trooper since last month, when Shallie and Dad threw that barbecue."

"I really appreciate this, Carly," J.P. said. It revisited him then, that pang of disappointment he'd felt when the results of the DNA test had come in, and he'd learned that this lovely, spirited young woman wasn't his biological daughter.

"Anything for the Troopster," Carly answered sweetly. "Our dogs will be happy, too. They love company, two-legged or four-legged."

"See you in a few, kiddo."

Trooper, who knew the drill, livened right up at J.P.'s beckoning whistle, trotted over, jumped onto the bales and then leaped from there into J.P.'s arms.

They traveled overland, since that was the most direct route, and Trooper, perched in front of J.P., took every bump with more ease than a lot of humans would have.

When they reached the Hollister ranch, Carly and the two family dogs were waiting in the front yard, none too patiently.

Trooper gave a happy yelp and jumped gracefully to the ground, racing toward the girl and her canine companions, a streak of fur and delight.

J.P. smiled at the sight, but remained in the saddle, having spotted Cord leading a saddled gelding out of the barn. The sun was still high, but the Hollister ranch was big, and they needed to make the most of the daylight.

Carly approached, looked up at J.P., shading her eyes with one hand, surrounded by eager dogs. "It's terrible, what's been happening to the mustangs," she said. "And the deer, too."

"Yeah," J.P. agreed, adjusting his hat,

remembering that Eric, Sara's boy, could be involved.

"Eric has nothing to do with this," Carly said, having apparently read his mind. "He still regrets last time. He's changed."

J.P. hesitated before he offered his reply. "I hope you're right," he said very quietly.

"But you're not sure," Carly responded somewhat sadly.

J.P. adjusted his hat, pulling the brim down lower over his eyes, since he'd left his sunglasses in his truck. "Seems like you might be sure enough for both of us," he observed gently.

He loved this girl as much as he loved his nieces. Maybe more, since he knew her a lot better, and it hurt to see her looking downcast.

"Do you really think I'd still be going out with Eric if I thought he'd gone back to his old ways, Uncle J.P.?" she asked. "Like I said, he's different now. He's planning to go to college and everything."

"I don't know the boy very well," J.P. admitted. "But I trust your judgment, Carly. If you say he's all right, then in all likelihood, he is."

Carly looked slightly happier, but when she glanced in Cord's direction, her face fell a little. "I think Dad has his doubts,"

170

she confessed. "And he thinks Eric and I ought to take a break, since I'll be going off to college in September and Eric will have to stay behind and finish high school."

Privately, J.P. thought his friend was right, but he wasn't fool enough to say so. He didn't want to alienate his honorary niece any more than he already had.

Carly would be living a whole new life when she started college. She'd make new friends, too, and some of those friends would be male. It wasn't hard to imagine a romance sparking between her and one of those guys.

There would be several, most likely, over the course of her college career, and she was hoping to go on to veterinary school after she'd earned her bachelor's degree.

A lot could happen.

She would grow and change.

Eric, left behind in Painted Pony Creek for another year, would, hopefully, do the same.

Young love, J.P. thought sympathetically, *can hurt like hell.*

"I can't predict the future," he said aloud, "but I know this much — you'll be fine, Carly, and Eric will, too. He's got a good mother and a damn fine uncle to steer him in the right direction."

Carly nodded and gave a nod as Cord joined them.

"Good luck," she said, addressing both men and already steering the dogs, Trooper included, away toward the house. Trooper looked back once, but at J.P.'s nod, he followed Carly.

"We're going to need luck," Cord said, sounding a little grim.

Eli was meeting them at the natural spring in the middle of the Hollister ranch. This time, instead of riding, he'd travel in the SUV. His deputies were busy elsewhere, and the feds were still holding back, grousing about budgets and being short-staffed.

J.P. and Cord had learned all this during their lunch meeting in the back room at Sully's, and plenty more. Melba and her people had been keeping their ears to the ground, counting on the acknowledged fact that most criminals aren't too bright, and usually can't resist bragging about their exploits.

Naturally, if the local police department turned up any useful information, they would share it with Eli and his deputies.

J.P. and Cord rode in silence across the Hollister range toward the springs.

When they arrived, Eli was already there, standing beside his rig.

The springs fed a small pond, and the horses strained in that direction, thirsty.

Both riders dismounted and let the animals drink while they went to meet Eli.

"I thought you might bring the chief along," Cord said, with a grin.

Eli smiled, shook his head. "Chief Summers," he replied, "is in labor, as we speak. Dan called me about twenty minutes ago."

Melba and Dan Summers had remarried six months before, after being divorced for some years. They had two young daughters.

"Is Melba okay?" Cord asked.

"She's fine," Eli replied. "I have that on good authority."

"And Dan? How's he doing?" J.P. asked.

Eli chuckled. "He's beside himself, but he's holding up for Melba and the girls."

It was hard to imagine Dan Summers, former navy SEAL, FBI special agent and, most recently, the head of his own international security firm, *beside himself.* He was big as a grizzly bear and twice as tough.

"Guess he's out of practice," Cord remarked. He and Eli swapped knowing glances. "Not that either of us had it all together when it was crunch time in the delivery room."

At that, they both looked at J.P.

"What?" he snapped, feeling unaccountably testy.

Cord laughed. "Touchy," he said.

"Let's get this show on the road," Eli interceded patiently. "We can hassle the Creek's most eligible bachelor later. Maybe over a game of poker."

J.P. said nothing, but his thoughts were snarky.

"Maybe you should go on that TV show," Cord suggested over one shoulder, heading for his horse. "The one with all the beautiful women competing to marry one guy."

J.P. kept pace, mounted Shiloh, gathered the reins in his left hand. "That your favorite program, Cordelia?" he chided.

Cord gave a gruff laugh and swung up into the saddle. "Shallie and Carly never miss an episode," he replied. "I picked up the gist of it by osmosis."

"Sure you did," J.P. retorted.

"Sounds like *you're* a faithful viewer," Cord challenged, adjusting his hat and grinning.

Eli stood there, shaking his head, obviously waiting for them to shut up so he could tell them what to do.

Nothing new there.

"All right, Sheriff," Cord said, giving their friend a brisk salute and a mocking grin. "Let's hear your orders for the day."

Eli sent them in two different directions, reminded them that there could be traps hidden along grassy trails, warned them to be careful.

The idea that his horse, or Cord's, might be injured in such a savage way cast a dark shadow over that otherwise sunny afternoon.

J.P. rode for several hours, stopping to let Shiloh rest when needed, kept a close eye out for traps and coils of barbwire, and found nothing. He was about to turn around and head back to the springs to meet Cord and Eli when he heard the first rifle shot.

Two more followed, then silence.

J.P. swore. He'd been a rancher long enough to know a signal when he heard one.

Three shots in sequence meant one thing: trouble.

With the sounds of that gun still vibrating in his bones, J.P. turned Shiloh and rode hard in the direction of the noise.

Ten minutes later, he reached the top of a small hill and searched the expanse of waving grass and brush until he spotted Eli in the distance. The sheriff waved both arms in the air, and J.P. headed toward him at top speed.

The SUV was nowhere in sight, but Cord was visible, approaching from the northeast.

He reached the scene at about the same time as J.P. — and what a scene it was.

A dead man lay in the tall grass, so coated in dried blood that it was impossible to tell whether he was facedown or lying on his back. A few bones jutted through torn flesh, and the flies and maggots were having a heyday.

J.P. felt bile surge into the back of his throat, turned his head and spit.

"Christ," Cord said, going pale. "What the hell happened here?"

"Stay back," Eli instructed calmly. Wearily. "Alec and Sam are on their way."

Alec Stone was the county coroner, and Sam Wu was his assistant. They were the closest thing Wild Horse County had to crime-scene techs.

"Somebody either beat this poor bastard to death with a sledgehammer or he's been trampled," J.P. speculated. He wasn't going to hurl or anything like that, but he wouldn't be eating supper that night, either. Breakfast might be off the table, too.

Literally.

"Look around," Eli said, crouching beside the corpse.

J.P. and Cord complied, noticed hundreds of hoof prints, gouged into the ground, flattening the grass.

"I guess this rules out the sledgehammer theory," J.P. remarked.

"Do either of you recognize this yahoo?" Eli asked, still studying the body.

"You're kidding, right?" Cord retorted. As J.P. had moments earlier, he turned his head and spit.

"No," J.P. said. "Isn't he carrying a wallet or something? There'll probably be ID inside."

"Thank you, DCI Barnaby," Eli replied amiably enough. "He probably *is* carrying a wallet, but I'm not going to be able to get to it without disturbing the body and thus pissing Alec off big-time."

Sirens sounded in the distance, growing closer and louder by the second.

The horses began to nicker and prance. No doubt they were more troubled by the body than the sirens, and they were nervous as hell.

"Where's your SUV?" Cord asked Eli.

"Just over that rise," Eli answered, pointing. Beyond that low rocky hillside was the dirt road that bisected both the McCall and Hollister ranches. "The ground is pretty soft out here, so I left the rig on the road. And before you ask how I knew there was something out here, look up."

Both Cord and J.P. tilted back their heads.

Saw the circling buzzards.

"Damn," J.P. said, wondering why he'd even bothered watching all those Westerns growing up if he hadn't even learned to be on the lookout for those nasty birds. "What a god-awful way to die."

Eli huffed out a sigh. "Yeah," he agreed glumly.

He seemed to be taking this in stride; he was cool and calm, sitting on his heels within a foot or so of a dead man.

From J.P's viewpoint, the only thing worse than the gore was the stench.

Shiloh grew more fretful, and J.P. backed the animal up a few paces, swung down from the saddle, kept his distance.

"How long do you think he's been dead?" he asked.

"I'll have to wait until Alec and Sam check him over to know for sure," Eli answered, "but if I had to guess, I'd say a couple of days."

"You think he was one of the people you've been looking for?" asked Cord.

"Probably," Eli answered. Then he reached into the tall grass and drew out a steel bear trap, the kind with teeth, and held it up for the others to see.

Cord swore again.

The sirens grew louder.

"I'm going to go over every inch of this place," Cord said. He meant the entire Hollister ranch, not just the immediate area. Like J.P., he owned horses and several hundred head of cattle, but he had an additional concern, since he taught students and often led them on trail rides.

"You'll need a crew," Eli said. "And it will be dangerous work. I'll help, and so will my deputies."

"I'll lend a hand, too," J.P. said, well aware that his own land might have been sprinkled with the cruel traps. If necessary, he'd hire on as many temporary ranch hands as he needed.

"I thought traps like that were outlawed a long time ago," Cord put in. Like J.P., he'd dismounted. Now they both inspected their immediate surroundings for more of the things.

"They're available if you know where to look," Eli said. "Watch your step, will you?" He stood up straight as they heard tires on the dirt road, male voices and the slamming of doors. "Be careful!" he shouted to the coroner, his helper, two paramedics and three deputies. "There might be traps planted in the grass."

"God Almighty," J.P. sighed, taking off his hat, wiping the back of his neck with one arm and then resettling the hat. "Who *does* shit like this?"

Eli was focused on the approaching group, so he didn't answer.

"Who does what?" Cord retorted. "Gets themselves trampled to death by a herd of wild horses?"

"That, too. But I was talking about the barbwire and the traps. Who gets up in the morning and says to themselves, *Today, I'm going to do as much damage and cause as much pain as I possibly can?*"

Cord moved to stand beside J.P., carefully avoiding the body and the pockmarked earth around it.

He rested a hand briefly on J.P.'s shoulder. "Probably somebody who's damaged and in a lot of pain themselves," he answered. "You doing okay, my friend?"

J.P. knew Cord was referring to the severe case of PTSD he'd suffered after the explosion in Afghanistan. Though he'd been ambulatory within six weeks, the psychological effects of seeing seven of his friends blown to a red mist had lasted a lot longer. He and Trooper had gotten together soon after he'd come home, and the therapy, both physical and mental, had gone on for a long, long time.

Gradually, with the help of his family, his

friends — especially Cord and Eli — his service dog, the sprawling Montana sky and the land beneath it had healed him.

Seeing the body, gruesome as it was, hadn't triggered him.

Yet.

He might get through this without a flashback, a nightmare or a killer headache.

Then again, he might not.

He felt tension tightening his neck and shoulders.

"Yeah, I'm okay," he assured Cord, his tone gruff. He was determined to keep it together, but he appreciated his friend's concern, too. Like Trooper, Eli and Cord had helped him cope when memories swamped him, tried to take him under.

They'd sat up many a night, the three of them, swilling coffee and playing poker, and when PTSD struck in the daytime, they dug fence-post holes and chopped wood.

"Good," Cord responded. "As for me, I'm still not sure I won't lose my lunch."

"You know," J.P. said, "I'd feel a lot better if we got these horses out of this deep grass and onto the road."

"Me, too," Cord agreed.

Alec and Sam were pulling on gloves, masks and paper shoe-covers, while the EMTs and the deputies hung back, prob-

181

ably on the sheriff's orders.

The buzzards had retreated, but they probably hadn't gone far.

"You need us for anything?" J.P. asked Eli.

Eli shook his head. "Thanks, but no. I'll be in touch."

J.P. and Cord led their horses over the path the new arrivals had worn in the grass and onto the hard-packed dirt road. The animals were still jumpy, but they were calming down.

The two men rode together until the road forked, one way leading to J.P.'s ranch house, the other toward Cord's. It wasn't a shortcut, which was why they hadn't used it to reach the springs, where they'd met up with Eli earlier in the day.

All of a sudden, J.P. felt as though he could fall face-first onto his bed and sleep for a month.

Unless, of course, he could convince Sara to join him.

He wouldn't sleep in that case, but a month would be just about long enough.

He turned his thoughts back to the problem at hand.

As a landowner, in charge of more than five hundred cattle and a dozen horses, he didn't have that luxury. Even if his own acres were clear, he wouldn't be able to sit back and relax, because his neighbors would need all the help they could get.

That was the way things worked in and around Painted Pony Creek and a thousand Western towns just like it — if someone's house burned to the ground, folks pitched in, provided food and shelter and what consolation they could.

Ranchers and farmers helped ranchers and farmers, and the townspeople did what they could.

If somebody's child got sick, fundraisers were held all over the county.

Livestock lost to a blizzard, a wildfire or a flood?

People gave till it literally hurt.

The current crisis would be no different.

This time around, it wasn't a matter of money. But once the word got out, volunteers would show up and comb the land.

The thought gave J.P. a lot of solace as he rode slowly toward his place.

Once he reached home, he put Shiloh in the barn, rather than turning him out to pasture. He whistled in the other horses, too, and put them in stalls.

After feeding them and making sure the electric watering system was working, he climbed into his truck and drove toward Cord and Shallie's place.

The moment he parked the truck, Trooper came running to greet him.

His eyes burning a little at the welcome, he crouched to ruffle the dog's floppy ears.

"Hey, old buddy," he said gruffly.

Trooper licked his face and then grinned in that goofy way dogs do.

Cord came out of the barn to wait for J.P., and he and Trooper walked over to meet him.

"Long day," J.P. said.

"You've got that right," Cord agreed. "Ours will be a lot shorter than Eli's will, I guess."

They entered the barn together, Trooper trotting along at their heels.

"What's the prognosis?" J.P. asked, after he'd gotten as close to the wild horse as he dared and taken a good look at the animal's injured leg. The colt didn't kick up a fuss; he just nipped behind his mama and then began to nurse.

"Good. We'll have to keep an eye on the wound, though. Make sure there's no infection."

"And when she's well again?"

Cord patted the mare's neck gently. "She'll go back to the herd, where she belongs." He paused. "Provided Eli and Melba and their people have been able to put a stop to the harassment, that is."

"Yeah," J.P. agreed on a long sigh. The sight of that trampled corpse bloomed in his mind, and he felt sick. "I'm not leaving it all up to them, though."

Cord shook his head. "No," he said. "Neither am I."

CHAPTER EIGHT

As she drove away from Sully's, Sara was struggling to recover her composure.

The encounter with J.P., innocuous as it had been, had left her feeling a mite jittery.

There was so much going on in her usually quiet life: Zachary's return had thrown her for the proverbial loop, and she was worried about Eric, too.

Deep down, she was *always* worried about Eric, had been ever since he'd gotten himself into all that trouble the summer before last. Once caught, he'd admitted his guilt, and he'd accepted his punishment — a year of community service — without complaint. He'd apologized to everyone who'd been affected by his actions and, where possible, he'd made restitution.

In fact, Eric had behaved like a new person, no longer moody and sullen, applying himself at school and keeping a civil tongue in his head, with his teachers and other authorities and at home with Sara and Hayley.

Seeing his father again, however, had flipped some kind of inner switch in the boy, or so it seemed to Sara.

Eric was only seventeen, she reminded herself as she drove toward the boutique for her intended shopping experiment, and he'd sorely missed having a dad like most of his friends did. Now, without warning, his father was back in his life and he would need to process that, figure out what that would mean for him and how he ought to respond.

Sara didn't want to overreact to Eric's change in temperament, but she didn't want to hide her head in the sand, either.

If there was one thing she'd learned about raising children, it was that parents — especially single ones — had to stay engaged at all times, no matter how tired or discouraged they were. They had to stand toe to toe, ready and willing to hold the line, and to somehow find a balance between enforcing the rules and being reasonably flexible.

Lost in thought, Sara parked in front of the small elegant shop she rarely visited.

The place had changed owners — and names — several times over the past couple of decades, starting out as Buttons & Bows and evolving from there.

A year ago, two sisters had purchased the building, renovated it completely, filled it with stylish, high-quality clothing, designer shoes and handbags and artisan-made jewelry.

Its new name was Fancy That, and it had proved surprisingly popular with the women of Painted Pony Creek and the surrounding area. The shop did a brisk trade with tourists, too, but Sara suspected the bulk of the profits came from online sales.

The Merriman sisters, Kate and Melody, had both earned their living in public relations, before leaving Los Angeles to settle in a comparative wide spot in the road, and they knew how to work social media in particular and the internet in general.

Melody, the younger of the two, was working alone when Sara entered the shop, causing the little bell over the door to jingle as it had been doing since the days of Buttons & Bows.

That bell, Sara reflected, was probably the only thing in the store that had ridden out two decades of near-constant change.

"Sara," Melody sang with a smile. She was slender and tall, with shoulder-length strawberry blond hair and emerald green eyes.

Colored contacts? Speculation was rampant in the Creek, even after a year.

Did *anyone* really have eyes that vividly green?

A little surprised that Melody recognized her, Sara shifted mental gears and smiled back. "Hi, Melody," she said.

Melody drifted gracefully from behind the glass counter, with its lit display of shimmering jeweled evening bags, Italian silk scarves and bright baubles. She was wearing a cornflower blue dress, made of soft cotton, and her feet were bare, pink toenails gleaming.

So California, Sara thought, and then reprimanded herself for indulging in a snarky thought. She hardly knew either of the Merriman sisters, and she had no business judging them for their un-Montana-like ways.

"How can I help you?" Melody asked.

"I need to update my wardrobe a little," Sara said, almost apologetically, glancing down at her jeans, tank top and blazer. She looked around and was nearly overwhelmed by the variety on offer — tailored pantsuits, spectacular evening gowns, cashmere jackets, gossamer blouses. "I'm starting small," she added hastily, blushing a little.

Which was silly. There was no way this poised, well-mannered young woman could

189

guess that she was embarrassed because she wanted to impress a certain man.

Not that that was the *only* reason she was there.

"What's the occasion?" Melody wanted to know. Her voice was low and smoky; rumor had it that she sang karaoke on the occasional Friday or Saturday night over at Sully's.

Sara, being secretly terrified that someone would force a microphone into her hand and shove her onstage, steered clear of karaoke nights.

Easy enough, since she rarely went anywhere on the weekends, except to see a movie now and then.

"No occasion," Sara replied somewhat belatedly. She began to feel foolish, and then felt foolish for feeling foolish. She wasn't a hermit, after all. She attended weddings and funerals and church potlucks, among other things.

The upcoming picnic with J.P. sprang to mind and, for a crazy moment, she was drawn to the rack of lovely, floaty sundresses. Then she remembered that she would be arriving at said picnic on horseback.

Melody, having followed her gaze, stepped over to the rack and showed Sara a gloriously feminine and subtly sexy pink floral dress. The pattern was muted, reminiscent of a watercolor painting.

"This would be fabulous with your dark hair and peaches and cream complexion," she said. She lifted a second hanger from the metal bar and held up another dress, this one turquoise, made of soft cotton.

She had a peaches and cream complexion? That was news to Sara.

Her skin-care routine consisted of washing her face with Dove and moisturizing with Noxzema.

"I'd like to try them on," she heard herself say, somewhat to her surprise.

"I'll start a room for you," Melody replied with another smile. "Why don't you browse on your own for a while? See what jumps out at you?"

"Okay," Sara said. Was she *really* paid to work with words? At the present moment, most of her vocabulary seemed to have deserted her.

She needed to go home and lie down with a cool cloth on her head until she was herself again.

"Would you like a bottle of water?" Melody inquired. "Or a cup of tea?"

Sara shook her head, murmured a "No, thanks," although she knew the water would have been a good idea. She was probably dehydrated.

Yes, that explained everything.

Except it didn't.

The encounter with *J.P.* explained everything.

She approached a display of silky blouses, sexy ones with low-cut necklines, short-sleeved sporty ones that tied at the waist, full lacy ones with long sleeves that reminded her of angel wings.

Concentrate, she ordered herself silently, admiring a bright red top bedecked in tropical flowers. When had she ever owned a blouse like that?

Never, that was when. For nearly twenty years, she'd mostly worn T-shirts and shorts or jeans in summer, sweaters and sweatshirts — and jeans — in winter. She owned two decent suits, reserved for rare meetings with her publisher and agent, in New York, church services and the aforesaid weddings and funerals.

Her wardrobe was, in a word, *pitiful.*

Ninety-nine times out of a hundred, she dressed like what she was — a mom.

But, damn it, she was *more* than a mother — wasn't she?

Okay, she was a writer, and a successful one at that, but she worked at home and that meant the dress code was casual.

Worse than casual.

Sometimes she worked in pajamas and didn't bother to brush her hair.

Sara held on to the red blouse, added one of the flowing lacy ones and then selected a third, a simple long-sleeved affair in amber silk.

She chose a couple of skirts, a pair of black slacks and some outrageous rhinestone-studded jeans in a deep shade of magenta.

Finally, telling herself she was crazy the whole way, Sara retreated into a changing room and slipped out of her clothes.

She tried everything on, and everything fit.

Amazing.

She put her own clothes back on and, having weeded out the doubtful prospects and misfits, carried her selections to the counter, where Melody was waiting with a smile.

Sara, tallying prices in her head, silently questioned her own sanity.

Again.

The total was scary, even though it would barely make a dent in her bank balance.

Sara regretted turning down that bottle of water, though, frankly, she thought a stiff G&T or a martini — dirty, with extra olives

— might be called for at the moment.

Melody, having rung everything up and swiped Sara's credit card, chatted amiably as she wrapped each deliciously lovely garment in pale gold tissue paper stamped with the store's logo.

Like her older sister, Kate, Melody was beautiful.

Did she have a significant other?

Sara stole a glance at the woman's left-hand ring finger.

No wedding band or engagement ring.

Melody was, most likely, *available.*

Sara felt the faintest whisper of paranoia.

She wondered if J.P. knew Melody — decided he must, given the size of the town — and then took the question further into the territory of the ridiculous.

Had J.P. noticed Melody?

How could he *not* have noticed her?

She was breathtaking.

Smart and sweet-natured.

Just the type of woman most men found attractive.

Hayley's nickname for Sara landed in the center of her chest.

Momster.

Sara began to feel flushed, even a little light-headed.

And, of course, because it was the last

thing Sara wanted, Melody noticed immediately.

She rounded the corner, took Sara gently by one arm and squired her to the velvet settee under a bay window.

"Stay put," the other woman ordered kindly. "I'll get you some water."

Sara closed her eyes, mortified. Perspiration tickled between her shoulder blades and she was slightly queasy.

Melody returned quickly with the promised water, unscrewed the cap and handed the ice-cold bottle to Sara, who took it gratefully, muttering an embarrassed, "Thanks."

"Shall I call someone?" Melody asked. "Maybe you shouldn't drive."

"I'm all right," Sara insisted. She always said that when asked, but this time it was true. The first few sips of water had done a lot to restore her equilibrium.

Water, she thought, *is a wonder drug, right up there with Imodium, Tylenol and Vicks Vapo-Rub.*

Melody's laugh was soft, sudden and musical. "I hope it wasn't the prices," she said.

Sara laughed, too, and nearly spit a mouthful of water onto the hardwood floor in the process. "They're definitely not typi-

195

cal around here," she replied, "but then, neither are the things you sell."

"We're thinking of expanding the store, adding a line of bridal gowns, bridesmaid's dresses, et cetera," Melody confided with a touch of excitement. "Now that Brynne Garrett's offering wedding-planning services, we're getting inquiries. So far, mostly from mothers of the bride or groom."

Sara thought of Brynne's luncheon/interview with David Fielding. Brynne's business, though relatively new, was already beginning to thrive, and unless Sara missed her guess, things would pick up even more if he was on board.

The man was class personified.

"Not a bad idea," she mused between sips of water. "Maybe you've heard. Brynne has a big splashy wedding booked — triplet brides. Evidently, the theme is medieval, so there will be lords and ladies and knights in shining armor — quite a shindig."

Melody's mouth rounded in surprise and wonder. "Wow," she said. "I *hadn't* heard."

"You might want to meet with Brynne," Sara suggested. "You and Kate. Hear her plans for yourself."

"Do you think she'd be interested in some kind of cooperative effort?"

Sara had finished the water, and Melody

took the empty bottle from her. "It couldn't hurt to talk to her," she told the shopkeeper. "There are no bridal shops in town, so people have to buy elsewhere. Brynne likes to make things as easy for her clients as possible, so I think she'd be pleased if they could make their purchases locally."

"Hmm," Melody said.

Sara got to her feet, gathered her shopping bags and her purse.

It was time to go home, get centered, prepare herself for another run-in with Zachary or an attitude from her son.

"Let me help you." Melody took two of the bags and followed Sara outside.

Her car looked dusty and very Mom-ish as she unlocked it, opened the back door and stowed her purchases.

Melody added two more bulging bags to the mix.

"Thank you, Sara," she said. "For shopping with us, I mean. And for giving me something to think about. Selling wedding gowns and other bridal goods might give the shop a real boost."

Sara merely nodded. She was talked out — and hoping she hadn't overstepped by mentioning the possibility of crossover business with Brynne's company.

She drove home, conscious of the booty

in the back seat, and hoped with all her heart that the house would be empty when she arrived.

She loved her children, but she needed a little time to collect herself.

She wasn't exactly rattled — that had worn off, thank heaven — but she was something of an introvert, and she'd had enough sensory input to overload her circuits.

The house was blessedly quiet when she entered.

No teenagers arguing.

No TV or computer blaring gaming sounds.

No shouts of triumph or outrage when one avatar defeated another.

Sara carried her bags to her bedroom and set them carefully on her neatly made double bed.

Her room was a haven of sorts; she'd spent a chunk of her first advance check bringing it from the last century into the present one, changing out the dated wallpaper and painting the walls a faint shade of grayish green.

She'd replaced the furniture, too, since it all reminded her of her married days.

The bed, dresser and mirrored bureau had been billed as Country French when Sara had come across them one day in the town's one and only furniture store.

Ever so slightly distressed, the pieces seemed particularly well suited to belong to her. She had tiny cracks here and there, too, and some of her natural luster had worn away, and yet she was solid and strong. Functional.

She'd learned, after Zachary's departure, that she certainly *could* take care of herself and of her children, despite her former husband's efforts to undermine her confidence and convince her that neither she nor Eric and Hayley could possibly survive without him.

Looking back, she wondered, as she often had before, how she'd ever bought into that line of bull; she had *always* been the strong one in the partnership, right from the very first.

With a sigh, Sara kicked off her shoes and put them away in her beautifully designed walk-in closet, with its lit cabinets and racks and shelves.

Pretty fancy, she thought, with no little amusement, for a woman who lived in blue jeans, T-shirts and sweatpants.

Well, no more.

It was a new day, and Sara had new clothes to go with it, clothes that would be right at home in her custom-built closet.

She was taking the tissue-wrapped bundles out of the bags when she heard the front door open, and she braced herself.

She was feeling hopeful and potentially glamorous, with all these great garments to choose from, and frankly, she didn't want to spar with Zachary or fend off a lot of snotty questions from Eric.

Mercifully, the new arrival turned out to be Hayley.

The girl's smile was dazzling as she stood in the doorway of her mother's bedroom. "Look!" she cried, and lifted her summery top to reveal a beautiful, intricately designed rendition of a dream catcher — the temporary tattoo. "I do NOT want to wash this thing off!"

Sara laughed and stepped closer to inspect the marvel. The lines were subtle, the colors bright, and the decorative feathers looked as though they would move in the slightest of breezes.

"It's gorgeous," she said.

Satisfied with that much approval, Hayley lowered her shirt and let her gaze stray to the bags and bundles on the bed.

"You went *shopping!*" she cried, in benign accusation. *"For clothes!"*

Sara was vaguely insulted. "I *do* buy new

clothes now and again, Hayley," she reminded her daughter, who was already folding back tissue and peering into bags.

Hayley made a dismissive sound. "Oh, *please,*" she said. "Ordering the same old shirts and tops from Amazon every other blue moon isn't *shopping.*"

"Whatever," Sara said, pleased because her daughter was pleased.

Was it possible that she'd actually done something teen-approved?

A rarity, indeed.

"Can I look?" Hayley pleaded. "I promise I'll be careful!"

"Look all you want," Sara replied.

"I could have gone with you, you know," the girl prattled on. "Given you fashion advice. Made sure you didn't buy anything stretchy, or with an elastic waistband. You didn't, did you? You didn't buy soccer-mom stuff?"

Sara laughed. "Judge for yourself," she said.

Hayley held up the magenta jeans bedazzled with rhinestones. *"Seriously?"* she crowed. The word was usually a reprimand of sorts, but this time, well, it sounded almost like a compliment.

"Mistake?" Sara asked cautiously.

Hayley held the jeans to her front. "Defi-

nitely not," she replied. "Can I wear them?"

"In a word," Sara replied, "no."

"Why not?"

"Because one, they belong to me, and two, they wouldn't fit you anyway."

"Did they have any in my size?" She indicated the name printed on the shopping bags. "At Fancy That, I mean?"

"Probably," Sara answered with a slight smile. "But unless you've been saving your allowance since you were in first grade, you can't afford them."

That remark inspired Hayley to peek at the price tag and then exclaim, "Holy crap!"

"Hayley," Sara said. "Language."

"Mom, *crap* is a perfectly acceptable word. Google it."

"Save it for people who aren't me," Sara replied. "And I don't *need* to Google it."

Hayley's blue eyes twinkled with mirth and a kind of effervescent well-being. She looked so much like Zachary, and yet she was nothing like him.

We all have our better angels, Sara thought.

Even Zachary Worth.

Mother and daughter spent a pleasant half hour or so unwrapping the clothes, remarking on them, putting them on padded hang-

ers and placing them in the central wardrobe.

Remarkably, Hayley approved of everything,

They were in the kitchen, cooking supper — pasta with chicken and garlic sauce, a green salad, banana pudding for dessert — when Sara's phone went through its default riff.

Since Eric had his own ringtone, as did Hayley and Eli, Sara figured the caller must be Brynne calling to report any further developments concerning David Fielding and his prospective employment as a wedding planner.

"Tell me you hired that beautiful man!" she cried instead of saying hello.

She heard a low masculine chuckle in response.

So, not Brynne.

"Competition already?" J.P. asked. "Damn."

Sara laughed, but her cheeks were burning, and she felt, not for the first time that day, like an idiot.

"I thought you were Brynne," she said, after spending a few moments struggling with her own mortification and, at the same time, basking in the warm echo of his voice. "You met David Fielding today at Sully's, and I imagine Eli has told you all about him. Can you possibly describe him as anything less than beautiful?"

"Actually," J.P. drawled, "he didn't do a thing for me."

Sara laughed again. Then sobered. Was J.P. calling to cancel on the picnic and the horseback ride?

"So," she prompted lightly, "what's up?"

There was a smile in his voice when he answered, as though he'd considered saying something other than what he did.

"I'm calling about our date on Saturday."

"I see," Sara said, hoping the wave of disappointment that rolled over her wasn't audible in her tone.

"I'm not sure you do," J.P. replied. "Horseback riding is out of the question right now, but we can still have the picnic. I have a great patio with what amounts to an outdoor kitchen. Suppose I grill up some steak or chicken — whatever you prefer — and we do the packed-basket-and-blanket thing another time?"

Sara's first reaction was relief out of all proportion to the situation. J.P. hadn't called to cancel their date.

Her second was a rush of joy.

Now that she wouldn't have to navigate a saddle, she could wear one of her new sundresses, dig out the strappy sandals she'd bought to wear to an Easter dinner a few years before, shave her legs, put on a little makeup and a very light misting of perfume.

"Sounds good to me," she managed after the silence stretched so far that Hayley made a say-something face at her, widening her eyes, raising her brows and inclining her head to one side.

Okay, so it wasn't exactly snappy repartee. She was paid to *write,* not speak.

"Great," J.P. responded. "We can make this lunch, or we can make it supper. Up to you."

Sara turned away, so Hayley couldn't read her face.

Anything could happen either way, of course, but supper was definitely riskier than lunch. The sky would be splattered with bright stars, and there would be wine and possibly soft music.

She recalled the kiss, the feel of J.P.'s strong work-hardened body against hers.

Heat surged through her, and a peculiar ache, warm and sweet and heavy, settled in her nether parts.

"Supper," Sara said decisively, blushing at her audacity.

"Supper it is," J.P. replied.

"Shall I bring anything? Dessert? A salad?"

"Just yourself" was J.P.'s answer. There was something intimate in his choice of words, or maybe it was the way he said them, all smooth and easy.

"What time?" she asked.

"How does seven sound? I'm going to be on the range most of the day, and I'll need a shower when I get home."

Sara allowed herself to imagine J.P. McCall in the shower.

Her knees went weak and she had to plop down onto the seat of one of the kitchen chairs.

Hayley looked at her with concern and, as Melody had done earlier, fetched her a bottle of chilled water.

"It's him, isn't it?" Hayley asked.

Sara held up a hand to silence her daughter. She could only manage one emotional riot at a time.

"Seven sounds perfect," she said at long last.

"I was beginning to think you'd ended the call," J.P. remarked with that same sexy warmth.

The sound made Sara want to get naked.

With J.P.

In his bedroom.

She was absolutely positively going crazy.

"No," she said, giving Hayley a look. "I wouldn't do that. Not without saying goodbye, anyhow."

The truth? She could have sat there, allowing this man to caress her with his voice, for hours.

"Good," he said.

Suddenly, it occurred to her that other people might be invited to J.P.'s to share in Saturday night's barbecue and, before she could stop herself, she blurted out, "Just us?"

"Just us," J.P. confirmed. "Is that a problem?"

Sara realized she was smiling. "No," she replied.

He laughed again, a low rumbling sound that was, somehow, deeply reassuring. Almost nurturing, which was insane.

"I'm glad we're on the same page," he said.

Sara began to feel nervous again. "Me, too."

"See you Saturday," J.P. told her.

"See you then." She looked around. "I guess I'd better get back to making supper," she added.

"Goodbye for now, then," J.P. said.

"Goodbye, J.P.," she answered.

And then she pressed the end button on

her phone.

Sat staring blindly at the nearest wall.

Hayley jolted her out of her reverie by jumping up and down, then punching the air with her right fist.

"Yes!" the girl cried joyfully. "I *knew* it! You're going out with J.P. McCall!"

Sara came out of her trance and smiled at her daughter. "I take it this is good news?"

"It is for me," Hayley said, settling down a little, but still breathless. "Eric's going to shit a brick, though."

Sara sucked in her smile and tried to look stern. *"Hayley,"* she warned.

"Sorry, Momster," Hayley told her, bending to kiss the top of Sara's head, "but *not* sorry. *Shit a brick* is part of the modern vernacular — power to the people — and, anyway, I've heard Uncle Eli say it a million times."

"Uncle Eli says a *lot* of things you shouldn't," Sara said. Her tone was prim, but she knew she wasn't carrying it off.

She was in too good a mood to be pedantic.

Hayley raised her eyebrows. Picked a cherry tomato from the salad and popped it into her mouth. Chewed and swallowed.

"I've never heard him use the *F* word," Hayley admitted.

"Trust me," Sara said. "He uses it. But that doesn't mean you get to. Not in my presence, anyway." She drew a breath, let it out. "Show a little respect for your aging mother."

"My *aging mother*?" Hayley challenged, apparently delighted. "If J.P. McCall, one of the best-looking men this town — heck, this *country* — has ever produced, thinks you're hot, then you are *definitely* hot!"

"Stop it," Sara said, but without much conviction. Secretly, she was flattered.

Did J.P. think she was hot?

Would he still think that if he took another look at Melody Merriman?

"*You* stop it, Mom," Hayley shot back. "Hasn't anyone ever clued you in to the fact that you're *beautiful*?"

Zachary had told her she was beautiful, once upon a time, and she'd believed he meant it.

Once she realized, in a very painful way, that everything he'd ever said to her had been a lie, she'd discounted the whole idea.

Brynne was beautiful.

Shallie Hollister was beautiful.

She, Sara Garrett Worth, was passably pretty.

Smart. Competent. Sensible.

But beautiful? No.

209

Zachary had disabused her of that notion long, long ago.

Besides, it was better, wasn't it, not to be conceited, full of oneself, vain and entitled?

Brynne and Shallie weren't like that — of course they weren't. They were wonderful, generous women. They *celebrated* their femininity.

And they were exceptions to the rule, Sara decided, with a touch of sadness.

She was who she was, and that was good enough.

It had to be.

CHAPTER NINE

J.P. had been on the range, on foot no less, checking for traps of any kind, since shortly after dawn, along with several deputies, his dad and about a dozen volunteers — mostly ranchers and farmers, but also a few townspeople.

Eli had helped out intermittently, going back and forth between J.P.'s place and Cord's, where Melba's people and more volunteers were covering as much ground as they could, as safely as they could.

Nothing had been found, but there was still a lot of ground to cover, not only on the McCall and Hollister ranches, but on the surrounding properties as well. Who knew how far this malicious mischief reached?

The work was hot, dull and tiring, not to mention discouraging, and when, after completing his usual chores, J.P. peeled off his dusty, sweat-stained clothes and climbed into the shower, just before 6:00 p.m. that evening, he figured he could have fallen asleep standing up, like an old horse.

The thought of Sara kept him upright.

In more ways than one.

He finished off the shower with a blast of ice-cold water before getting out, drying himself off and pulling on clean jeans and a relatively new green T-shirt. After pulling on a decent pair of boots, he went back into his bathroom to assess himself in the mirror.

Wiping away enough steam to make out his general condition, he peered at the image of a very tired man in sore need of another shave and a few swipes of a comb.

He used the comb, then brushed his teeth.

Trooper meandered into the foggy room to see what his primary human might be up to.

J.P. grinned down at the dog. Rubbed his own stubbled chin.

"So a little scruff is considered fashionable these days," he explained amicably. "They say women find it sexy — who the hell ever *they* is. What do you think, old buddy?"

Trooper tilted his faithful head to one side, as though considering a reply.

Of course, none was forthcoming.

"You're right," J.P. said. "It's a good time to find out."

Trooper backed out of the bathroom and disappeared.

J.P. hoped that wasn't a judgment on his decision to forgo shaving.

He splashed on some woodsy, leathery-smelling cologne — a gift from one of his sisters several years before — and sat down to inspect the soles of his boots, just in case.

The ones he'd worn to scour part of his land with a metal detector were on the back porch, caked with dirt and manure, waiting to be hosed off before he wore them again.

He went out to the patio, where the fancy brushed-steel grill took up a considerable amount of space, raised the lid and inspected the racks.

They were clean, thanks to the housekeeping service — they were nothing if not thorough. Then he lowered the lid again, turned on the propane to fire the thing up.

Barbecuing was a questionable endeavor, given that the heat of the day still lingered, but J.P. had made the offer of an outdoor meal to Sara, so he was going to follow through.

He headed for the kitchen, washed his hands at the sink and carried the still-packaged steak and chicken breasts outside.

After warning his shadow — Trooper — that the food was off-limits, he made another trip inside to fetch a pair of sizable baking potatoes wrapped in foil.

God bless his mother. She'd stopped by, at his request, earlier that day to look in on Trooper and make sure he wasn't too lonesome.

Since J.P. had mentioned plans to entertain Sara Worth that evening, Sylvia had taken the figurative bull by the horns and whipped up two salads, one pasta and the other green, with all kinds of vegetables.

For good measure, she'd baked her famous rhubarb/strawberry crumble.

Her thoughtfulness had saved J.P. some work and, after the day he'd had, he was more than grateful.

He made a mental note to send her flowers, to supplement the thank-you he'd already offered.

Her response, via telephone, had been a cheerful, "I *like* Sara."

"So do I," J.P. had responded honestly. "You're the best, Mom. I can't thank you enough."

"Sure you can," Sylvia had responded with a mischievous note in her voice. "You can come over here one day soon and roto-till a space for a new flower bed. That kind

214

of work is too hard for your father."

That remark had worried J.P. a little. "Is something going on with Dad that I ought to know about?"

He'd heard the smile in his mother's tone. "No, honey, he's fine — I promise. But he *is* getting older. He needs to slow down a bit."

J.P. had thought about the plan he and his dad had hatched to hack away and haul off the brambles covering those old graves over at the homestead cabin, and wondered if he should just go on ahead and do the job himself.

Trouble was, they'd made an agreement, and circumventing that might chafe the old man's pride.

Since he wouldn't be getting around to that particular task for a while, considering the wild horse/trap problem, he'd have time to think it over.

He'd been about to thank his mom again, hang up and go take his shower when she'd asked about the body Eli had found.

The sheriff's office hadn't issued a formal statement yet, though the corpse had been identified as a local kid, Randy Becker, recently graduated high school football star and well-known bully. Becker's parents, vacationing in Europe, had been notified, of course, but otherwise the identity of the dead boy was still being kept on the down-low.

J.P. had explained patiently that the deceased was a local and his name would be released when the initial investigation was complete.

"You know and you won't tell me," Sylvia had accused but good-naturedly.

"Yep," J.P. had confirmed. "That's about the size of it."

"Which just goes to show that we raised you right," his mother had said.

J.P. had grinned. "Flattery will get you nowhere, Mom," he'd replied.

"Nonsense," came the chipper response. "It gets me everywhere — except with you."

He'd laughed. "Goodbye, Mom," he'd said. "And thanks again."

The call had ended on that note, though J.P. knew his mother would have liked to ask more questions, beyond whether or not he'd heard when her granddaughters were expected — Tuesday or Wednesday of the coming week — and whether this evening with Sara was just a casual get-together or the start of something.

Damned if he knew what would happen after tonight.

Now J.P. returned to the patio and placed

the foil-wrapped spuds on the grill, since they'd take a while to cook through.

When that was done, he brought out a couple of bottles of wine: a decent red, to be served at room temperature, and a good chardonnay, chilling in a fancy ice bucket that had belonged to his folks. They'd left it behind, along with a lot of other stuff, when they'd moved to the A-frame, where space was obviously limited.

He'd been going back and forth between the kitchen and the patio for a while by then, and Trooper, who had been keeping pace, finally decided he'd had enough traveling and lay down in a shady spot to keep an eye on the steak and chicken.

If either one of them tried to make a run for it, Trooper would be there to prevent their escape.

J.P. brought out wineglasses and splashed some red into one before dropping into a patio chair to check his phone.

As was his custom, he scanned his portfolio, then read the latest financial news. He took in the pertinent information, but his mind was only half fixed on the numbers.

He kept thinking about Sara.

Wondering about her.

His knowledge of the woman was wide, but it wasn't deep.

217

For instance, he didn't know how she'd feel about getting married again, since the first go-round had been such a shit show. Practically everyone who'd lived in or near the town of Painted Pony Creek knew Zachary Worth as a spoiled rich kid, a pathological liar and a cheat.

J.P., Cord and Eli had not been all that well acquainted with Worth, to be fair, because he hadn't gone to school locally. He'd been a boarding student at an expensive and prestigious institution back East, visiting his divorced and famously reclusive father for part of every summer and quickly proving himself to be a narcissistic prick.

What Sara Garrett had seen in him, besides his slick good looks and way with words, was anybody's guess. She'd been a serious student back then, shy but popular, planning to go on to college and get her teaching credentials.

Instead, after a few heavy dates, the summer after graduation, she'd eloped with Worth.

Rumors of pregnancy had arisen right away and, as often happens, they proved true, when Sara gave birth to a full-term baby after too few months as a bride.

Nothing unusual, especially in a small town, where secrets were harder to keep, but that it happened to Sara? That *was* a surprise to the locals.

J.P., being a kid himself at the time, hadn't paid a lot of attention.

Zachary and Sara had broken up a few years later, when he'd run off with one of the barmaids at Sully's. At the time, Zachary'd been out of work for a while, and he'd left Sara practically destitute, with two young children to support.

She'd filed for divorce immediately.

Presently, things had gone south between Sara's ex and the waitress, and he'd returned to the Creek, full of sloppy remorse and broke on his ass.

Rumor had it, Richard Worth, Zachary's wealthy father, had refused to fund the prodigal.

No fatted calf for him.

For a while, Zachary hung around, probably bed surfing between girlfriends, trying to cajole Sara into taking him back, but she'd been adamant.

As Eli had said at the time, when Sara was through with somebody, she was through. End of story.

Most people had expected Sara to remarry, once she'd had time to get over Worth's betrayal. But for all his faults, she'd evidently loved him more than anyone could have guessed.

He'd broken something in Sara, taught her not to trust.

Since then, she'd lived quietly, working a low-paying job, mothering her kids, teaching Sunday school. She'd had a tight circle of friends, and according to Eli, she'd tried dating a few times, though nothing much had come of it.

She'd been burned too badly.

The thought made J.P.'s jaw harden.

He'd never understood people who signed up for a relationship and then decided to risk everything — partner, children, home, reputation — for a roll in the hay with somebody else.

During his hitch in the military, prior to the explosion, he'd seen soldiers of both sexes get breakup letters and emails from people who'd promised to love them forever and to wait for them. That, among other things, had soured his confidence in human nature; maybe it was even one of the reasons he'd never married.

At seventeen, he'd *thought* he loved Reba Shannon, Carly's mother.

He'd been super pissed off when he'd learned she was playing him, right along with Cord and Eli, but he hadn't suffered a broken heart or anything like that.

No way.

He'd almost lost his two closest friends over Reba, and that was a mistake he'd never made again.

For a long time, he'd been content to date a lot of different women, with no intention of settling down. But after Cord fell in love with Shallie, and then Eli with Brynne, he'd begun to feel a little restless, at least on the romantic front.

He'd known happy marriages existed, obviously — his parents had one and so, as far as he knew, did both his sisters, though it seemed things might be a little rocky in Josie's partnership, given that she was sending her daughters to the ranch for an indefinite visit.

His folks were older, and his sisters had settled down far from home, so marital bliss had seemed pretty ordinary to J.P.

Cord and Eli, however, were his age.

He'd grown up with them. Watched them take up with various women, then move on. Cord, in fact, had been married before; *that* had been a train wreck.

J.P. had chalked that up as one more reason to keep playing the field.

For a long time, he'd loved chasing women, and truth be told, he still had all the opportunities he could use, when it came to hot no-strings sex.

He'd lost interest, though. Not in hot sex, never that — but in sleeping around the way he used to do. He'd basically played fast and loose with too many women, often forgetting their names after he'd stopped by the florist's, chosen a bouquet and signed a card.

The message had been, in so many words, *So long, see you around, it was fun, have a nice life.*

He'd been a selfish bastard, plain and simple.

Albeit a clean and very careful one.

Some of those women had been, like him, looking for a good time and nothing more, but others, surely, had hoped to find someone to truly love. It didn't sit right with him now, knowing he'd used them. Never taking the time to get to know them and never allowing them to get close enough to know him.

All of them were human beings, and they'd deserved better.

Better treatment.

Better men.

Nope, he wasn't proud of what he'd done, hadn't been at any time, but he saw no point in beating himself up. He'd faced his shadow side — part of it, at least — and changed

222

his ways, and that was what mattered.

If there was one thing J.P. had learned, lying in a military hospital bed for months, it was that holding on to the past, ruminating over what could have been, *should* have been different, was a fool's game with no winners.

Naturally, he had some horrible memories, stemming from the roadside bombing in Afghanistan, and he didn't resist or repress them. He let them come, rode them out and moved on when they'd passed.

The other side of that coin was that he didn't dwell on anything he couldn't actively change.

Life was too full of good things to sweat the small stuff, or the big stuff, either, for that matter.

He believed in letting life be life, and so far, the philosophy had served him well.

He took another sip of wine, savored it.

Heard a car pull up in front of the house.

Sara.

He swallowed, nearly choked.

With a grin, J.P. got to his feet, set aside his wineglass.

Time to welcome the woman he very much wanted to know, and know well.

CHAPTER TEN

Something leaped inside Sara as she parked her car in front of J.P.'s ranch house and saw him approaching, the dog at his heels.

She'd been full of nervous excitement all day, deciding what to wear and then changing her mind and deciding on something else, choosing to put on a little extra makeup and then choosing to go with her usual mascara and lip gloss.

She wanted to look good, not just for J.P. but for her own gratification. She *didn't* want to look like somebody she wasn't, though, or as if she might be trying just a smidge too hard.

In the end, with Hayley's largely unnecessary but greatly appreciated assistance, she'd settled on one of the new sundresses — pink with spaghetti straps and a built-in bra. As for the makeup — well, she'd stuck with a minimalist approach.

Now, wanting the driveway dust to settle

on the ground instead of on her, she sat behind the wheel, admiring J.P.'s physique, his sexy stubble, his grin.

Like many cowboys, he walked with a slow, easy motion, ambling as though his hip sockets had been greased.

In those moments, Sara felt fiercely feminine and not the least bit wary.

To put it bluntly, she wanted to eat J.P. McCall right up.

Yum.

He reached her side of the car and opened the door. The dust had shimmered its way back to earth, mostly, but he seemed oblivious to the stuff, as though it had never billowed up beneath her tires.

"Hello, Sara," he said, and his voice was gruff.

His eyes took in her face, her hair and what was visible of her dress, and his perusal felt like a full-body caress.

She shivered, which was weird, because she'd expected to spontaneously combust. Just burst into flames right there on her car seat.

J.P. held out a hand to her, and Sara remembered to unfasten her seat belt before letting him help her from the car.

She wasn't used to her high-heeled Easter shoes, and the driveway was rough, so she stumbled into J.P.'s chest.

Just the way she had after their dinner date at Bailey's.

What if he thought she'd done it on purpose?

She decided not to go down that particular rabbit hole.

His arms closed around her, strong. Warm steel covered in flesh.

"Oops," she said, feeling the dreaded blush rise into her face. "Sorry."

J.P. didn't release her right away. "Don't be sorry," he said. "I don't mind catching you when you start to fall. In fact, I kind of like it."

Sara willed her throbbing cheeks to chill out.

For a long moment, she was incapable of speech. Then, ever the wordsmith, she blurted out, "I brought wine."

"Good," J.P. said. He held her back a little way so he could look at her, and Sara got the distinct feeling that he wasn't referring to the bottle of Shiraz she'd pulled from her personal collection before leaving the house.

When Trooper began trying to nose his way between them, J.P. laughed and let go of Sara, only to take her left hand in a loose grip. He started for the side of the house, which was sheltered by tall fruit trees.

"The wine —" Sara protested weakly.

"Later," he replied.

He led her through the trees and onto a spacious covered patio paved in red brick. There were several tables, with cushioned chairs, and the grill was a huge, shiny thing accompanied by an actual stove, what looked like an ice machine, a small refrigerator and a double sink.

"Very fancy," she said. "Do you give a lot of parties?"

J.P. grinned as though she'd said something funny, and she truly hoped she hadn't.

"No," he replied easily. "Mom and Dad used to entertain a lot when they lived here. I've only used it a couple of times."

Sara looked around, imagined the tree limbs festooned with fairy lights, or loaded down with colorful Chinese lanterns. "It's lovely," she breathed and, once again, felt something quicken inside her.

"Thanks," J.P. said. "Wine?"

"Yes, please," Sara replied.

"Red or white?"

Ridiculously, she looked down at her expensive pink sundress. "Red would be risky, since I'm such a klutz," she deliberated. Then she smiled. "I'm feeling reckless, though, so I guess I'll take the pinot noir."

J.P. filled a wineglass, held it out to her. "I

like reckless," he told her.

"Wait," she said hastily, distracted. "Maybe I should sit down first."

The grin returned. "Okay," he replied, holding the glass in one hand and drawing back a chair at the center table with the other. "Have a seat."

Sara obliged. Settled herself.

Accepted the wine.

"Thank you," she said.

J.P. quirked an eyebrow. "Could we be a little less formal? We've known each other for a long time, after all." He joined her at the table, taking the chair directly across from hers. Took a sip of his own wine.

"We have," Sara agreed quietly. "But this is different."

He nodded. "Yes," he agreed. "It is."

Suddenly, she couldn't hold it back any longer, the question she had been dying to ask ever since that unforgettable kiss.

"J.P., what's happening here?"

He reached across the table, took her hand again. "Damned if I know," he replied, "but I'm all about finding out."

She was at a crossroads, and she needed more information. Like was she about to take a wrong turn?

"You're not helping," she pointed out.

"Is it my imagination, or am I getting the

impression that my reputation has preceded me?" J.P. asked mildly, settling back in his chair.

"Sort of," Sara admitted. Then she added, "Well, yes."

"I'm not especially proud of that part of my life," he said. "Looking back, I think it might have been some kind of reaction to the explosion. It was as if, on some level, I was afraid to stand still, take stock of myself and the way I was living, and figure out what I really wanted." J.P. paused and shook his head slightly, as though shaking off memories he didn't want to face. "That's no excuse, of course."

Sara studied him for a long moment before confessing, "I was pretty good at running away myself. Funny thing is I did it standing still. I was so focused on my children all the time — and I don't regret that — that I guess I couldn't see myself in any other role than Hayley and Eric's mother."

She thought she saw a flicker of something in his eyes. Not anger but — sorrow?

"I don't pretend to know," he ventured quietly, "but being a single mother has to be damn difficult."

"It is," Sara confirmed gently. "But I don't imagine being so seriously injured was a day in the park. Seems as though that would do things to the mind, not just the body."

Again, something moved in J.P., this time in his face. It was very subtle, the slightest of shifts, but it was definitely there. "I still want to run away from that sometimes," he admitted.

And Sara wanted to weep. To lay all this man's ghosts to rest.

Wanted to put her arms around J.P. McCall, big and strong as he was, and tell him everything would be okay and hold him until it was.

But *would* things be *okay*? If she'd learned anything along the rocky way, it was that life didn't come with a warranty. All a person could really do was suit up, show up and do what they thought was right.

Fate would decide the rest.

"I'm sorry about what happened in Afghanistan, J.P.," she said softly.

"Don't feel sorry for me," he warned, but his tone was easy, gentle. Practiced. "I was one of the lucky ones, after all. I came home. I've still got two arms and two legs. Seven of my buddies — and a hell of a lot of other soldiers — drew the short straw and were shipped back in boxes."

"Still," Sara murmured, wanting to hug him more than ever, "I reserve the right to wish you hadn't been hurt at all. You didn't deserve to suffer like that. No one does."

"Thank you," he said, and though he smiled, he changed the subject. "What about you, Sara? Were you happy raising kids?"

"Sometimes I felt like tearing my hair out," she answered honestly, "but, yes, I was happy. Exhausted, flat-ass broke most of the time and lonely as hell after they went to bed at night — but happy. Grateful, even. Sound convoluted?"

He shook his head again, and the smile faded to a sad remnant of itself. "Would you do it all over again?"

Sara didn't hesitate. "Yes," she said. "If I could still have the kids and cut Zachary completely out of the picture."

"Do you think you'd want more children? In the right circumstances?"

That gave her pause. After a long time, she replied, "Maybe. I'm not sure, actually. Parenthood is a big responsibility, but it's rewarding, too."

J.P. looked thoughtful, as though he were weighing her words.

Another silence settled between them, but it wasn't an awkward one.

Then, after the interval, J.P. spoke again. "How do you want to play this, Sara? Will it be fun and games, or something more serious?"

"I don't know," Sara replied honestly. "Do we have to decide tonight?"

He laughed. "No," he said. "But I have one more question."

Sara braced herself. "Shoot," she said.

J.P. took a sip of wine, thought for a moment. "Do you think all men are like your ex?" he finally asked.

"God," Sara said with a shudder. "I hope not."

"You never miss Zachary at all? You must have loved him once."

"Zachary," Sara stated firmly, "ran me over with an emotional bulldozer, then backed up and ran me over *again.*" She blew out a breath. "So, yes, I guess I *do* think about him, on bad days. Now that he's back in town, trying to play the devoted parent, I can't really ignore him the way I'd like to."

"No tender feelings at all?"

"I have feelings, all right," Sara blustered, fiddling with the stem of her wineglass. "Though, where he's concerned, they're mostly homicidal."

J.P. laughed. "Good to know," he said.

"And that was more than one question," she pointed out. Then because, damn it, J.P.

McCall didn't have a corner on questions, she decided to ask a few of her own.

Sara narrowed her eyes. "Are people saying I'm still in love with him?" she asked. "And don't say you don't *know* what people are saying, because this is Painted Pony Creek, Montana, we're talking about, and *everybody* has heard *something.*"

"Sara," J.P. said reasonably, gently. "I heard the guy was back in town. Eli told me. And that's *all* I've heard."

Realizing she'd gotten a little riled up, Sara calmed herself by taking several slow deep breaths.

"Are you?" J.P. prompted. "Still in love with the Boy Wonder?"

Sara, having just taken a sip of wine, nearly snorted the stuff through her nostrils. *"No,"* she answered. Then, after a few more restorative breaths, she added, rather archly, "And how many times do I have to say it?"

J.P.'s gaze was level, clear. He didn't give a direct reply.

Instead, he said, "In all this time, you haven't dated seriously, or fallen in love with someone new. Yeah, I know you've been busy bringing up your kids, but single mothers remarry all the time. A man can be forgiven for thinking you might be carrying a torch."

"*You* haven't dated seriously, either," Sara reminded him. "You've been playing the field since puberty."

Again, he laughed. "True enough," he said. "But you, Sara Garrett, have been living like a spinster schoolmarm since your divorce."

"You don't know that!"

"Yes, I do," came the unruffled response. "Your brother is one of my two closest friends, remember? Eli's no gossip, but he *does* mention you from time to time."

Sara sighed. Drank more wine. "I'm the fool who chose Zachary Worth for a husband," she said softly, sadly, after swallowing and setting the glass down carefully. "So I guess I didn't trust my own judgment. The man had fatal flaws, and I thought he was Prince Charming. If I'd made the same mistake all over again, it might have destroyed me."

J.P.'s gaze was sympathetic, but there was no pity in it. Only respect. "You were what, Sara — nineteen when you met Zachary?"

"Seventeen," Sara recalled ruefully. "I was eighteen when Eric was born."

"Give yourself a little credit, why don't you? Your frontal lobes weren't even fully developed back then. You made the decision you were *capable* of making at the time —

234

and you got a son out of the deal."

Sara relaxed a little. Smiled. "*And* a daughter."

"So why beat yourself up?"

Sara considered the question, then quipped, "It's my hobby?"

Again, J.P. laughed. "Get a new one," he said.

"Such as?"

"Such as, I'm not touching that question with the figurative ten-foot pole."

Now it was Sara who laughed.

And it felt so very good, laughing with a man.

Laughing with *this* man.

Another silence fell then, and it was comfortable, something to nestle into, to wrap around one's heart like the softest of blankets.

The daylight, though still bright, was beginning to fade, promising yet another breathtaking Montana sunset, and a cool breeze made the leaves of the fruit trees shift and whisper.

There had been a lot of questions that evening, and there would be plenty more, if they kept seeing each other, but Sara didn't worry about that.

Tonight, she was entirely content just to be in J.P.'s company.

"I'd better get the food on," he said presently and with happy resolve. "I promised you a meal, and I am a man of my word."

Sara was deliciously relaxed. "Yes," she said, "you are."

"Chicken or steak? Or both?"

Sara chose steak. She ate a lot of chicken at home, and she was rather tired of it.

J.P. set two large T-bones on the grill. "More wine?" he asked over one broad shoulder.

Even through the back of his T-shirt, she could see the powerful play of his muscles.

Dear God, he was so uncompromisingly masculine, though not in a toxic way.

He simply *liked* being a man, it seemed to her, didn't need to prove himself to anyone.

Sara could admit it to herself, if not J.P. — she wanted to go to bed with him.

Wanted him to hold her, kiss her, drive her to distraction.

Who *was* this reckless person who called herself Sara?

Where was the *Momster* Sara?

The ambitious, independent Sara, determined to make it on her own, financially and in every other way?

She'd gone underground, that other Sara, so practical, so disciplined, so dignified, replaced by a slinking jungle cat, ready to

236

mate and damn the consequences.

They ate dinner, once the steaks were ready, and talked about wild horses being harassed, rusty coils of barbwire and wicked steel traps lurking in tall grass.

They drank more wine, and when J.P. turned on the sound system, they danced to slow smoky-smooth jazz that drifted across the patio like the receding daylight, full of sex and shadow and sweet surrender.

Sara, always so cautious, relaxed into J.P.'s embrace, loving the feel and the smell and the sight of him.

All her life, she'd prided herself on being *enough,* in every way, needing no one to make her feel whole, but in those moments she was, for the first time she could remember, ready, even eager, to let down her guard, to be truly vulnerable.

Never, not even in the early days with Zachary, had she felt the way she did now, swaying gently in J.P.'s arms on a dusky patio, aware in every fiber of her being of his muscular chest, his hard thighs, the gentle power in his hands.

This was a man who could ravish her, yes, but he was also one who would shelter her when she needed sheltering. He was country born with a heart as big and as elemental as the broad Montana plains, a heart where some lucky woman, someday, would find sanctuary.

Much to her surprise, Sara felt a tear slip down her right cheek.

She hoped J.P. wouldn't notice but, of course, he did. He brushed it tenderly with the side of one thumb.

"What's this?" he teased in a hoarse whisper. "Did I step on your foot?"

Sara sniffled inelegantly. Grabbed a cloth napkin from the nearby table to repair any damage. "I was thinking silly thoughts, that's all."

"Such as?"

Such as how much I want you to make love to me, J.P. McCall. Not just tonight, but every night, for the rest of my life.

"I guess I'm feeling a little sentimental," she replied. It wasn't a lie, but it *was* a deflection. How was she supposed to tell him she wanted him to kiss her again, remove her clothes and *have* her as she had never been had before? "I think I need more wine."

He didn't answer.

As if he had somehow divined her thoughts, intuited her deepest desires, he kissed her, very lightly at first and then with a depth and a hunger that splintered her road-weary soul.

And Sara kissed him back with everything she had to offer.

"Well, then," J.P. said, sounding breathless, when they were forced to come up for air. "I guess that answers *some* of my questions."

"What questions are those?" Sara asked very sweetly and quite shamelessly, too.

"You tell me," J.P. countered with a sly grin and a flash of mischief in his eyes.

That ruffled Sara, although she was every bit as aroused as before. She flattened her hands against the breadth of his chest and pretended to push. "Oh, no, you don't, J.P. Answer my question!"

He chuckled, caught her wrists in his hands, held them gently. "All right," he said. "My question — one of them, anyway — was, does Sara want me as much as I want her?"

Sara blushed hard again, and supposed that was answer enough, but she pressed for more. "What were the others?"

He caressed her palms with the pads of his thumbs, sending a ragged need ziplining through her entire system. "There was only one other," he said, playing dumb.

Then, after a long, long moment, he went on. "Not to tank a romantic moment or anything, but I was wondering if you're on birth control."

"I have an IUD," she replied. And that was true enough, though it was something she rarely thought about — just a precautionary measure she'd taken several years before during a fit of unbridled optimism. She'd never been able to tolerate the pill.

"Okay," J.P. said with a resigned sigh. "And I have condoms."

"I'm sure you do."

"Was that a gibe?"

"Actually, yes," Sara said with a smile. She pulled her hands free, slipped her arms around his neck. "Now," she added, "kiss me again."

The second kiss was more dizzying than the first, so much so that Sara swayed in J.P.'s arms, and that prompted him to sweep her up into his arms, Rhett Butler–style.

Oh, for a grand stairway.

But there was none, since the ranch house was all on one level.

"Where?" he asked in a gravelly voice.

"Anywhere," Sara murmured in reply.

J.P. laughed throatily, his face buried in the curve of her neck. His mouth moved against her flesh as he spoke, driving her nearly insane with wanting him. "Lady," he said, "I like your style. *And* your body."

They made it all the way to his bedroom,

which seemed, to Sara, like a minor miracle. She wanted him *inside* her, and she didn't care where it happened.

Setting her on her feet next to the bed, J.P. steadied her for a few moments, then reached around to unzip her dress.

It fell away, built-in bra and all, and left her naked except for her shoes and a pair of ridiculously expensive lace panties.

J.P. surveyed her, almost in wonder, then let out a long breath.

Sara kicked off her shoes, ready for action. *More* than ready.

J.P. hauled his T-shirt off over his head, revealing a spectacular chest, scarred from his injuries in Afghanistan but still beautiful, a vee of honey-colored hair. His stomach was wash-board-lean.

He took off his boots, realized Trooper was in the room, swore affectionately and ushered the animal out, closing the door behind him.

Sara, feeling wilder than wild, waited for J.P.'s return, and when he reached her, hooking his thumbs under the narrow waistband of her barely-there panties, she opened his belt buckle.

After that, things happened very rapidly. Sara, for her part, would gladly have skipped the foreplay, at least that first time, but J.P.

had other ideas, as it turned out.

He wanted to drive her batshit crazy, and that's what he did.

He laid her on the bed sideways and, after tossing his shorts, fell to her the way a man dying of thirst might fall into a cold, clear stream.

He nibbled at her breasts, each in turn, until her nipples were hard and wet from his tongue, and she was whimpering, begging for *all* of him.

Now.

J.P. only chuckled at her pleas and went right on tormenting her.

He moved from her breasts to her earlobes and her neck, and then back again, tasting, teasing until she thought she might actually, for real, go completely insane.

But even that didn't satisfy him.

He pulled her to the edge of the bed, slid her panties down her thighs, over her knees and calves and ankles.

Afraid she truly wouldn't be able to bear the pleasure of what she knew he was about to do, Sara tried to sit up, whispered a raspy, "J.P. —"

"Preview of coming attractions," he murmured, parting her thighs, revealing her most intimate, most vulnerable parts. "Stay tuned."

She moaned. "Oh, God —"

He parted her, kissed her, his touch soft as a breath, and she cried out, tangling her fingers in his hair, tossing her head from side to side.

She could *not* bear this. She *could not.*

She would catch fire, implode, disintegrate.

"Please," she whispered, and if J.P. had been waiting for a cue, that must have been it. He played her, with his lips, with his tongue, with the muffled groans that vibrated through her.

The orgasm was endless and shattering, wringing shout after shout from her throat; she felt herself splinter and rain down from the sky in flaming shards of utter satisfaction.

Sara melted into the mattress, its linens crisp against her bare skin, and waited, waited, until finally she settled back into herself.

J.P., meanwhile, was still between her legs, lightly kissing the quivering insides of her thighs.

When she could speak, her voice was sultry. Sated. "If that was a preview —" He stroked her upper thighs, her belly, her breasts. Laughed quietly.

She wondered if she would *ever* need sex

again after that apocalyptic experience.

Then J.P. parted her again, stroked her.

She gave a low helpless moan. "That — feels — so *good.*"

"It's supposed to," he murmured, and then he took her into his mouth again, and made her climb and climb toward another release, tossing and pleading and raising her hips high off the bed as he suckled her, once again, into madness.

That second orgasm was sharper, more intense than the first one, high and thin like a scream of pure, delightful surrender.

When the last shuddering tsunami of ecstasy had subsided, J.P. lay down on the bed, hauled Sara up beside him and held her, just held her.

She wept.

He kissed away her tears. "What is it?" he asked.

She, a professional writer, didn't have words to express the things she felt. She only knew that he'd made her fly apart in pieces, body and soul, and now, simply by holding her, he was putting her back together again.

"I'm all right, really," she assured him.

He kissed her forehead, her eyelids, her cheek. "Sara," he persisted, "if something's wrong —"

She cupped his handsome face between her hands. "Believe me, J.P.," she responded, still misty-eyed, "*nothing* is wrong about this."

And then she kissed him.

The buildup was slow and sultry, deliciously, endlessly sweet.

When Sara finally got what she wanted, she was a tigress, now on her back, now astride J.P., holding him in that most primitive of ways, working him relentlessly until he stiffened beneath her, giving a shout of mingled triumph and defeat.

His release went on and on, playing out in his face, in the corded muscles of his neck, in the driving force of his hips.

The power of his thrusts drove Sara over the edge, and she joined him in the fire, flexing upon him again and again, her head thrown back, her cries unrestrained.

When it was over — *finally* over — they were both struggling to breathe.

The echoes of that third orgasm boomed through Sara like thunder rolling across a stormy horizon.

She was winded, exhausted, *bamboozled.*

Why had no one told her sex could be like this?

Nestled deep inside herself, almost like a person under water, she found no answers to her question.

So she rested there, J.P. beside her, one leg flung across her thighs, one arm resting across her middle.

She traced the scars on his back, not wishing to smooth them away but to revere them as a part of him.

She dozed and dreamed, and when she woke, J.P. was holding her again, the way he had earlier.

With one fingertip, he traced her mouth, the length of her cheek. "Hey," he said. "Practicality rears its ugly head. It's after midnight. Are the kids waiting for you?"

Sara shook her head, touched by the concern she saw in his night-shadowed face. "No. Eric is spending the night with a friend, and Hayley babysits for Eli and Brynne practically every Saturday evening, provided she doesn't have a date. She's there now, and she'll sleep over."

J.P. smiled. "Good," he said. "We'll have a sleepover of our own."

Sara giggled like a girl. "I don't know if I have the strength," she admitted. "Making love with you, Mr. McCall, is a real workout."

He kissed her lightly. "Let's be fair here," he teased. "You rode the buck right out of this bronco."

That time, she laughed outright. "You enjoyed it," she reminded him.

He traced her mouth again, this time with his tongue. "So did you," he retorted.

"Oh, yeah," Sara sighed, still floating languidly in a sea of residual pleasure. "I certainly did."

J.P. leaned over, reaching for something on the floor, and came back with her new panties hooked on the tip of his index finger. He gave them a spin.

"When I saw these, I knew it was going to be a wild night."

"Very perceptive of you," Sara replied, taking the panties and tossing them aside again. The dim light and the mood emboldened her a little — or maybe a lot. "I almost bought crotch-less ones, if you must know."

J.P. raised both eyebrows. Gave a low shrill whistle.

Outside the bedroom door, Trooper whined.

"Not now, buddy," J.P. called to the dog.

Trooper's tags jingled as he settled down again, keeping his vigil.

J.P.'s attention shifted back to Sara. "About those crotch-less panties —"

"What about them?"

"Next time, wear them."

Sara felt a faint flexing between her legs.

Next time? There was going to be a next time?

Hallelujah.

"Why?" she asked, feigning innocence.

"Because I'm going to want to get right down to business," he replied.

"Is that so?" She was getting hot and achy again. Squirmy.

He was stroking one of her nipples with an expert thumb. "It's so," he affirmed. "It's going to happen. You won't know where, you won't know when. And I guarantee you this, Sara Garrett — you'll howl like a she-wolf."

More heat. More ache.

"You're trying to seduce me again. Right here, right now."

"Whatever you say," he replied, and with that, he replaced his thumb with his mouth, suckled at Sara's hardened nipple until she moaned.

Another few moments of *this* and she'd be pleading again, thrashing about on the bed.

And here she'd thought they were through making love for the night.

"I'm not *trying* to seduce you, Sara. I don't *have* to try."

"Now, *that* is arrogant," she said.

J.P. answered by sliding his hand down

over Sara's belly, stroking her.

Again.

Her hips began to rise and fall with his caresses.

He kissed her neck, nibbled at her earlobe, told her sexy stories, broken and breathless in places, about a woman who wore crotchless panties and the man who meant to take full advantage of that, at the most outrageous times, in the most outrageous places.

It was glorious.

CHAPTER ELEVEN

Sara sneaked into her house, into her own kitchen, like a guilty teenager, at 6:05 a.m. the next morning, hair askew, shoes in one hand, purse dangling from the opposite wrist.

It came as a less-than-fabulous surprise to find her son and her ex-husband seated at the table, drinking coffee.

"Mom," Eric blurted, clearly shocked. He actually went pale.

Zachary, for his part, smirked and raised one eyebrow but said nothing.

Sara decided, in a moment of pure desperation, that the best defense was indeed an offense. "What are *you* doing here?" she demanded, setting aside her handbag with a thump.

"I *live* here, remember?" Eric snapped, furious and faintly contemptuous.

"I wasn't talking to you," Sara said evenly. It was a struggle not to react to her son's mood, but she managed, mostly.

Zachary shambled easily to his feet, obviously enjoying Sara's predicament.

"I guess I'd better be on my way," he said.

"Good idea," Sara affirmed, glaring.

"Dad brought me home," Eric all but whined. "And he has a *right* to be here!"

"The hell he does," Sara countered without taking her eyes off her ex. "Get out, Zachary."

"Don't you think you're overreacting just a little bit?" Zachary replied. "You've always been so *dramatic.*"

"Isn't that what narcissists always say?" Sara shot back. "When someone calls them on their bullshit, they say they're overreacting, being dramatic. *Get the hell out of my house.* Now."

Zachary, still smugly jovial, raised both palms, playing the peacemaker. "I'm going," he said indulgently. "No need to lose it in front of our son, Sara."

She was supposed to feel guilty.

She didn't.

She folded her arms, shoes still dangling from one hand, and waited.

Zachary finally left, going through to the living room and then out the front door.

It slammed behind him.

In all that time, neither Sara nor Eric

spoke. They were both royally pissed, and it was a standoff.

Finally, Eric slammed one fist down onto the tabletop, causing the coffee mugs to jiggle. Then he shoved back his chair, got to his feet and stormed out of the kitchen.

Welcome back to the real world, Sara told herself silently.

Thanks to the encounter just past, her delicious night with J.P. seemed like a distant dream.

And she was wide-awake now.

"Crap," she muttered, and headed for her own quarters on the other side of the house.

There, she dropped her shoes, took off her sundress — with some difficulty since it zipped in the back — and let it fall to the floor.

After that, she padded into her bathroom, loosening her hair from its braid as she went. She showered thoroughly, shampooed and conditioned her long tresses, and after drying off and wrapping her head in a towel, she donned regular clothes — ordinary jeans, a plain short-sleeved cotton blouse and flip-flops.

She was sitting on the back patio, brushing her hair before re-plaiting it, when Hayley appeared in the doorway, her eyes round.

"Eric is *freaking out,*" the girl announced.

252

"Eric," Sara answered coolly, "needs to mind his own business."

"He said you were out all night, with *some guy*," Hayley went on with delight. "I didn't tell him you were with J.P. McCall." A pause. "You were with J.P., weren't you?"

"That," Sara replied, a bit tersely, "is no more *your* business than it is Eric's."

Hayley pulled up a patio chair and plopped into it. "Okay," she answered companionably, "that's fair."

In that moment, Sara imagined a scene from her good-natured daughter's future career as, Hayley hoped, the first female sheriff of Wild Horse County.

You're under arrest, she heard Hayley say cheerfully, *but I hope that doesn't make you feel bad. You can* definitely *turn this thing around. In fact, I'll help.*

Inwardly, Sara smiled.

"How was the babysitting gig?" she asked, partly to change the subject and partly to get her mind off the prospect of searching the internet for a source of crotch-less panties. She certainly wasn't going to buy local in *this* case.

Hayley's face, already bright, lit up even more. "It was *great.* Those baby cousins of mine are *beyond* cute. Smart, too."

Sara smiled. She loved her brother's twin

sons as much as her daughter did.

"Did your uncle Eli take his gorgeous wife out for a glamorous evening?" she asked pleasantly.

"Yes," Hayley answered. "Dinner and dancing."

Dancing.

Sara remembered slow dancing with J.P. on his darkened patio and a jolt of passion zigzagged through her.

"Very romantic," she said.

Hayley picked up the conversational thread without a hitch. "Speaking of romantic," she teased, "is this thing between you and J.P. going anywhere? Eric says you were out all night and came in carrying your shoes."

"Back to Eric again," Sara said with a sigh, and began weaving her damp hair into its customary single braid. She loved her son, but right about then she could cheerfully have throttled him for his attitude.

Hayley, probably realizing that the conversation would go no further, at least for now, rose to her feet, stretched her long arms toward the sky, yawned and said, "I think I'll catch a couple of hours of sleep. I binged on episodes of *Virgin River* between the time I put the babies to bed and Uncle Eli and Brynne came home."

Sara smiled. She liked the show herself.

"Sleep tight, kiddo," she said as Hayley went back into the house.

Anticipating a few minutes of sunshine and peace, Sara was a little disappointed to hear the French doors open again.

"Mom?"

This time, it was Eric.

"What?" She spoke patiently, gently, though it was an effort.

Eric took the same chair his sister had occupied only minutes before. "I'm sorry," he said glumly. "I acted like a butthead."

Sara suppressed a smile. "Yes," she agreed. "You did. But I accept your apology."

"Thanks," he answered, splaying his fingers through his hair and lowering his forehead to his palms.

Sara's finely honed mother's intuition kicked in. "What's up, Eric?" she asked quietly.

"It's Dad," Eric confessed. "I thought he was going to try to get you back, but instead he's getting married. To some bimbo."

"Eric," Sara corrected her son, "the word *bimbo* is sexist."

"So I have to be politically correct, even with my own mom?" The whine was back, though it was mild.

"We don't call other people names like

that, ever. It's wrong to slap a simplistic and insulting label on another person, especially when we barely know them."

Eric looked up, drew his hands down his face, distorting it comically in the process. A wicked grin tilted one side of his mouth.

"So you've never labeled Dad with an insulting name?"

"I have, actually," Sara confessed. "I'm working on that."

"Who did you spend the night with, Mom?"

"That is an intrusive question," she said.

"I'm your son. Don't I have a right to know if there's an incoming stepfather?"

"If there's ever any indication that he's about to become your stepfather, I'll give you a heads-up right away."

Sara hadn't pictured J.P. as a stepfather to her children.

Or as a husband to her.

What would that be like, adding a fourth person to their small family circle?

A chain of questions followed that one.

Did J.P. want kids of his own?

Did *she* want little ones when her own children were nearly grown?

Eric would be going away to college in just a year and, though Sara would definitely miss him, she saw his departure for school as a finish line of sorts.

One she meant to fling herself across, figuratively speaking.

He'd be homesick when he left, for about five minutes.

Then he'd be into college life, busy with classes and new ideas and new friends.

Hayley would not be far behind; she was already planning to enter the University of Montana. She, too, would be preoccupied with her studies and boyfriends and the sports — softball and swimming — she loved.

Would she, Sara, even *want* to start over, have more children?

Or was she past it, past sleepless nights and changing diapers and all the other things that went with raising little ones?

Frankly, she didn't know.

She wanted more sex with J.P., that was for sure. She'd never been more alive than when she was entwined with him, soaring in an ecstasy she couldn't have imagined before last night.

"Mom?"

Sara realized she'd been drifting. Brought herself up short. "Yes, sweetheart?"

Eric cleared his throat. "I know it doesn't seem like it sometimes, but I love you."

Tears burned behind Sara's eyes. She was

an emotional basket case, loved senseless the night before, confronted with her ex-husband and angry son the next morning.

"I love you, too, Eric. And don't you forget that."

She leaned over, gave her son a one-armed hug.

"So, tell me about your father's engagement. In fact, tell me where he's been all these years, and what he's been up to."

Eric seemed pleased by this invitation, and that touched Sara's heart in very tender places. She wondered what he'd told Zachary about her — a lot, probably.

"He met her in a nightclub down in LA," he began. "That's where he's been. He was trying to break into the movie business."

Sara bit her tongue. *Don't say it,* she warned herself.

"As an actor?" she asked when she could speak moderately. Without inflection.

"No," Eric answered with a shake of his rumpled head. He needed a haircut, and Sara barely resisted pointing that out to him. "He wanted to be a producer."

"I take it that didn't work out," Sara observed cautiously.

Again, Eric shook his head. "He couldn't get a break. Everybody was against him. Jealous, he says."

Inwardly, Sara rolled her eyes. Outwardly, she was every bit the good listener. "Okay," she said in a tone meant to lead her son into further revelations. "How did he make a living?"

God knew Zachary Worth, would-be movie mogul, certainly hadn't paid child support.

Not that she intended to point that out.

This connection with Eric was too precious, and too tenuous, for that.

"I guess he had a trust fund or something. It ran out, so he changed his career plans and came back here to see if Grandfather would make a place for him in the family business. You know, the commercial real-estate thing."

Eric, Eric, Eric, Sara thought, but what she said was "I see."

"Grandfather isn't a very nice man," Eric confided.

Ah. A clear space in the shifting fog.

It closed immediately, of course.

"I know," Sara agreed, remembering her own confrontation with her ex-father-in-law. He had been old then, which meant he was ancient by now. Probably not long for this world. "Isn't there another son?"

"Wyatt," Eric supplied, with a sympathetic sigh. "He's Dad's half brother, actually.

He's not a Worth — his mother was the second wife, and when she divorced dear old Granddad and remarried, Wyatt took his stepfather's name. Anyhow, he and Dad don't get along. Wyatt's a couple of years younger, and he's the head of his own corporation, wants nothing to do with Worth Enterprises. He thinks Dad is a waste of skin. That's what he said once when Dad asked him to invest in a film project."

"Hmm," Sara breathed.

"And what do you think my grandfather plans to do?" Eric challenged.

"I have no earthly idea," she said.

Indignation flared red in Eric's cheeks. He was such a good-looking boy, and so smart. Sara hoped he wouldn't ruin his life by patterning himself after his father.

She'd worked hard to keep her son on track, but stranger things had happened.

"He's leaving the company to Wyatt, not Dad. Even though Wyatt doesn't want it, and he doesn't even go by our last name!"

"Ouch," Sara said. The old man was crafty, that was for sure. He hadn't built a multinational real-estate investment firm by being a sucker.

And he obviously wanted to stick it to Zachary, financially at least.

Plus, he surely knew his elder son would

run the company into the ground, given the chance.

"Your dad gets nothing?"

"A pittance by comparison," Eric huffed. "It isn't right."

"The money belongs to your grandfather, Eric, and so does the company. He gets to decide who inherits what."

Eric tensed. "You love this, don't you?" he accused, riled up again. "Seeing Dad get the shaft!"

"Calm down," Sara counseled. "I do *not* love this. And kindly watch what you say and how you say it. The truth is I don't actually care what happens to your father, one way or the other."

"Don't you have any feelings for Dad at all?"

"I'm sorry, Eric, but the honest answer is no."

"Didn't you *ever* love him?"

"I did, way back when. I was a naive young girl with a head full of dreams."

"You stopped when he left us? Loving him, I mean?"

"Yes." That answer was close enough to the truth. To be more accurate, she'd stopped loving Zachary Worth the night she caught him with another woman.

Things had come to a head one soft summer night when a friend had called to tip her off that her husband was down at Sully's making out with a barmaid.

Sara, who had suspected something was going on but refused to consciously accept the fact, had asked a neighbor to watch Eric and Hayley, both toddlers then, and driven her ancient rattletrap of a truck across town to the popular bar.

She'd hurtled into the parking lot, tires flinging up gravel, gotten out and raged into Sully's with angry sparks flaring before her eyes.

Sure enough, there was Zachary, drunk, draped all over his latest lady friend, plying the old cliché when Sara snatched a mug of beer from an unoccupied table and tossed the contents in his face.

"Sara," he'd said in a tone of sugary condescension, "it isn't what it looks like."

The hell it wasn't.

She'd told him to pack his shit and hit the road.

The other patrons of Sully's, looking on, had slow-clapped.

After repeatedly protesting that he was innocent, that she was blowing this whole thing *way* out of proportion, yada yada yada, Zachary had finally done what she asked and gone away.

Over the next couple of months, he'd returned to the Creek several times, swearing he was a changed man, begging for a second chance.

But Sara had stood firm.

She held on to a quote attributed to Maya Angelou, one of her all-time favorite poets. Paraphrased it to suit her situation: "When somebody shows you who they are, believe them."

"There's more," Eric said with a note of petulance in his tone, and Sara had to flip back through her mental files to remember what they'd been talking about.

Oh, yes.

Zachary and how everyone had done him wrong. Such a victim.

Sara held back a sigh. Wondered randomly what J.P. was doing at that moment.

Wished she were still with him, lying naked in his arms.

Last night almost seemed like a fantasy now. After making love into the wee small hours, they'd both fallen into a deep sleep.

Just as the sun rose, J.P. awakened her with a kiss, then made love to her again, this time slowly, so very slowly.

Her responses had left her languid, wanting to snuggle down and go back to sleep, but J.P. wasn't having that. He half dragged, half cajoled her out of bed, across the room to the bathroom door, into the shower.

They lathered each other in soapsuds, but they were still weak-kneed from the last round, so there was no sex.

J.P. had dressed in the bathroom — jeans, a blue chambray shirt, old boots — while Sara struggled back into her sundress. She had to search awhile to find her discarded underpants.

He'd rejoined her just in time to zip up her dress.

After that, he steered her toward the spacious kitchen.

There, he let the ever-present Trooper outside, then filled the dog's water and food bowls.

Sara had looked down at her crumpled sundress, wishing she'd brought a change of clothes along with that bottle of Shiraz. But then, she hadn't expected to spend the night.

Or had she?

J.P. had kissed her forehead and told her to smile. That this was Painted Pony Creek, not Lake Woebegone.

She'd laughed.

He'd set about brewing coffee, and then he'd made a rancher's breakfast — pancakes, eggs, bacon and toast slathered with sweet butter and strawberry jam.

The meal had been delicious and filling, and thus it had restored her wavering confidence, too.

Without that food, she knew, she would have been weepy.

Lake Woebegone, indeed.

After they'd eaten, she'd helped with the cleanup.

Trooper was readmitted to the house and treated to the last remaining strip of crisp bacon.

And then it was time to leave.

Time for her to go home.

Time for J.P. to attend to his chores.

He'd walked her to her car. Kissed her.

Sara had waited for him to mention seeing each other again.

He hadn't, exactly. But he *had* promised to call.

She'd driven home in a daze.

Parked her car in the garage and taken off her shoes, just in case.

And there was Zachary, the last person she had expected — or wanted — to see.

She'd been stunned.

Now, sitting on her shady patio with her son, Sara shivered.

Last night had been a journey to a shimmering world hidden somewhere far beyond time and space. Population: two — herself and J.P.

This morning, in the bright and uncompromising light of day, it was almost as if the whole thing had been a dream. Sweet and sultry, but still a dream.

Suddenly, she wanted to cry.

Eric must have read her expression, because he actually reached over and rested a hand on her shoulder.

"Is everything okay?" he asked.

Sara blinked a couple of times, and the threat of tears subsided. Thank God.

"Yes," she answered. "Don't worry about me."

"You're not upset because Dad is getting married?"

An inelegant snort of laughter was Sara's reply.

Eric chuckled. "I guess that *was* a pretty dumb question."

Sara poked him lightly in the ribs. Raised both eyebrows when he looked at her.

He laughed, but his expression turned solemn pretty quickly.

"Let me turn your question around, Eric," Sara ventured. "Are *you* upset that he's getting married?"

"Yeah," Eric admitted with a heavy sigh. "I don't think he's going to stick around

266

the Creek much longer — not unless Grandfather relents and leaves him more in the
will than he plans to right now."

Although Zachary couldn't leave town
soon enough to suit her, Sara knew Eric
was cherishing certain hopes that were
probably going to be dashed, simply because
of who Zachary was.

The man probably couldn't change even
if he wanted to — which she was sure he
didn't. He *liked* being a selfish asshole;
almost surely prided himself on it.

It was then that Sara realized that all the
anger she felt toward her ex-husband had
nothing whatsoever to do with what he'd
done way back when. She'd been over that
for a long time.

No, what infuriated Sara about Zachary's
sudden reappearance in their lives was the
certainty that he wanted something —
money, most likely — and he was willing to
use his own children to get it. *Her* children.

He had to know she wasn't going to give
him a nickel.

But his elderly father? Better chance there
that Daddy Dearest hoped for a last-minute
connection with the grandchildren.

Sure, the old man was bitter and hard,
not to mention stubborn, but he was a mil-
lionaire many times over.

Over the years, Zachary's father had made no effort to get to know his grandchildren, but that might have been, at least partly, because of Sara herself. She had told the chauvinistic old coot to take a flying leap — albeit in more colorful terms — and she'd definitely meant it.

He hadn't reached out to Eric and Hayley, it was true, but that didn't mean he'd written them off.

Perhaps *that* was Zachary's game: his father was purportedly dying, and it was at least *possible* he wanted to see Eric and Hayley before he crossed over. Zachary could make that happen — with Eric, anyway — and that might be a very valuable bargaining chip.

Then again, given the old man's apparent disinterest, it might not.

"Have you actually seen your grandfather? Visited him in person?" Sara asked. She was fairly sure her son would have told her about such a momentous meeting, but then, with kids, one never knew.

Eric shook his head. "Not yet. He's in a hospital in Seattle, I think. Dad says he's coming home, though. Maybe he wants to die in the mansion or something."

"Does it make you sad? That your grandfather is dying?"

Eric shrugged, somewhat disconsolately. "He's old," he said, sounding forlorn. "And I don't know him. So I guess I'm only losing the grandfather I wanted, not the one I had. Or *didn't* have."

Sara felt another pang of sympathy for her son. When it came to blood kin, she and Eli had been all the kids had, since their folks had died a long time ago. "Has he asked to see you and Hayley?"

"Dad's trying to arrange something," Eric replied.

"Do you *want* to meet him?"

"I guess," Eric said.

"You guess?"

"Well, I suppose I ought to say thank you, if I get the chance."

"Thank you?" Sara echoed, trying not to sound ironic. *For what, exactly?*

"I've been waiting for the right moment to tell you," Eric said very cautiously. "Grandfather is leaving a chunk of money to Hayley and me. It'll be held in trust until we turn thirty-five — *thirty-five,* can you believe it? We'll be too *old* to have any fun."

This news rocked Sara to the core. "Your dad told you this?"

"He showed me the paperwork. It's seven figures, Mom. For *each* of us."

Although Sara had never wanted anything

269

from Richard Worth, wouldn't have asked him for a penny, even when times were hard, she didn't begrudge her children an inheritance. They were closely related to the man, after all.

"When were you planning to mention this?" Sara inquired.

Again, the desultory shrug. "When you and I weren't fighting. I haven't said anything to Hayley yet — Dad wants to do that." Eric huffed out a sigh. "I told him she might not want to see him for a while — maybe she *never* will, because she's Hayley — but he thinks she'll come around. Want to meet our grandfather."

"Who's managing these trust funds?" Sara asked. Damn, but she'd almost worn herself out, asking all these questions.

Right about then, she could have crawled into bed and pulled the covers up over her head.

"That's the crazy thing, Mom," Eric replied. "It's Wyatt, *not* Dad."

Sara had been quietly clicking the pieces of the puzzle into place for several minutes, but this last statement completed the picture.

Zachary wanted to manage — read *spend* — his children's inheritance, and he was hoping a visit from Eric and Hayley would smooth the way. Charm their grandfather and, with luck, persuade him to put their devoted dad in charge of the trust funds.

Not on my watch, you bastard, Sara told her ex-husband silently. *Not on my watch.*

"So, Mr. Moneybags," she said, crinkling her eyes even though she was shading them with one hand. "Any plans for this fine Sunday in June?"

Eric smiled. "Carly and I are going to the movies. Two o'clock show. What about you?"

Sara closed her eyes, sat back in her chair and allowed the sun to kiss her face. She wasn't into tanning, but a few more minutes of blissful warmth couldn't hurt.

"I'm going to do some laundry," she replied. "Whip up something simple for supper and go to bed early."

Oh, and I plan to go online and order crotchless panties.

And erase my search history immediately afterward.

Blushing slightly at the thought, Sara opened her eyes, turned her head to look at Eric. "You can invite Carly to join us if you want. For supper, I mean."

"I'll ask her," Eric promised, pleased. "She might want to get home early, though. I guess J.P. McCall's nieces are coming for a visit soon. They're younger than Carly, but she wants to make sure they feel welcome. You know, because they'll be so far from their friends and everything."

J.P. hadn't mentioned the imminent arrival of his nieces, but then, it wasn't as if they'd done much chitchatting the night before.

They'd been too busy swinging from chandeliers.

So to speak.

"That's nice of Carly," Sara said sincerely. "Very thoughtful."

"She's golden," Eric agreed, rising from his chair. "Guess I'll grab a shower and have something to eat." With that, he disappeared into the house.

Sara decided she'd had enough sun — at least, without sunscreen — so she followed.

She was sorting laundry when her cell phone, tucked into the pocket of her jeans, began to pulse.

J.P.?

She peered at the screen. Nope.

Brynne.

"Hey," she said. "Did you and Eli have a good time last night?"

Brynne gave a throaty laugh. "We had a *very* good time."

Sara wanted so much to confide in her sister-in-law, but it was too soon for that.

Things were still far too fragile between her and J.P., outside of his bedroom, anyway. "What happened with David Fielding?" she asked. "Did he accept your job offer?"

"Yes," Brynne said, clearly happy about David's decision. "He's quite the business-man. Wants the option to buy into the wedding-planning part, if it turns out we can work together effectively. He'd be a full partner."

"What's your take on that? Would you consider a deal like that?"

"Definitely," Brynne replied. "He's already given me about a thousand new ideas, all of them excellent, and he wasn't expecting a New York salary in backwater Montana."

"Sounds good," Sara said, happy for Brynne, who needed all the help she could get when it came to her wedding business. Although it wasn't common knowledge, Brynne and Eli were trying for another baby. They didn't want too big of an age gap between the twins and their little sister or brother. "When does he start?"

"Not for two weeks," Brynne said, this time with a sigh. "He and Evan are closing on their farm. They want to renovate the house — it's the old Wilkins place, you remember — and replace the barn, too. Plus, Evan is buying sheep and cattle and a few horses —" Her voice fell away, and when she went on, she sounded sad. "Livestock isn't such a good idea at the moment, what with all the traps they've been finding all over this part of the county."

"I hear there was a body," Sara said, knowing Brynne couldn't give her the details, if indeed she knew any of them. Eli wasn't one to spill information that hadn't been released to the public yet, even to his wife.

"Yes," Brynne replied. "And that's all I know."

"Of course it is," answered Sara. "This is Eli Garrett we're talking about here."

"Tell me about it," Brynne said. "Listen, I have another reason for calling. You might have heard already, but Melba and Dan's new baby was born a couple of days ago. Everybody's healthy."

"I hadn't heard," Sara said, and she felt some degree of chagrin, because Melba and Dan Summers were good friends. "Boy? Girl?"

"Boy. Nine pounds, twelve ounces. Dan calls him the Hulk, but his actual name is Daniel Martin Summers Jr."

Sara teared up, happy and a little relieved. The Summerses had two daughters, a teen and a preteen, and they'd been divorced for several years when little Daniel was conceived.

Mending their relationship hadn't been easy, Sara knew, but really, when was *any* relationship easy?

"And," Brynne said, drawing out the word, "there's the matter of you and J.P. and that picnic you were planning. How did that turn out?"

Sara blushed, standing there in front of her washer and dryer, glad her sister-in-law couldn't see her. The two of them went way back, and if they'd been face-to-face, she wouldn't have been able to hide much of anything.

"We had to change it up," she said with a deliberate no-big-deal note in her voice. "You know, because of the traps and all. J.P. barbecued steaks on his patio and we had fun."

"*Fun* fun?" Brynne wanted to know.

Sara remembered dancing with J.P., their bodies swaying together. She remembered him carrying her to his room . . .

Heat surged through her bloodstream, and she ached.

Everywhere.

"It was very nice," she said at last.

"I'll just bet it was," Brynne answered.

"If you did," Sara told her, "you'd win."

"Good for you. Good for *both* of you."

"Don't start planning things," Sara warned. "This might not go anywhere."

"Whatever you say," Brynne responded sweetly. "Listen, when can we visit Melba and Dan and the newest member of the family? The chief says she doesn't want a fuss made — as in, no baby shower — but Shallie and Emma and I think we ought to do *something.*"

"Melba doesn't want a shower?" Sara asked. "But the girls are practically grown, and their hand-me-downs wouldn't do for a boy. I say we get presents, anyway. We just won't do the cake and the games or the balloons and streamers."

"I'm on board with that idea, and I know Shallie and Emma will like it, too."

They agreed on a tentative date, a few days away, and ended the call.

Sara was humming as she stuffed a load of towels into the washing machine, added soap and pushed the button.

That done, she sneaked into her office, closed and locked the door, logged on to her computer and did a little online shopping, quite unrelated to the baby shower that wasn't one.

CHAPTER TWELVE

It was Sunday, which meant the flower shops were closed, and J.P. wasn't about to give Sara supermarket roses.

She deserved the best.

So he loaded Trooper into the truck and drove over to the A-frame, where he found his mom working in her vegetable garden and his dad sitting on the deck, whittling on a piece of wood with his pocketknife.

Trooper, always delighted to pay a visit to extended family, slithered past the gearshift and the steering wheel and jumped out of the truck as soon as J.P. opened the door. The mutt ran around the yard in happy circles, barking for joy.

Not for the first time in his life, J.P. reflected that human beings would be a lot happier if they were as easily delighted as the average dog.

Talk about living in the moment.

"Hello!" J.P.'s mom called, straightening

and pulling off the gloves she wore to weed the rows of carrots and turnips and other good-tasting things.

His dad set aside his whittling and got to his feet, beaming.

J.P. wasn't normally the sentimental type, but it warmed his heart to be welcomed with so much enthusiasm. He hadn't realized it, but he'd been pretty lonesome for a while now.

A *long* while.

Leaving his hat in the truck, he crossed the yard to plant a kiss on his mom's cheek.

"I need flowers," he told her. "Can you fix me up?"

"Flowers?" Sylvia echoed, grinning impishly. "For a lady, I presume?"

"Yes," J.P. answered, well aware that the one-word answer would nettle his mom, she of the romantic heart.

Sylvia's eyes twinkled. "And that lady's name?" she inquired.

He sighed, shoved a hand through his hair. There was no point in trying to throw his mother off the trail. She'd find out he was getting serious about Sara sooner rather than later all on her own.

"Sara," he said simply.

"Sara Garrett?" Sylvia asked, face alight.

"She's Sara Worth now, but yeah. She's

278

the one."

"You go and visit with your dad," Sylvia urged, giving her son a light nudge with one elbow. "Let me handle the flowers."

"You won't get an argument from me, Mrs. McCall," J.P. replied.

He turned and headed toward his father, who was standing on the grass at the foot of the deck steps, greeting Trooper.

"Get me a vase before you settle down to swap tall tales," Sylvia called after him. "A big one. I keep them in that cabinet in the laundry room above the folding table. Wash it out in the kitchen sink, too, while you're at it."

J.P. looked back at her over one shoulder, grinning. "Anything else I should take care of while I'm in there? Maybe mop and wax the kitchen floor or paint the living room?"

"Oh, shush," Sylvia said with a dismissive wave of one hand. She was already heading for the flower beds, clippers in hand.

J.P. went inside, found a suitable vase, dutifully sloshed it around in some warm soapy water and went outside again. Gave it to his mom, who had already gathered an armload of pink and white roses and was now adding a variety of other blossoms to the mix.

"It's empty," she said with a slight frown.

J.P. went over to the spigot on the back wall of the house and filled the vase.

Tried again.

"That's better," Sylvia said.

J.P. only chuckled and shook his head. "*Now* can I hang out with Dad for a while?"

She swatted at his arm and missed.

John was seated on the deck again, Trooper lying at his feet.

J.P. pulled up a chair and sat down across from him.

"When are we going to clear out those blackberry bushes over at the cabin?" his father asked. "The ones you said were covering those old graves?"

"Soon," J.P. replied. "Right now, it probably isn't safe."

"They still haven't caught those thugs? Found all the booby traps?"

"No," J.P. answered, "but I think Eli has an idea who the culprits are, at least. You know we found a body out there, right?"

"Everybody's talking about it, at the feed store and everywhere else in town," John McCall answered. "Rumor is it's the Becker boy."

"The rumor is right," J.P. admitted. "But don't spread it around, okay?"

"What do you take me for?" his dad retorted, feigning indignation. "I'm not some blathering fool, you know. I can keep a secret."

"Don't get your boxers in a twist, Dad. Eli asked me not to say anything and, until now, I haven't."

"When that boy's folks get back from wherever they are, all hell's going to break loose." John paused, shook his head sadly. "Never much cared for those people — the Beckers, that is. Too high and mighty for my taste — but I wouldn't have wished this on *anybody*. No, indeed. Worst thing that can happen to somebody, losing a child. Especially like that."

"Yeah," J.P. agreed.

"Eli figures it was an accident? Something just spooked a bunch of those mustangs and they stampeded right over the kid?"

J.P. remembered the steel trap found near the body, winced. "Sometimes," he said, more to himself than to his father, "stupidity is fatal."

"You can say that again."

J.P. sighed. "In any case, we can't ride out to the homestead and walk around in the tall grass until there's some kind of resolution where the traps are concerned."

"You didn't find any on our place?"

"No," J.P. said. He'd be taking up the search again in the morning, checking mes-

281

sages periodically to see if the girls were arriving that day. Their mother was the type to book last-minute flights. "But that doesn't mean they're not out there, so stick close to the house. No long walks across the prairies."

"Give me a *little* credit, son," his dad urged, though without the flare of annoyance this time. "I didn't just fall off a hay truck."

J.P. chuckled. "I know, I know. I don't want you to get hurt, that's all."

It was then that the shriek of a siren splintered the calm summer morning, blaring along the inter-ranch road that snaked between the McCalls' place and the Hollisters'.

"What the hell?" John muttered, half rising from his chair, then sitting down again, hard.

More sirens ripped wide gashes in the peace.

J.P. stood up. "Keep Trooper here, Dad. Don't let him try to follow me, whatever you do."

"Maybe you ought to stay right here, too, son. Let Eli and his people do their jobs."

"No possible way," J.P. replied. With that, he put an anxious Trooper inside the house, closed the screen door tightly and told the dog to stay, his voice stern. "This is our land, Dad. We need to know what's going on."

His mom was coming toward them, carrying the vase in both hands, frowning over the glorious bouquet she'd picked and arranged for Sara.

"Not more trouble," she said, sounding forlorn.

"I'll be back for the flowers," J.P. told her, heading for his truck.

When he spotted the cluster of vehicles — Eli's SUV, an ambulance and two of the town's outdated Crown Vics — J.P. parked on the side of the road and deliberated on what to do.

He wanted to know exactly what was going on, but he knew better than to get in the way.

A couple of the volunteers who'd been out searching the ground for traps saw him and walked in his direction, following a path of trampled grass.

J.P. got out of his truck.

He recognized the pair — Jim and Dottie Fillmont, a young couple working a nearby farm. The small place had been in Jim's family for generations.

Jim put out his hand and J.P. shook it.

"What happened?" J.P. asked.

"A kid from town stumbled across a trap and sprung it. He's in a bad way."

J.P. swore, and then swore again. Apologized to Dottie, who was pale under her bright pink sunburn.

"Don't be sorry, J.P.," she replied. "I feel the same way. That poor boy is going to be lucky if he doesn't lose his leg."

"You found him?"

Jim nodded. "Heard him screaming and came as quick as we could. Dottie hurried over to the road, where the cell service is better, and called for help while I stayed with the kid. He passed out right about the time we reached him, which is a good thing, because that thing bit into him like a grizzly."

J.P. winced. In the distance, he could see the paramedics loading a stretcher into the back of the ambulance.

"You know the kid's name?" he asked.

"Yes." Dottie answered this time, hugging herself as though she felt cold, even though it must have been eighty degrees out, at least. "It's Eric Worth — the sheriff's nephew. He wasn't on the volunteer schedule, so he must have shown up anyway, to own — to help with the search? We didn't see him this morning, when Deputy Canfield briefed us all at the town hall."

Eric Worth. Eli's nephew.

Sara's son.

J.P. swore again, silently this time.

"It's bad," Dottie added, albeit unnecessarily. "Sheriff Garrett is fit to be tied."

"I need to talk to him," J.P. said, thinking aloud more than addressing Dottie and Jim.

He followed the pathway, his strides long.

Eli, speaking to one of his deputies, noticed his approach and turned to walk toward J.P. He was sheet white, Eli was.

J.P. figured his friend would either puke or pass out in another second or two.

"What the hell?" he asked when he and Eli were facing each other, a few feet apart.

"Eric —" Eli began. And then his voice fell away.

"Does Sara know?" J.P. rasped.

Eli looked even sicker than he had a moment before. "She knows he's hurt — I didn't give her the details. Brynne's picking her up, driving her to the hospital. I'll meet them there."

"I'm coming along," J.P. informed his friend.

Eli moved to load a bicycle — Eric's, of course — into the back of the SUV.

"Good," he replied, his voice hoarse with suppressed emotion.

A few minutes later, J.P. was in the pas-

285

senger seat of Eli's SUV, and they were bumping and jostling overland to the dirt road and then speeding toward the highway beyond the western fence line of the McCall property.

Eli's knuckles were white where he gripped the steering wheel. "Sara's going to take this hard," he said. "She thought he was going to a movie with Carly. What the *hell* was he doing out here?"

"Trying to help?" J.P. wondered aloud.

"Dottie and Jim thought so. I just hope to God they weren't wrong. If he's involved, that will half kill Sara."

J.P. figured Sara was going to be shattered either way.

And he wanted to be there for her.

"Any reason to think he is?" J.P. asked moderately.

Some of the tension in Eli's shoulders released. Up ahead on the highway, the ambulance siren screamed for right of way.

He shook his head. "No," he said gruffly. "But some of the townspeople might have a different opinion, given his history."

"If I were you, I wouldn't worry about that right now. You've got a big enough load to carry as it is."

Eli sighed, nodded.

"Any new developments since Randy

Becker was identified?"

"Yes," Eli replied after a few moments. "We're pretty sure Becker was part of the gang. Some of his former classmates claim he's been hanging out with thugs. Guys they didn't know."

"You're bringing them in?"

"We need warrants. Those are in the works — should be ready this afternoon." Eli steered the rig onto the main road, practically on two wheels. "They're lying low, these pals of Becker's, but we'll root them out in no time. It's hard to hide yourself in or around a place like the Creek, especially if you're a stranger."

J.P. pondered that, but only superficially. His mind was still fixed on Sara.

He wanted to find those bastards himself, beat a confession out of them.

"You're going to be busy today," J.P. told his friend. "Tell Sara what happened — she needs to hear it from you — and I'll take it from there. Look after her as much as she'll allow."

Eli gave him a distracted glance. His jawline was tight, and it glowed red. "That would be good," he said. "Thanks."

"Don't worry about it," J.P. replied, then realized how damned glib that sounded, given the situation, and wished he could take the words back. Swallow them or some-thing.

Eli flipped on the lights and siren, driving at top speed. "So," he said without looking at J.P. "It's true."

"What's true?"

"You and Sara."

"Yes," J.P. answered, because he'd never lied to Eli or Cord, or pretty much anybody else, in his life. "Me and Sara."

It took ten minutes to reach the hospital in Painted Pony Creek. J.P. used part of the interval to call his folks and fill them in on what had happened.

Naturally, they were horrified.

And they agreed to look after Trooper for as long as necessary.

The ambulance stood, rear doors open wide, in the special bay allotted to such vehicles when they arrived, tires screeching on the asphalt of the parking lot, but there was no sign of Eric.

He was inside by now, probably being rushed upstairs for emergency surgery.

Silently, J.P. prayed the kid would make it.

Come out of this ordeal with two legs instead of one.

Eli shoved open his door and jumped out of the SUV just as Sara's compact car sped into the lot, driven by a pale-faced Brynne.

Sara sat trembling in the passenger seat while her daughter, Hayley, leaped from the back, ran to Eli, sobbing, and flung her arms around him.

He spoke soothingly to her, then released her and approached the car.

Sara and Brynne got out, Brynne moving to embrace Hayley, who was still falling apart, Sara standing woodenly on the hot pavement, looking as though she'd fallen into a trance.

Eli gripped her shoulders as J.P. drew near, took up a position a few feet behind Sara. Waiting to be needed.

"Eli," Sara whispered, agonized. "What happened to Eric? What in *God's name* happened to my son?"

Without Eli's hands holding her up, J.P. knew Sara would have collapsed.

"One of the traps —" Eli began gravely, his voice hoarse.

Sara's scream of anguished protest sundered J.P.'s soul. *"Nooooo!"*

And with that, she shook free of her brother's hold, tried to go around him, meaning to rush inside the hospital and find her son.

"Sara," Eli murmured, stopping her. Restraining her.

She struggled in his arms, emitting a

piercing wail, shaking her head.

Eli caught J.P.'s gaze.

J.P. got the message. He moved closer to Sara and wrapped one arm loosely around her waist, ready to catch her if she fell.

"Go," he said in response.

Eli went, passing Brynne, who was already steering a still-sobbing Hayley inside.

Sara tried to follow her, but J.P. tightened his hold on her.

"Easy," he whispered, a raspy sound like a file scraping the edge of a horse's hoof. "Everything's going to be all right, Sara. For Eric's sake, you need to get hold of yourself. The staff will help him."

Sara whirled in J.P.'s arms, tried to slug him. *"Let me go!"*

"I will," J.P. replied with gentle reason. "As soon as I'm sure you're not going to take two steps and then fall flat on your face."

He felt her trembling against him. Thought how different this was from the last time he'd held her close.

"Breathe," he instructed her quietly.

A shudder went through her, but she seemed a little calmer.

"The trap —" she managed "— did someone take it off? My God, is that horrible thing still —"

J.P. closed his eyes for a moment, seeing the same horrific, bloody image in his mind that was probably playing out in Sara's.

"It's off," he said. The word was scraped from his throat, and it left him raw. "Eric was unconscious when the ambulance arrived. The paramedics freed his leg and applied a tourniquet to slow the bleeding."

"I need to go inside, J.P.," Sara whispered, almost pleading now. *"Please."*

J.P. spoke into the soft ebony of her hair, which smelled of sunlight and shampoo. "I know. Let's do this together, okay?"

The reply was a soft sob and, "Okay."

With that, J.P. escorted Sara across the ambulance bay, around the rig — its lights were still flashing, though blessedly the siren had gone silent — and into the waiting room serving the ER.

There was a trail of blood on the floor, leading toward one of the exam rooms in the back, and a janitor was in the process of mopping it up, his expression suitably morose, while various future patients watched in horror from the plastic chairs lining the walls.

Brynne and Hayley came out of the women's restroom, Brynne supporting the girl with one arm around her waist, the same as J.P. was doing with Sara.

Brynne seated Hayley in one of the chairs and crossed the room to meet Sara.

Her gaze linked with J.P.'s for a moment, then shifted back to Sara's face.

"Marisol is with Eric, Sara," she told her sister-in-law tenderly, taking Sara's hands in hers. Squeezing. "He's on his way up to the OR right now, and you know as well as I do that he couldn't be in better hands."

Dr. Marisol Stone, the daughter of the county coroner, was a skilled surgeon and chief of staff at Painted Pony Creek General Hospital.

Between them, Brynne and J.P. squired Sara to a chair next to Hayley's.

Sara rallied enough to wrap an arm around her daughter's trembling shoulders.

J.P. stood back a little, to give them space, and so did Brynne.

Brynne handed Sara and Hayley a box of tissues, taken from a nearby table, and J.P. crossed to the watercooler and filled two paper cups, brought them back.

Sara and her daughter accepted them gratefully.

"Is Eric going to die?" Hayley asked plaintively, the cup shaking in her hand as she raised it to her mouth.

"No," answered a feminine voice.

It was Marisol, dressed in scrubs. Eli

stood beside her, looking as though he could use a stiff shot of whiskey.

"How bad is it?" Sara asked, almost pleading for an answer she could endure.

"It's not good," Marisol responded in her kind but direct way. "But I'm *very* sure Eric will recover. We're stabilizing him now, treating him for shock, and he's had pain medication. Dr. Reynolds, a colleague of mine, is flying in from Helena as we speak. He's one of the best orthopedic surgeons in the country, and if your son's leg can be saved, Sara, he'll save it."

"If?" Sara echoed, holding her free arm close to her middle and rocking slightly in her chair. *"Eric could lose his leg?"*

"It's possible," Marisol replied, "but let's focus on what we're dealing with right now, at this moment. An amputation is the worst-case scenario, and it probably won't happen." She paused, sighed, though her brown eyes held Sara's without flinching. "Eric is going to require several more surgeries in the coming months," she went on. "And, of course, he'll need a lot of physical therapy, too. There's a rough road ahead, Sara, but Eric's *alive,* and that's what counts."

Tears trickled down Sara's cheeks as she absorbed Marisol's words, and J.P. wished he could smooth them away, gather Sara into his arms and hold her until all the sorrow, all the fear, was gone.

"Is Eric awake?" Sara asked after a long painful silence that encompassed all of them. "Can I see him?"

The conversation was punctuated by the distinctive sound of an approaching helicopter.

J.P. was all too familiar with the noise; he caught himself on the dark precipice of a flashback and mentally stepped away, back into the light.

"I'm sorry, Sara," Marisol answered quietly, lifting her eyes toward the ceiling. "That'll be Dr. Reynolds coming in for a landing. Eric will be taken into the operating theater within the next few minutes. We'll let you know as soon as he's in recovery."

Just then, the doors of the emergency room burst open, and Carly rushed in, flanked by Cord and Shallie.

The girl was frantic.

Marisol said she'd keep them up to date on Eric's progress and took her leave.

Carly rushed into the center of the group.

Cord caught up to his daughter and gripped her shoulders from behind, much as J.P. had done with Sara out in the parking lot.

Sara started to rise from her chair, wobbled and sank back into it. "Carly," she blurted. "What *happened*? Eric told me the two of you were going to the movies!"

Carly's pretty face was tear-swollen. "We had a fight," she half sobbed in response. "We went for coffee before the movie was supposed to start, since we had some time to kill, and he was going on and on about what a great guy his bio-dad is, and how everybody misunderstood him."

"And?" Eli prompted.

Fresh tears filled Carly's eyes. "I was fed up, *really* tired of hearing about his loser of a father," she said with a mixture of spirit and regret, "and I told him he was being delusional. I said if Zachary Worth was so terrific, he would have stayed around and raised his kids. Eric got mad and left." She stopped to draw in a long shaky breath and exhaled in a huff. "That was the last I saw of him. He just took off!" The girl's gaze held Sara's. "This is all my fault!" she cried. "I shouldn't have said what I did about his dad!"

Sara attempted to stand again, and this time she succeeded. She put her arms around Carly and hugged her tightly.

"This *isn't* your fault, Carly," she assured the girl. "You couldn't have known what would happen."

"What *did* happen?" Carly cried once Sara let her go and sat down again, clearly still weak in the knees. "All I know is that Eric is badly hurt, and he was brought here by ambulance!"

Nobody asked how she'd known even that much. This was the Creek.

Enough said.

It was Brynne who explained.

Eli caught J.P.'s eye, then Cord's.

By tacit agreement, all three of them went outside, where they could talk in relative privacy.

Eli looked, as the old-timers used to say, like death warmed over.

"How can we help?" Cord asked, breaking the silence.

"By standing by Sara and Hayley," the sheriff replied grimly. "The warrants came through, so I'll be meeting up with my deputies and a couple of Melba's people in a few minutes. We'll be making some arrests, and it might get ugly."

"Did you get a chance to talk to Eric when you went inside?" J.P. asked Eli.

"No," Eli answered.

"How did he get out there?" Cord asked.

Eli sighed. "He rode his bike. We found it nearby."

"Somebody lured him out there," J.P. mused.

"Possibly," Eli agreed.

"Why?" J.P. wanted to know.

"Could be somebody was trying to tell *me* something, and they used my nephew as the messenger," Eli answered. "An indirect way of saying *back off*? I'm not sure whether the trap was placed there deliberately or if Eric simply had the bad luck to stumble across it. Which is why I don't want Sara and Hayley — *or* my wife and children — left alone until we've rounded up these ass-holes."

"Sara will want to stay here, wait for news about the boy," J.P. said. "I'll stick around. Make damn sure nothing happens to her or Hayley."

"Shallie and I will take Brynne and the twins home to our place," Cord put in. "Hold them hostage there until you give the word that the danger is past."

"Thanks," Eli said, trying for a smile and not quite getting there. "Follow Brynne over to Bailey's — the twins are there, with their grandparents, Mike and Alice, and she'll head there first to pick them up. Don't let her out of your sight, Cord," he reiterated. "Not until you hear from me."

"You've got it," Cord affirmed, resting one

hand briefly on Eli's shoulder. "We'll gather up Mike and Alice, too, if they're amenable."

"What about you?" J.P. asked Eli, frowning. "You don't look so good, old buddy, if you don't mind my saying so."

"I have a job to do," Eli said flatly. "And I mean to do it."

With that, he nodded farewell and headed for his SUV.

J.P. and Cord went back into the hospital.

Over the next couple of hours, as the ER filled with people seeking medical treatment, mostly for simple illnesses and injuries, the place got crowded.

No word came down from on high.

The OR.

Eventually, Brynne and the Hollister gang trailed out.

Carly — with some help from Sara — had persuaded Hayley to go back to Cord and Shallie's place as well and spend the night there.

The girl was reluctant but she was also exhausted, so she agreed.

J.P., who had been pacing in order to stretch his legs, sat down beside Sara, reached for her hand.

She didn't look at him, but she didn't pull away, either.

"You don't have to stay, J.P.," she said after a long time.

"Oh, yeah," he replied. "I do."

"Did you see him?" Sara asked. "Eric, I mean? Before they brought him in?"

"Only from a distance," J.P. answered. "When they were loading him into the ambulance."

"I suppose I should call Zachary," she mused, staring straight ahead, still in a daze. "But I can't bring myself to do it."

J.P. figured Sara's ex would be less than useless, but he *was* Eric's father, so he supposed the man had a right to know his son had been hurt.

"You have the number?" he asked.

Sara groped for her handbag, which was on the floor under her chair, then rooted around inside until she found her phone. She fumbled with the thing, scrolled until she found the pertinent information.

J.P. pressed the appropriate buttons and waited.

After three rings, a woman answered. She sounded high — or drunk.

"I'm looking for Zachary Worth," J.P. said. No matter what ended up being said here, he promised himself he wasn't going to lose his cool.

"And who would *you* be?" the woman

asked in a distinctly flirtatious way.

"My name is J.P. McCall," J.P. answered, without inflection, "and I need to talk to Zachary. It's about one of his children."

He heard her set the phone down with a thud and call out in a wheedling, sickly sweet voice, "Zachary! Zachary, honey, there's a call for you."

A silence followed.

Then the syrupy voice was back. "He's in the shower."

"Well, tell him to get out," J.P. snapped.

So much for keeping his cool.

"You don't need to go all *grumpy* on me, J.P. McCall," Zachary's wife/girlfriend whined. "You and I can just visit until he gets here, can't we? You sound kind of — *hot.*"

And you *sound kind of — stupid.*

"Get him," J.P. ordered. *"Now."*

"Well, for pity's sake," the woman complained.

Two minutes later, Zachary was on the line.

J.P. told him, in the fewest possible words, what had happened to Eric and where the boy was now — i.e., in emergency surgery at the local hospital.

"All right," Zachary said when J.P. was finished.

" 'All right'?" J.P. repeated. "Are you coming over here or not?"

They might have been discussing a golf date, going by Zachary's tone.

"I'll stop by tomorrow," Zachary answered. "It's not as if the kid's going anywhere, is it?" He was silent for a beat. Then he asked, "Are you the guy who kept Sara out all night?"

J.P. ended the call without another word.

CHAPTER THIRTEEN

Eric regained consciousness at 6:17 p.m.

He was definitely in pain, but he was alive and he still had both his legs.

Win-win, as far as Sara was concerned.

Standing beside his bed in the recovery room, she brushed his dark hair back from his pale face.

"Hey," she said, the word catching in her throat.

"Hey," Eric croaked in response.

Sara leaned over, kissed her son's forehead. His flesh felt cool and a little clammy against her lips. "Welcome back."

Eric tried to lift his head, failed and let it fall back to his pillow. "Do I still have both my legs?" he asked.

"Yes," Sara said, blinking to ease the burning sensation in her eyes. This was not the time to cry.

Eric needed her to be strong.

His next question broke her heart.

302

"Is Dad here?"

Sara closed her eyes briefly, gathering her scattered resources. She was exhausted, relieved, frightened and, yes, angry.

"No, sweetheart." Her throat felt like dry knotted rope pulled tight, and that made her sound gruff. "I'm sure he'll come to see you tomorrow, though." She swallowed, tried for a lighter tone. "You're still in recovery, and that means you can't have a lot of company."

"He isn't *a lot of company,* Mom. He's my dad."

Sara felt helpless in the face of her son's disappointment. There was nothing she could do about the situation, at least for the moment, and that hurt.

She considered telling Eric that even though Zachary hadn't troubled himself to show up, *J.P.* had been present throughout the vigil she'd kept in the hospital waiting room, but decided against it.

Clearly, the circumstances weren't right. Besides, she wouldn't have been able to explain her bond with J.P. to herself, let alone her son. J.P. had, after all, lost livestock when Eric, Freddie Lansing and the others were running wild.

During the brief silence that fell between Sara and Eric, tears brimmed in his eyes, and his face contorted slightly, as though he were trying to brace himself against inevitable suffering.

She would gladly have borne Eric's pain for him, if that had been possible. But, alas, it wasn't.

Sara put a small cylinder device, dangling from a tube connected to a pump, into his palm, placed his thumb on the button. "Press this," she said gently. "It will help with the pain."

Eric swallowed visibly. Pressed the button so hard that the muscles in his forearm corded.

After a few moments, he seemed to breathe more easily. He even relaxed a little. "What happened to me, Mom?" he asked hoarsely, after visibly gathering the momentum to speak. "I don't remember anything after Carly and I got into a fight at the coffee shop. We were supposed to go to a movie —"

Sara explained as best she could, though her own knowledge was limited.

By the time she'd finished, Eric was drifting. Going under.

He was better off asleep, she thought, praying that his memories of the ordeal would not haunt the rest he needed so desperately.

She kissed his forehead lightly, blinked back another rush of tears and turned to leave the room.

Marisol and Dr. Reynolds, a tall, studious-looking man with an early receding hairline, were waiting in the hall, talking quietly.

Sara joined them, limp with fatigue and gratitude and a myriad of other emotions that were not so easy to identify.

"He's sleeping," she told the two doctors.

Marisol reached out a hand, lightly squeezed Sara's shoulder. "You need to go home," she said. "Have something to eat. Get a good night's sleep."

Sara knew her friend and personal physician was right, but she wasn't sure she could make it to the parking lot under her own power, never mind get back to the house.

She longed for a shower, though, and a soft place to lie down.

And strong arms to hold her.

"Shouldn't I be here?" she fretted. "In case — in case something happens?"

"You live five minutes from the hospital," Marisol reminded her kindly. "Eric is stable, but if that were to change, you would be notified immediately. Right now, Sara, the best possible thing for *both* of you is rest."

"You'll need all your stamina," Dr. Reynolds interjected, "to help your son get through the next few months. You *must* take care of yourself."

Sara nodded. She knew the doctors were right, but the instinct to protect her wounded son ran deep like some invisible river, wild and primitive, full of whirlpools and swift eddies. If she didn't let her better judgment prevail and go home, she wouldn't leave Eric's bedside until he was completely healed.

And even though he was the focal point in this particular equation, she needed to think about Hayley as well. Though they bickered almost constantly, her children were close.

Hayley was shaken at best, and traumatized at worst.

For tonight, thankfully, she was safe in Cord and Shallie's care, with Carly lending extra support.

Tomorrow would be a new and very demanding day, on all fronts.

"Do you need to call someone to pick you up?" Marisol asked, gently steering her away from Dr. Reynolds — and Eric — toward the elevator bank.

Sara shook her head as Marisol pressed a button and elevator doors swished open right away. "J.P. is downstairs. He'll drive me home."

He was waiting for her in that easy, no-pressure way of his. Giving her space and, at the same time, solidly present.

Now he would take her home.

Make sure she was settled and safe.

Beneath the tangle of weariness, sorrow and residual fear, Sara felt her personal equivalent of Camus's invincible summer.

Had it always been there?

Yes.

It had sustained her when her and Eli's parents died, and when Zachary shattered her heart, and in all the ups and downs in between.

It would sustain her always, no matter what, if only she remembered to tap into it.

She stepped into the elevator and watched numbly as the doors closed between her and Marisol and the room where her son lay, sore but mending.

It would, as the doctors had warned, be a long and difficult process, but it was there to do, as the old-timers liked to say.

Sara would push up her figurative sleeves and do whatever it took to aid in Eric's full recovery, both physically and emotionally.

When she reached the first floor and the large waiting area outside the emergency room, J.P. was there, standing before one of the windows, his hands braced against steel dividers, his head lowered.

Sara felt a pang of something sweet and terribly tender as she looked at him.

Was it love?

Probably not. But whatever it was, it was far more complicated than ordinary affection for another human being.

He turned, as though sensing her presence, and she saw that, strong as he was, J.P. was tired, too.

He came to her, caught her hands in his very gently.

"How is he?" he asked, his voice husky.

"The doctors say he'll recover completely." She smiled, and it was an effort. "They also informed me, in so many words, that if I don't take care of myself, I won't be much good to anybody."

"I agree," J.P. said with a weary smile of his own. "Let's get you home."

She nodded.

"My place or yours?" he asked, after he'd helped her into the passenger seat of his truck and slipped behind the wheel.

"Mine," Sara replied. "It's going to sound crazy, but I need to be where Eric's things are — his room, his clothes, his books and the like. And I want to be around if Hayley needs to come home tonight for some reason."

J.P. made no protest. "Okay," he said, "but

unless you tell me to get lost, I'm going to stick around and make sure you're all right. You shouldn't be alone."

"Eli and the others haven't made the arrests?" she asked, wondering what kind of monster a person had to be to set steel traps for animals and other human beings. If she hadn't been so worn out, she would have exploded in the kind of fury only a mother can feel.

"They've gotten them all," J.P. informed her. "Eli called while you were upstairs with Eric. The arrests were made, and the feds are pressing charges of their own, in addition to those of the sheriff's department. There are five people involved, so far — four men and a woman."

Sara put a hand to her mouth. Muttered something unintelligible.

J.P., already pulling out of the hospital parking lot, reached over to touch her arm. "They're being held without bail, Sara. They can't hurt anybody else — for the time being, anyway. And the National Guard is sweeping practically the whole county for more traps. In a week or so, things should be pretty much back to normal."

Since no reply seemed necessary, Sara didn't make one.

Storefronts slipped past on either side of

the road, then houses as they entered Sara's neighborhood.

Again, she longed to be inside her own house, with her own things around her and her children's things.

"What about your nieces? Aren't they supposed to arrive soon?"

"They'll be here soon," J.P. answered, signaling for the left turn into Sara's driveway. "They usually stay at the A-frame with Mom and Dad, but Mom likes to close ranks when there's trouble, so I expect they'll all bunk in at the main house instead."

"What about your horses? And Trooper?"

"Dad will feed the horses, and Trooper is almost as at home at my folks' place as he is at mine."

"Sounds like you're missing a lot," Sara said.

J.P. parked the truck, shifted out of gear and shut off the engine.

Every motion was subtle — and resolute.

"As I said, Sara, I mean to stay unless you want me to do otherwise."

"I don't," Sara said. "Want you to do otherwise, I mean."

He grinned, but it was a very slight grin, a mere tilt at one side of his mouth. "That's good," he answered. "Now, let's get you inside. You're a wreck."

"Gee, thanks," Sara replied.

He laughed. "Woman," he told her, once he'd climbed out of the truck and come around to open Sara's door, "you need food and a good night's sleep."

"I had a sandwich from the vending machine," she reasoned as they headed for the front door. The lock was digital, so no key was necessary.

"You had one bite of a stale sandwich," J.P. corrected good-naturedly. "Which was probably worse than nothing."

Sara had to agree.

They were inside by then, and she closed the door behind them.

"I want to call Hayley," she said, thinking aloud. "And then I'm going to take a long hot shower."

"I'll check out your refrigerator and see what I can find for your supper," J.P. told her. And, with that, he headed for the kitchen.

Sara sank into her favorite living room chair and speed-dialed her daughter, feeling mildly guilty for not placing the call as soon as she'd stepped out of the recovery room.

"Mom?" Hayley trilled after two rings, dispensing with her usual *talk to me!*

"Hi, babe," Sara said, her eyes smarting

again as she pictured her lovely woman-child, being brave and afraid, both at once. "Eric's going to be okay. They didn't have to amputate."

Hayley's reply was a grateful sob.

"It's going to be a long time, though, before he's up to speed physically. He'll need more surgery, as you know, along with lots of physical therapy and counseling for PTSD. Your brother is going to need all of us — you, me, Uncle Eli, Brynne —" Silently, she added J.P. "All of us."

Kids are resilient, and Hayley proved no exception. She laughed through her tears. "He's going to be a royal pain in the — Well, he's going to be a royal pain. Period."

"I'm sure you're right," Sara agreed, smiling even as a tear trickled down a cheek chafed by its predecessors. "We'll just have to deal."

"Does that mean he gets his way, no matter what?" Hayley wanted to know. Judging by her tone of voice, she *very much* wanted to know.

"Absolutely not," Sara promised. "What it *does* mean is that we'll have to be extra patient with him at first, because he's going to be in considerable pain. That will make him grumpy."

Hayley sighed audibly. "All right," she

312

said, "I'll be as patient as possible, but I'm *not* going to put up with any garbage, either. I love my brother, but he can be a sexist asshole."

Sara recalled her son's use of the word *bimbo,* in reference to Zachary's current partner, and the reprimand she'd issued. Had that really been just this morning out on the patio? "We'll work on that," she promised. A pause, a shifting of conversational gears. "Right now, I'm concerned about you, Hayley. Are you okay? And would you even tell me if you weren't?"

"I am and I would," Hayley answered. "Cord and Shallie are looking after me, and so is Carly. She's a great friend, Mom. I hope she marries Eric someday, so we can be sisters, too."

Let's not get ahead of ourselves, Sara thought, tired to the bone.

But what she said was "That would be nice." If there was one thing Hayley didn't need right now, it was a lecture on the importance of finishing the long process of growing up — Eric, especially, had a long way to go on that score — going to college, finding a good job, demonstrating responsibility.

"What about you, Mom?" Hayley asked, sounding concerned. "Is somebody taking care of you? And don't say you can take care of yourself, because I already know that and it isn't what I meant to ask you, anyway."

"Convoluted," Sara observed with a smile. "I'm fine. J.P. is starting supper as we speak." She could hear him rummaging around in the kitchen, rattling plates, opening and closing cabinet doors. If the steaks he'd served the night before were any indication, he was a very competent cook.

"Carly is going to bring me to town tomorrow for visiting hours," Hayley added. "If there are any."

"I'm not sure how that will go," Sara admitted. No one was going to keep her away, but it was possible that restrictions would be in place.

Visiting hours, as she recalled from her brother's long stint in the hospital a year before, were carefully regulated in cases of serious illness or injury.

Eric had not, after all, had his tonsils removed.

He had undergone major surgery.

Once again, the implications of that washed over Sara, and she shuddered, chilled and spent in every way.

"We'll have to see," Sara finished.

"Is it okay if I stay here with Carly for a few days?" The question was tentative. "If

I'm at home, I'll probably think too much."

"If staying with Carly helps you in any way, sweetheart, then that's what I want you to do."

J.P. pushed open the kitchen door and stood in the gap, holding up a block of cheddar cheese. "Everything else is frozen," he told her. "How about grilled cheese sandwiches and canned soup?"

If J.P. had offered filet mignon or any other out-of-the-ordinary food, Sara wouldn't have been happier to accept.

"Sounds good," she said.

"Say hi to J.P. for me," Hayley put in, obviously cheered.

"I will," Sara promised, touched.

It was a safe bet that if things went further between herself and J.P., and she devoutly hoped they would, Hayley would be amenable to the idea.

Eric, on the other hand —

But she didn't have to think about that. Not now.

She and Hayley said their goodbyes, and Sara joined J.P. in the kitchen.

He was standing at the stove.

She resisted an urge to step up behind him, wrap her arms around his lean waist, rest her head between his shoulder blades.

Then she thought, *What the hell?* and did

it anyway.

"Thank you," she said very quietly.

"Anytime," he replied without turning around. "Sit down, Sara. Let me wait on you."

Reluctantly, she drew back from him, walked to the table, sat down in her usual seat. The chairs where Eric and Hayley normally sat were emptier than empty, and her throat tightened at their absence.

When J.P. served their soup-and-sandwich supper, Sara simply stared down at the food.

J.P. had opened a bottle of red wine earlier; he filled two glasses and then joined her at the table.

"Eat," he said.

Sara sighed, remembered she hadn't washed her hands. Got up and went to the kitchen sink to run warm water and lather up.

When she sat down again, she reached for her wineglass first. Decided against taking so much as a sip until she'd eaten at least part of her sandwich.

"Tell me about your nieces," she said, hoping to distract herself from Eric's situation, at least for a few minutes. The girls were coming for a visit in the near future, she knew, and she didn't want to keep J.P.

from his family. "They're Josie's daughters, right?"

"Right," J.P. confirmed, watching her closely. After a few moments, he went on. "The truth is I don't know them very well. Josie's lived and worked in Virginia since I was in middle school. The girls came out here to stay with Mom and Dad for a couple of weeks most summers, but I didn't spend much time with them."

"Why not?" Sara asked, after savoring and swallowing a spoonful of soup.

J.P. executed a half shrug. "I guess I was busy with other things. I regret it now."

"Umm," Sara said, noncommittal. "Does Clare have children?" she asked.

She'd known J.P.'s eldest sister in school, though not too well, given the difference in their ages.

J.P. shook his head. "She's *child-free,* as she puts it. No interest in raising kids."

Sara looked up from her plate. "You don't approve?"

"I don't have an opinion on the matter, one way or the other," he replied. "It's Clare's decision to make, not mine."

The question arose naturally after that. "What's *your* plan, J.P.? Do you want kids of your own?"

He set down the section of sandwich he'd

317

been about to bite into, caught Sara's gaze and held it. "Yes," he said. "I do."

It struck Sara then, the sticking point between them, the thing that might erase any possibility of sharing a future.

Children.

She'd already raised two, but J.P. was new to the game.

"I see," she replied.

Even before the tragedy that had almost taken one of Eric's legs, the tragedy that might actually have taken his *life,* Sara had found parenting her temperamental son a challenge, and she was honest enough to admit that, love that boy though she did, there had been times when she'd looked forward to the day he'd go off to college.

Hayley had been, and remained, easy to deal with.

Easy to love. But, still, there had been that sense of constant vigilance, unflagging engagement.

The experience had been fulfilling, certainly.

But, at times, it had also been exhausting.

Sara did *not* regret having either of her children; indeed, she cherished them, took pride in them, would quite literally have died to protect them from harm of any sort.

Raising Eric and Hayley had been wonderful, even sacred at times.

And yet —

Could she — *would* she — give J.P. the babies he wanted? Could she conceive a child, or was she past that, biologically speaking?

And would she be able, or even willing, to start all over from scratch?

Handle diaper changes and night feedings and everything else that came with rearing small children? Small children who would eventually become teenagers?

She honestly didn't know.

In fact, she was too frazzled and run-down at the moment to consider these questions properly, let alone answer them.

"Big subject," J.P. said with the slightest of smiles. There was something wistful in that expression. "Finish your sandwich."

Sara obeyed. Ate what remained of the grilled cheese, spooned up the rest of her soup.

Sipped from her glass of wine.

Gave up on it halfway through.

She was so ridiculously tired that she couldn't even summon the energy to stand up. "I need a shower," she lamented.

J.P. didn't reply. He got to his feet, cleared away their plates and bowls, placed them in the sink.

Then, still without saying a word, he leaned down and scooped Sara up into his arms. He carried her through the house, found her bedroom and then the bathroom beyond.

There, still silent, he set Sara on her feet, steadied her when she swayed and reached into the shower to turn on and adjust the water.

As steam began to billow up around them, he undressed Sara, gently, garment by garment.

She said nothing. Instead, she allowed herself to be vulnerable, to be taken care of. For once, she wasn't in charge. Nothing was expected of her, nothing at all.

It was poignantly luxurious, being able to let go like that.

To simply allow things to unfold as they would.

When Sara was naked, J.P. removed his own clothing, tossed it aside.

Taking her hand, he led her into the shower, under the warm pounding spray. Turned her so that the water struck her back, easing her taut shoulders, softening them.

He lathered her with soap, his hands firm but making no demands as they passed over her breasts, her belly, her hips, her thighs.

Most of the tension gathered in her muscles drained away.

She gripped his shoulders first, then wrapped her arms around his neck and clung to him shamelessly, not because she wanted to seduce him, but simply because she knew her knees would buckle and she would sink to the shower floor if she didn't hold on.

She was like a weakened climber, clinging to the edge of a cliff.

J.P. somehow managed to shower himself, while keeping Sara upright with one arm, and then she slipped into a sort of standing stupor.

They got out of the shower, and he shut off the water, dried them both with a single towel, carried Sara into her bedroom, threw back the covers on her bed and laid her down to rest.

At last, she could rest.

The sheets were clean and cool and smooth.

Deliciously so.

"Don't go," she whispered once she was settled, reaching for J.P.'s hand, holding on tight.

"I wasn't planning on going anywhere," he replied gruffly. And then he lay down beside her, drew the covers up, wrapped her in his arms. Kissed the top of her head. "Go to sleep, Sara. When you wake up, I'll still be here."

"Promise?"

"Promise."

She closed her eyes, drifted off. Sank into the deep and silent refuge of sleep, the dreamless, restorative kind.

When she woke up, hours later, night had fallen.

The pounding ache of fatigue she'd suffered earlier was gone, and she lay nestled against a still-sleeping J.P., her head resting on his strong scarred chest. She listened to his steady heartbeat, matched the rhythm of his breathing.

Suddenly brazen, she slid her hand downward, over his washboard belly, and gripped him, felt him grow stiff and hard within the warm circle of her fingers.

"Sara," he moaned, hoarse with need and recent slumber.

She made a purring sound, kissing each of his scars, honoring them, honoring him.

Sara continued her progress along the terrain of J.P.'s body, and when she took him into her mouth, he cried out and arched his back.

She teased him, and then teased him some more.

Finally, with a warrior's cry of surrender and triumph, he broke free, turned Sara onto her back, used one leg to part hers.

When he thrust himself into her, she was amazed to find herself already teetering on the edge of orgasm. In seconds, she shattered, flailing and bucking beneath him, clawing fiercely at his back, shouting his name.

J.P.'s release was simultaneous with Sara's, and just as powerful.

After the earth stopped undulating beneath them, they collapsed into the soft mattress, damp with perspiration, still shuddering with the aftershocks of consummation.

They lay in silence for a long time, recovering, content in the fog of mutual satisfaction.

"Sara?" J.P. asked when he'd caught his breath.

Sara's hand was splayed over his heart, her head nestled into the curve of his neck. "What?"

"We might have a problem."

Sara was not disturbed by this announcement. At the moment, she wasn't *capable* of being disturbed. "Like what?" she murmured, snuggling even closer.

"Like, I didn't use a condom."

She sat up suddenly, looked down at him, blinking. Not really alarmed, but definitely startled. "Oh," she said.

"I wasn't exactly planning on having sex when I left home this morning," he added without apology. He drew her back down, held her so tenderly that she melted into him again. He yawned. "You have an IUD, right?" he asked sleepily.

"Right," Sara confirmed, trying to remember the last time she'd seen her gynecologist. Was the IUD still in place?

Within five minutes, they were both asleep again.

When they woke up, it was morning.

J.P. got out of bed first, hauling on yesterday's clothes.

Sara, recalling how she'd behaved in the night, wanted to pull the covers up over her head and hide until J.P. went away.

Once he'd gone, she assured herself, she would get up, take another shower, get dressed and head straight for the hospital.

Only he didn't leave.

"I'm making breakfast," he told her. "Don't bother to argue."

"Okay," Sara replied tremulously, squeezing her eyes shut.

He leaned over the bed, bracing his hands on either side of her, his face less than an inch from hers. "Look at me," he said with a note of amusement in his voice.

She opened one eye.

He laughed and kissed her soundly but briefly on the mouth. "What happened between us last night was natural and good, Sara," he said. "Let's not pretend we have anything to be ashamed of, all right?"

"I was pretty forward," Sara reminded him.

He laughed again. "You were a wildcat," he replied. "I'm a changed man."

Sara's embarrassment hadn't abated. "Go," she said. "Start the coffee brewing. Whatever. I need a few minutes to collect myself."

J.P. stood, smiled, and before leaving the room, he said, "Don't waste too much time and energy on that, sweetheart, because I plan to love you into flaming pieces all over again first chance I get."

As soon as he'd gone, Sara bolted for the bathroom, where she showered, pulled on jeans and a short-sleeved cotton blouse, brushed and re-braided her hair.

She needed to concentrate on her son and his recovery.

She was not going to think about J.P.'s sexy remark.

Not much, anyway.

325

CHAPTER FOURTEEN

Once he'd driven Sara to the hospital and hung around long enough to make sure she wasn't going to be confronted with bad news, J.P. returned to the ranch long enough to complete his usual chores, shower and put on fresh clothes.

He didn't pack a suitcase — that seemed more than a little presumptuous under the circumstances, given that Sara hadn't invited him to settle in for a long stay — but he did toss a new toothbrush and a few toiletries into his shaving kit.

The nieces had not arrived yet, but his mom was in the kitchen, ready to welcome them with love and food and looking as though she'd never left the place, and his dad sat at the table, reading his newspaper.

Same story. It was as if time had rewound.

"I see they caught those trap-setting sons of bitches," the old man remarked. "I hope they throw the lot of them in the slammer and throw the keys down a mine shaft."

J.P. felt the same way, pretty much, but he couldn't resist a quip. "Guess *you* won't be tapped for jury duty."

"I wouldn't be a suitable candidate," John McCall admitted.

Trooper lay calmly at John's feet, looking as though he might have forgotten whose dog he was, since he showed no particular interest in J.P.

"How is Sara's boy doing?" J.P.'s mom inquired, looking worried. "Such a terrible thing to happen."

J.P. helped himself to a fat strawberry from the fruit salad Sylvia was making for her granddaughters and, peripherally, for her husband and son.

She slapped at his hand, but she smiled, too.

"Eric's in a bad way, but he has both his legs and he'll live. I guess that makes him lucky, all things considered."

"And Sara? Is she doing all right?"

J.P. remembered how she'd awakened him during the night, and felt his neck warm up a little. Among other things.

"As well as could be expected," he said hastily, turning away in the direction of the door. "Guess I'd better see to the horses." He glanced back, caught Trooper's eye.

"You coming out to the barn with me or not?" he asked the dog.

Trooper didn't move. He just lay there, muzzle resting on his forelegs, his mismatched gaze rolling upward to take J.P.'s measure.

"Horses have been seen to," J.P.'s dad interjected with another rattle of his newspaper. "And Trooper's already made his rounds."

J.P. grinned. "Meanwhile, back at the ranch, everything seems to be under control."

"Your mother has been cooking since yesterday," his dad remarked. "She could feed all those National Guard folks patrolling the range for traps and *still* have enough food for the granddaughters and half their friends."

"Oh, hush," said Sylvia.

J.P. tried for another strawberry, but she blocked him.

"You go on back to town now," she went on. "Look after Sara."

"What about the girls?"

"Don't worry about that. I'll call Josie and get some information out of her, no matter what it takes," she told him. "Right now, you need to be with Sara for as long as she'll have you. Your dad and I will take care of

328

things on this end." A pause for breath. "And don't forget to take those flowers I picked for her this morning. They're by the front door."

J.P. kissed his mom lightly on the forehead. "Well," he said, "I guess that settles it."

"I'm trying to read here," said his dad.

He left the house, leather shaving kit in one hand, picked up the lavish bouquet waiting where his mother had said it would be and headed for his truck.

Ten minutes later, he reached the hospital waiting room.

Sara wasn't there, so he took his phone from his shirt pocket and keyed in two words.

Need anything?

Yes, she wrote back. A decent cup of coffee. As in, not from the vending machine or the cafeteria.

J.P. smiled to himself.

You got it. Shall I fetch it for you or will you let me take you to Bailey's? And how's Eric doing this morning?

He's hurting. In a very bad mood and thus not sociable.

J.P. wrote, Sorry to hear he's in a lot of pain. Guess I'd be pretty surly, too, if I'd stepped in a bear trap.

This time, there was no immediate response.

Oops, J.P. thumbed into his phone screen. Sorry. You probably didn't need the reminder.

She texted back. Eric wants me to leave. If he can't see his dad, he doesn't want to see anybody. On my way downstairs.

Sara arrived a few minutes later, looking much stronger than she had the day before. Despite an apparent run-in with her son, she was smiling. Even a little pink in the cheeks.

And was that a sparkle in her eyes, or just the angle of the light?

He gave her the flowers.

Her eyes misted over for a moment, and she buried her face in them.

"Thank you," she whispered when she lifted her gaze to him again. "But where shall I put them?"

A nurse stepped up, volunteered to keep them safe until Sara returned.

"Will Bailey's work for you?" J.P. asked, wanting to pull her close, hold her, kiss her. Take her somewhere private and make love to her until they were both deliciously exhausted.

Whoa back, big fella. Rein it in.

"Bailey's serves the best coffee in Painted Pony Creek," Sara answered with a nod.

The sudden, overwhelming need of her had not subsided, J.P. discovered.

Thankfully, the front of his jeans hadn't turned into a tent.

"You're okay with being away from the hospital?"

"Yes," Sara answered with a note of humor. "I'll come back later, when, I hope, Eric won't be in such an ugly state of mind."

They left the hospital, side by side, and walked to J.P.'s truck.

He opened the passenger's-side door for her, and she climbed in on her own before he had a chance to help.

When he was behind the wheel, he noticed she was holding his shaving kit on her lap.

"So, cowboy," she teased, "you planning to spend the night again?"

"With your permission, yes, ma'am," he teased back, deepening his voice to a Sam Elliott pitch.

Sara pretended to fan herself, like an old-time movie heroine in a spaghetti Western. "Why, sir, you do indeed have my permission."

He laughed. "Stop it," he said, starting the truck engine up with a satisfying roar, "or I'll pass right on by Bailey's, head for your house, carry you inside and have you standing up with your back to the inside of the front door."

She turned a rich shade of peachy pink at the prospect.

"Promises," she said, nearly breathing the words. "Always promises."

He grinned, wondering if she was blushing all over, her supple flesh as delectable as ripe fruit. And damned if he wouldn't have given half his herd of cattle to find out right then and there.

Obviously, unless he wanted to get both of them arrested, that wasn't going to happen.

"Keep that up," he warned, "and I won't be able to go inside Bailey's without causing a public scandal. I'll have to sit in the truck with an ice pack in my lap."

She laughed. "You're deliberately trying to arouse me, J.P. McCall."

"Is it working?"

"Oh, yeah," she said.

"Hot damn," J.P. growled.

By some miracle of physiology, he was still presentable when they reached Bailey's. He parked in the side lot in approximately the same spot where he'd kissed her for the first time, the night of their awkward supper.

It seemed fitting, somehow.

Brynne was helping out, while her mother chatted with the row of regular customers lining the pie-and-coffee counter.

She crossed the room immediately, weaving her way between tables, and hugged Sara tightly.

The expected questions were asked, and Sara answered without mentioning Eric's current emotional state.

They took a table for two, over by one of the side windows, and Brynne brought them ice water and coffee.

"Mom made some wicked strawberry/rhubarb pies this morning," she said. "Can I interest you two in a slice?"

"I'm definitely interested," Sara replied.

Strawberry/rhubarb pie. J.P. saw that as a form of culinary justice, a do-over for not being allowed to raid the ingredients of his mother's famous fruit salad that morning in the ranch house kitchen.

"Same here," he said.

"Join us?" Sara asked her sister-in-law when she returned with two huge slices of pie.

Brynne shook her head and looked around the restaurant. "Too busy," she lamented. "Thank God the bar isn't open yet, or we'd be swamped. With the National Guard troops in town, we're doing a land-office business — so is Sully's. I'm only here because Dad is having a root canal this morning, and Mom needed a hand."

"Where are the twins?" Sara asked, making conversation.

J.P. was watching her, not Brynne, amused by the way she held her fork poised above her slice of pie, as though she couldn't decide from which angle she ought to approach it.

"Eli's home with them. He needed a mental health day."

"I can imagine," Sara said, solemn again. Remembering.

Brynne consulted her watch. "Miranda will be coming in to work soon, and so will Evelyn — she's the new waitress. When they get here, I'll go back home — Eli wants to visit Eric this afternoon."

"He might want to wear a suit of armor," J.P. remarked with a smile.

Sara made a face at him.

"Speaking of suits of armor," Brynne said, "the triplet wedding is beginning to take shape. The bridegrooms and their posses are wearing full armor to the ceremony. They'll ride up on horseback, no less."

"Sounds awkward," J.P. observed mildly, enjoying the pie and coffee.

Both women ignored him.

It seemed women did that a lot, ignored men, when they talked about weddings.

Which was fine with J.P.

He had nothing against marriage, but the idea of outfitting himself in a hundred pounds of clanking steel and climbing into the saddle gave him the willies.

First of all, it couldn't be good for the horse.

And second, it would be a great way to break a few dozen bones in very quick succession.

"What does David think of the medieval theme?" Sara was asking when J.P. started tracking the conversation again.

Brynne rolled her eyes. "He's horrified," she replied, "but he says he's seen worse, if you can believe that."

"Like what?" Sara asked, intrigued. Most likely, she was enjoying this brief respite from keeping her vigil at the hospital.

"Once," Brynne responded, with a touch of eager delight, "the bridegroom lifted a three-tiered wedding cake and upended it over his new mother-in-law's head."

"I hope he took pictures," J.P. remarked.

Both women looked at him as though he'd just materialized out of the ether.

"Who?" Sara asked. "The bridegroom or

David?"

"Does it matter?" J.P. wanted to know.

Brynne laughed. "It's all over the book of faces," she said. "I'll send you both a link."

"That's the Information Age for you," J.P. said, with a sigh. "Everything is recorded for posterity — the good, the bad and the ugly."

"True," Sara agreed.

"Listen," Brynne said, "I'd better get back to work. The pie and coffee are on me, and tell Eric we love him."

With that, Brynne walked away, busy again, pouring more coffee, serving pie, greeting everyone who came in off the street and bidding a bright farewell to everyone who was leaving.

"She's beautiful, isn't she?" Sara asked with nothing but admiration in her tone and manner.

"Yes," J.P. responded. "She is."

"Did you ever have a crush on her? Back in high school, maybe?"

"No," he answered, amused. "Brynne was Eli's girl. Until he got stupid and dumped her for Reba Shannon."

"Not his finest hour," Sara admitted.

"Not mine or Cord's, either," J.P. added. Of course, she knew the story of Carly's arrival, looking for her real father, who might have been Cord or Eli or J.P. himself, so he didn't expand on the statement.

"Have you ever been in love?" Sara asked quietly, serious now.

J.P. considered. "I don't believe so, not really. I *thought* so once — with Reba — but I was so young and stupid back then, I didn't know my ass from a hole in the ground, as my dad used to say."

Sara grinned. " 'Used to say'?"

"My mom pretty much broke him of the habit," J.P. explained with a grin of his own.

Sara put down her fork, apparently absorbed in thought. "I thought I loved Zachary," she said, "but now I realize I didn't even know what love was — not the kind between a man and woman, anyway. I was crazy about the kids from the first moment I saw them, though."

"Sounds right," J.P. said, picturing Sara with a newborn baby in her arms.

His baby.

Now, *there* was a subject he wasn't about to broach.

"Ready to get back to your post?" he asked, and his voice sounded gruff, so he cleared his throat self-consciously.

She looked up at him for a long moment, with her remarkable gray eyes, and he thought he glimpsed a flash of sadness there.

Little wonder, considering what she'd been through.

Eric wasn't the only one suffering. Sara was, too, and so was Hayley.

"Yes," she said in belated reply. "I'm ready."

When they arrived back at the medical center, J.P. accompanied Sara as far as the small waiting room outside the ICU. While Sara proceeded to Eric's room, he paced, scrolling through his phone.

There was a text from his mother — Becky and Robyn, his nieces, had arrived at the ranch in a hired car.

She just couldn't get over how grown-up they were.

And there was a thing or two she wanted to tell Josie, if she ever managed to get ahold of her.

Apparently, his sister wasn't taking calls.

J.P. smiled at that, shook his head.

He was in the middle of texting a mundane response when a male voice broke his concentration.

"What the hell are *you* doing here?"

J.P. glanced up and saw Zachary Worth standing in the waiting room doorway.

Like cheap whiskey, good ole Zachary hadn't aged well. He was thickening around the middle, his hairline was starting to

338

recede and there were deep grooves on either side of his mouth.

J.P. sighed, dropped his phone into his shirt pocket, rolled his shoulders back to stretch out the kinks. "I'm not aware of any rule compelling me to answer that question," he responded, his tone easy and smooth. Unruffled.

"I know you're seeing Sara," Worth accused.

As if he had any right to be pissed off by that fact, though he obviously was.

"And?" J.P. prompted, raising an eyebrow.

"*And* Eric is *my* son, not yours."

"Nobody's saying otherwise, as far as I know," J.P. responded.

"As soon as he's released from this hospital," Zachary Worth frothed, "I'm taking *my son* away from this Podunk town!"

"Sara might have something to say about that. Eric's still under eighteen, and she has primary custody." J.P. hadn't meant to say that much — he had no sway in the matter, one way or the other, but he knew how Sara would react to her ex-husband's plan to take Eric *anywhere.* "Sheriff Garrett — Eric's uncle — will no doubt have an opinion or two as well."

Worth thrust splayed fingers through his gel-stiffened, coiffed hair.

It barely moved.

What an irony it was, this man's last name.

"I'm here to see my son, McCall," Zachary said, the words forced through his teeth. "Not to listen to some yahoo cowboy who's been boinking my wife!"

"*Ex*-wife," interjected a third voice, this one female and razor-sharp.

Sara.

Her gaze collided so hard with Worth's that J.P. half expected to hear the clash of steel striking steel.

"Want some privacy?" J.P. asked Sara very quietly, though the last thing he wanted to do just then was leave her alone with this particular man.

"Stay," Sara replied without looking away from Worth's furious face. "Please."

Worth, already red to his creeping hairline, turned crimson. *"This,"* he steamed, "is a *family* matter."

"You're not family," Sara told him calmly. "You're a sperm donor."

"That isn't fair!" Worth raged, taking a step toward Sara.

J.P. stepped between them, arms folded.

Outwardly, he was calm, like Sara. Inwardly, however, he was a bear trap set to spring. "Stand back, Worth," he ordered quietly. "And keep a civil tongue in your head."

Worth deflated slightly, though he still looked as though he might bust a capillary any second now. "Sara," he said, shoving his hand into his hair again. "Would you mind calling off your dog? I have a right to see my son."

Sara stepped close to J.P., wrapped an arm loosely around his waist.

J.P. returned the favor.

"Eric isn't having a good day," Sara told her ex, her voice quiet but firm. "Tomorrow might be better."

"I have a meeting in LA tomorrow," Worth retorted grudgingly. "So I need to see Eric today. It's important."

"Fine," Sara conceded, very much in control of her emotions, which were raging inside her like a storm. J.P. knew this because he was standing in her energy field, and because she was shaking almost imperceptibly. "But I'm going to be there."

"Do you honestly think I'm a danger to Eric?" Worth demanded.

"I think you're basically a nonentity," Sara answered. "Eric will figure that out on his own, sooner or later — he's a smart kid — but, in the meantime, he's still a minor and I *will* look after him, Zachary."

"I want a *private* word with the kid," insisted the ex.

"So you can try to convince him to ask your father to appoint you as Eric and Hayley's trustee?" Sara's voice was a sheet of ice, smooth and ice-cold. "I know about the trust funds, Zachary. If you try to interfere in any way, I'll be happy to pass the word on to your brother. As I understand it, he's been appointed executor of the will."

Worth, flushed before, paled. "I'm their father," he blustered. "I *should* be the one to oversee their trust funds. Eric and Hayley will be rich in their own right, once their grandfather is gone, and I want to protect them!"

"The hell you do," Sara replied, somewhat tersely, letting her arm drop from J.P.'s waist to her side and straightening her shoulders. "You're broke, you're set to inherit very little money and you think you can make up for that, keep up your fancy lifestyle, by stealing from your own children. *That* is what you really want!"

"That's a lie!" Zachary barked.

A nurse appeared in the waiting room doorway.

"I'm sorry," she announced, not sounding sorry at all, "but you will have to leave now, Mr. Worth. We can't have disruption of any

342

kind in this unit."

"I'm staying," Zachary said, though not with much conviction.

"I'll have security remove you if necessary," the nurse warned.

She looked faintly familiar to J.P., though he couldn't place her.

Whoever she was, she had grit, like Sara.

Eli appeared beside her in full uniform. "What's the trouble?" he asked, eyeing his former brother-in-law with barely concealed dislike.

"Mr. Worth has been shouting," said the nurse. "Obviously, we can't have that here."

"Obviously not," Eli said dryly.

His gaze moved to Sara, then J.P. Gave a very slight nod of acknowledgment.

"I might have raised my voice," Worth admitted lamely. His hands were knotted into fists at his sides. "I just want to see my son, that's all. I'm leaving town tomorrow, and I'll be gone for a while. So I came here to look in on Eric, find out how he's doing."

"Took you a while to start wondering along those lines," Eli remarked. "Some fifteen years, by my calculations."

Worth heaved a great sigh. Glared at Eli. "So now you and Sara are going to double-team me, right? Make sure Eric goes right on believing I don't give a damn what happened to him?"

"On some level," Eli replied, "he already realizes that."

"Do you need security, Sheriff? As backup?" the nurse asked.

Eli shook his head, glanced at J.P. "I have all the backup I need, thanks," he said.

"Let me stay," Worth said, almost pleading now, looking winsome for the nurse's benefit.

She wasn't buying it. "You can visit another time," she informed him, "when your temper is under control. But for today, you've already created all the disturbance I'm going to allow."

Eli gestured toward Worth. "I'll walk you out," he said.

It wasn't an offer. It was a command.

"I *will* tell Eric what happened here today," Worth spouted, his gaze landing hard on Sara's face, though he had the good sense to keep his voice down. "You can *all* be sure of that."

"Let's go," Eli reiterated with less patience this time.

Worth was spitting mad, but he nodded sulkily and started toward the door, purposely knocking the nurse's shoulder as he passed her.

Sara turned to J.P. "I need to speak to my brother," she said. "Would you mind looking in on Eric? Just to make sure he didn't hear his father throwing a temper tantrum?"

"I'll sit with him until you come back," J.P. assured her. "I'm not sure the kid will be glad to see me, though."

Sara gave him a wan smile.

She'd been so bright and hopeful before Zachary Worth showed up. Now she looked tired and a little pale, and J.P. yearned to gather her to him, shield her from everything bad.

Impossible, of course.

Besides, Sara was an independent woman. She might enjoy tenderness and solicitude — especially in bed — but she also had a spine of steel.

She'd shown that today.

"If Eric says anything nasty," she counseled, "don't take it personally. He's as grouchy as a bear with a toothache."

"I can take whatever he wants to dish out, Sara," J.P. said. "And I can relate to what he's going through."

Her face changed, and J.P. knew she was remembering the scars on his back and chest. She'd traced them, after all, not only with a fingertip, but with her lips.

He felt a jolt of heat, recalling how she'd

345

approached those scars, not as the ugly marks of a critical war injury, but as something to be respected. Honored.

She gave him a small smile, then slipped away, following Eli and a reluctant, grumbling Zachary Worth out of the ICU waiting room.

J.P. waited a few moments, then realized he didn't know Eric's room number.

Obviously, he couldn't go poking his head into other patients' rooms, looking for the kid.

"I'll show you the way," the vaguely familiar nurse said.

Her name tag read Portia Reese.

Ah, yes. They'd connected on Tinder approximately a year and a half before and gone on exactly one date — dinner at a restaurant over in nearby Silver Hills. And they'd decided over dessert that they were a definite mismatch.

Zero chemistry.

Portia was looking for marriage, and J.P. for a one-night stand, essentially.

He'd respected the woman for telling him he was a dick for using the dating app as an escort service.

It was a fair assessment.

"I'm sorry about — the other thing," J.P. confided as he and Portia moved along a gleaming tiled hallway lined with numbered doors.

Portia gave him a sidelong look and a perky little smile. "No harm done, cowboy. I'm *very* happily married now, and my man and I will be starting a family soon."

"Congratulations," J.P. said sincerely.

"Thanks," Portia replied, coming to a stop in front of room eight. "This is the Worth boy's room."

J.P. nodded thanks of his own.

Pushed open the door.

Eric, with tubes entering practically every orifice, his injured leg supported by a sling, turned his head, saw J.P., frowned and asked the same question his father had minutes before in the waiting room.

"What are you doing here?"

J.P. raised both hands, palms out. "I come in peace," he said. "Your mother asked me to keep you company until she comes back."

"Suppose I don't *want* your company?" Eric rasped. His face was thin, sheet white and dappled with perspiration.

J.P. ignored the question. "You're in pain?"

"Duh," Eric replied. "I stepped in a fucking trap and it almost fucking cut my leg off."

"Shall I call a nurse?" J.P. asked. When it came to hospitals and surly patients, he was

347

pretty unflappable, having spent several months in such places after the explosion in Afghanistan.

Same old, same old.

Eric shook his head. "This drip-thing won't give me another shot of meds for fifteen minutes or so." He paused, groaned, tried in vain to shift into a more comfortable position. "Make that thirteen minutes and twenty-four seconds."

J.P. drew up a chair, sat. "You seem to be recovering pretty quickly," he observed. "They'll probably move you out of the ICU and into a regular room pretty soon."

"Maybe the day after tomorrow, if I don't get an infection," Eric said. "I wish I could just skip that part — the regular-room part, I mean — and go home."

"Yeah. I don't blame you."

Eric looked directly at him then, and his eyes were so like Sara's that J.P. was a little taken aback. "Are you fucking my mother?" he asked.

J.P. held the boy's gaze. "If I were," he answered, "it would be none of your business."

Eric flushed slightly, which was something of a relief, given his deathly pallor. "I was in the kitchen yesterday morning, when she sneaked into the house like a guilty teenager, carrying her shoes in one hand. I didn't know who she'd spent the night with until Hayley told me she was seeing you."

"Okay," J.P. said, noncommittal. *And* unfazed.

"The worst part was my dad was there, too."

"So?"

"*So,* it was awkward."

"I'll just bet it was."

"You need to leave my mother alone."

"Do I?"

"Yes," Eric snapped. "Hayley and I aren't in the market for a stepfather. We've *got* a father."

"You couldn't prove that to me," J.P. replied with a semblance of a shrug.

"Maybe he was gone for a long time — our dad, I mean — but that was partly Mom's fault. He made a mistake, but he apologized all over the place and she wouldn't give him a second chance. Not even for Hayley and me!"

"This is a conversation you should be having with your mother, not me," J.P. told the kid, but gently. He understood the anger the boy felt, even though he'd been raised in a two-parent home.

"My mother doesn't understand!" Eric complained.

"Calm down a little, bud," J.P. urged. "You might just angst yourself into some kind of setback if you don't."

"I'm hurting — a lot," Eric ground out. "You don't have a clue what I'm going through!"

"It just so happens that I do," J.P. countered. He stood up, hauled his T-shirt off over his head and revealed the splotchy scars that nearly covered his chest. Then he turned to give the kid a look at his back, which was even worse.

"Holy shit," Eric whispered.

"Yeah," J.P. said, pulling his T-shirt on again.

"You were hurt in Iraq or Iran or —"

"Afghanistan," J.P. corrected without emotion. He'd pitied himself plenty, back when his wounds were fresh, but he'd gotten past that a long time ago.

"I guess you know about pain," Eric conceded.

"We have that much in common, at least," J.P. said, sitting down again.

"I still think you ought to stay away from my mom."

J.P. sighed. Rested a booted foot on the opposite knee. "Tough luck, kid," he replied. "I'm not going anywhere."

Chapter Fifteen

Hayley's voice floated from the speaker of Sara's cell phone, cheery and full of bright energy, filling Eric's room in the ICU like sunlight.

"Mom?" she said. "You have a package. Shall I open it?"

It had been three full days since Eric's accident, and Sara had spent most of that time sitting with her son, keeping him company. Hayley had returned from Carly's house just that morning, and it seemed she was home to stay.

Which meant there would be no more sex with J.P., wild or otherwise, at least not at Sara's place.

"Hi, honey," she greeted her daughter, distracted because she'd been revising her book on her laptop. Eric was about to be moved to a regular hospital room and, at the moment, he was downstairs, having yet another CT scan.

Then, in an instant, Hayley's words registered.

A package.

Very likely, the parcel contained something embarrassing.

Like the crotch-less panties she'd ordered after J.P. had literally rocked her world that first time.

Sara blushed. Tried to speak calmly. With casual disinterest.

Ha.

"Er — no, sweetheart. I'll open it when I get home."

"Okay," Hayley said, ready, as always, to move on to whatever came next. Eric might not have been so cooperative had he been in his sister's place.

And *that* scenario would have been a disaster.

"How is my brother?" Hayley asked. "Nicer than he was yesterday, when Carly and I visited, I hope."

Eric's mood hadn't changed, at least not where his mother and sister were concerned. He was civil to Carly, his uncle Eli, and to Sara's surprise, he seemed to get along well enough with J.P., who spelled Sara for a few hours every day, so she could go home to eat, shower and grab a nap, if she needed one.

They usually played chess or cribbage, J.P. and Eric, but Sara knew few actual words passed between them.

Now that Eric's condition was improving, and Sara wasn't so frazzled, J.P. spent less time at the hospital than he had at first. He had company, after all — his two nieces — and, of course, he still had a ranch to run.

He visited Eric every afternoon, nonetheless, and he spent his nights with Sara. She was always wound up to the breaking point by the time she left the hospital, and J.P. was *very* good at *un*winding her.

Sara's blush deepened at the memory.

"Eric," she replied belatedly, "is Eric. We're looking into getting him a personality transplant."

Hayley laughed. "Good luck with that, Momster. With Eric, it's systemic. He's too much like the sperm donor for his own good."

"Don't say that," Sara whispered. "*Please* don't ever say that again."

Hayley's amusement had faded away. "You know it's true, Mom," she said. "Why else would he be so eager to fawn over a man who never cared enough to stick around and help raise his kids, divorce or no divorce?"

"It's transference," Sara answered, clutching at straws. "I'm pretty sure Eric has a fantasy father. And he's most likely projecting that ideal — and nonexistent — man onto Zachary."

"So now you're a shrink?" Hayley challenged. "Mom, you might have a fantasy *son*. Is this one of those Redditworthy scenarios where Eric is the Golden Child and I'm the leftovers? The kid who never makes trouble and therefore is mostly ignored?"

Sara was so stricken by Hayley's words that she actually shot to her feet, nearly knocking her laptop off the small table in front of her.

"Oh, my God, Hayley, is *that* how you feel? Ignored? Do you actually think I love you less than your brother? That simply isn't true!"

Just at that moment, J.P. entered the otherwise empty ICU waiting room.

He paused just inside the doorway and raised one eyebrow in unspoken question: *Go or stay?*

"Stay, please," Sara mouthed, beckoning him with one hand.

"I wonder sometimes," Hayley admitted sadly.

"Then you and I have some work to do," Sara replied, sounding the way she felt:

354

broken. "As soon as things settle down again, you and I are getting some counseling. Just the two of us."

"It's okay, Mom," Hayley answered, though there were tears in her voice. "I understand that you have to spend a lot of time with Eric right now and, I swear to you, I'm cool with that. It's that time of month, and I'm worried about my brother, and my emotions are all over the place."

"I love you, Hayley. You're precious to me."

"I know, Mom," Hayley sniffled. "And I love you, too. Really."

"I've never doubted it," Sara replied. "But your feelings matter, sweetheart. We're going to work this thing through with a professional, ASAP. If that's okay with you, of course."

"It's okay with me," Hayley said.

Sara realized she was trembling and so, apparently, did J.P., because he gripped her gently by the elbows and lowered her back into her chair.

He left the room without a word, and Sara and Hayley said their goodbyes.

When J.P. returned, he handed her an ice-cold bottle of water.

Sara unscrewed the top and drank thirstily.

"Thank you," she sputtered.

J.P. pushed aside the table, borrowed from the medical staff, drew up a second chair and sat facing Sara, their knees almost touching.

"I guess you heard," Sara said. It was an inane remark, she knew, but she didn't care. It was what she found when she reached inside herself for words.

"I caught part of the conversation, yes," J.P. admitted.

"Hayley thinks Eric is the Golden Child in our family and she's — well — second fiddle. It isn't true, J.P.!"

"I believe you, Sara. And you don't need to explain anything to me. What goes on between you and your kids — you and anybody else, for that matter — is yours to deal with, as you see fit."

"Do you *always* know the right thing to say?" Sara asked, weary and relieved, before taking a big gulp from her water bottle, swallowing.

J.P. grinned that wicked sex-against-the-wall grin. "Let's just say, I work at it."

Sara sighed. Sex against the wall, one of J.P.'s specialties, was off the table for the time being, now that Hayley was back home.

Even his place was out of bounds these days, because his parents and his two nieces were staying at the ranch house.

Sara was overjoyed that her son was well enough to leave the ICU, if not the hospital, and she'd missed Hayley something fierce.

But she was going to miss those crazy-gentle nights with J.P., too.

A tear slipped down her cheek.

J.P. wiped it away with the pad of his thumb.

"Hey," he said.

"I'm okay," Sara lied.

"Shhh," he told her.

"Why didn't this happen *years* ago, J.P.? When the kids were little and Eric would have been thrilled to have a stepfather?"

"Why didn't what happen?" J.P. countered, watching her.

"You know damn well what I mean," Sara bristled. "I love you, J.P. God help me, *I love you,* and, damn it, I'm not afraid to say so."

He chuckled, leaned forward to kiss the damp place on her cheek, where the tear had been. "Good," he said. "Because I love you, too."

Sara's heart leaped.

He loved her?

She hadn't expected that. J.P. McCall was a good man, no question about it, but he was a known player, too. He'd probably dated half the eligible women in Wild Horse County.

"Really?" she asked.

"Really," he confirmed.

"Why didn't this happen earlier?" Sara nearly wailed, so great was her frustration.

"Because neither of us were ready, Sara," he replied. "We were both busy becoming the people we are right now."

The conversation ended there, because the sound of voices and a rattling hospital gurney filled the hallway.

Eric was back from his scan.

"The doctor wants one more look at this guy," George Adams, a male nurse, announced as the little caravan came to a halt outside Eric's present room. "Then we'll move him out of here."

J.P. got up from his chair, and so did Sara.

"I'll be outside," J.P. told her.

She nodded.

J.P. gave Eric a thumbs-up before he left the room, and Eric returned the favor.

Because Eric would be changing rooms soon, George and the others chose to leave him on the gurney, with the rails up. Moving him from one bed to another was a difficult and very awkward process, and very painful for Eric.

Seeing him lying there, one leg full of

staples and stitches and other surgical detritus and raised at least a foot off the bed, made Sara's heart ache.

If she could have spared him all this, she would have done so.

She would have taken his place in a heart-beat.

Alas, that wasn't the way the real world worked.

"Go home, Mom," Eric said, sounding sleepy. "They're going to drug me up for the move, and that means I'll be out of it, probably until sometime tomorrow morn-ing."

Sara approached the gurney, and George, who, like much of the hospital staff, was a former schoolmate of hers, moved aside to make room for her.

"You're sure, honey? I can stay —"

"You've been here every day, Mom," Eric said, trying to smile. "And, frankly, you look like you've been dragged backward through a knothole. I'm getting worried about you."

Maybe that personality transplant had actually been performed.

"Who are you?" Sara teased. "And what have you done with my son?"

He laughed.

Sara couldn't remember the last time she'd heard Eric laugh.

"Go home," he repeated, sounding a little groggy now. One of the other nurses had just adjusted a knob on his IV bag, so he was probably about to go under. "Let J.P. and Uncle Eli fill in for a while. And this would be a good time to spring for a Switch and a few games, now that I think about it."

Sara smiled, kissed his forehead. They'd been arguing about the purchase of the portable gaming console for weeks now.

"I might just do that," she said softly.

"What? Take a few days off or buy your poor, lonely, bored son a Switch?"

"Both," Sara replied.

Eric's eyelids drooped. "Mom?"

"What?"

"I love you."

She planted another kiss on his forehead, this one a brief noisy smack. "I love you, too," she said.

After a few quiet words with George, Sara gathered her laptop and handbag and headed for the waiting room.

J.P. was there, arms loosely folded, handsome head tilted to one side, as if he were pondering some enigma.

One that intrigued and amused him just a little.

Had he really said he loved her, back there in Eric's room? And, if so, was he about to backtrack? Say he hadn't meant what he'd said, that he'd gotten ahead of himself, or something equally devastating?

He took the laptop from her, tucked it under one arm.

"I think it's about time you and I went for that picnic we planned," he said. "Back before the shit show started."

Sara liked the idea, but her daughter was at home and in need of some mothering, unless she was mistaken.

And she knew she wasn't.

"I'd like that," Sara said as they walked toward the elevator bank. "But Hayley's back home and I haven't seen her much in the last few days. Somehow, our paths hardly ever crossed during visiting hours."

"We'll have the picnic another time, then," J.P. said easily.

"Is it safe?" Sara asked as they stepped into an elevator. "Did they find all the traps?"

"Yes," J.P. replied, pushing the button. "The area was thoroughly searched, using metal detectors, and things have settled down considerably since the arrests were made."

Although Sara had seen her brother often since Eric's accident — if it could be *called* an accident, given that someone had summoned him to the scene, where the trap was waiting — they hadn't discussed the case.

Eli was notoriously reticent about such things, and he'd probably figured Sara didn't need any more reminders of what had happened to her son.

"What's going to happen now?" she asked, aware that J.P. had been following the case closely.

"The feds have taken charge of the prisoners, so that's off Eli's plate, anyway," J.P. replied, and for the first time, he sounded tired. "There'll be a memorial service of sorts at the high school, for Randy Becker. His folks don't want a funeral."

Sara gave J.P. a sidelong glance as the elevator came to a stop on the first floor of the hospital.

"That's odd," she commented. "Why not? Wasn't Randy their only child?"

J.P. sighed, placed one hand lightly on the small of Sara's back.

She loved it when he did that.

It made her feel cherished. Protected.

"Eli and Melba's people found a lot of evidence that he was the ringleader in this bunch. They *also* found half a dozen steel traps in the Beckers' basement, and Randy's name was on the invoices."

"My God," Sara whispered. "A person can

just *buy* those dreadful things?"

"They can," J.P. confirmed. "Probably on the dark web."

And Randy Becker, along with the others, had been responsible for hurting Eric, nearly killing him, in fact.

But she couldn't hate him.

All she felt for Randy and his parents was pity.

"They're ashamed of the kid," J.P. went on as he ushered Sara outside into the parking lot, which was bright with late-afternoon sunlight. "Most people would be, of course, but they've taken it to a new level. Did you know it's possible to legally disown someone postmortem?"

Sara stopped, stared up at J.P. in shock. "They *disowned* him? *Their dead son?*"

J.P. pulled his keys from his jeans pocket, pointed the fob toward his truck and thumbed it. "Absolutely. According to their lawyer, the late Randal Becker the Third is no longer a member of the family. They're selling their house and moving to Europe. In fact, they're already gone. End of story."

Sara was horrified. "They *just walked away*? As if *nothing happened*? As if they'd never had a child in the first place?"

"That's about the size of it," J.P. responded.

"I can't believe it." Despite her anger, Sara felt a stab of pity for the Becker boy.

J.P. opened the passenger's-side door of the truck and helped her inside, even though she didn't need help.

"Believe it," he said. "Not everybody loves their kids the way you do, Sara."

Until her first novel had sold, Sara had worked as the manager of the county's day-care center, and while most of the parents had loved their lively little offspring to distraction, there *had* been a few who gave another impression entirely.

Some had actually turned out to be abusive and neglectful, if not both, and Sara had reported several cases to CPS, when she or one of her staff members found suspicious bruises, cuts and once — she shuddered at the recollection — cigarette burns.

"I understand that," she told J.P. "I've seen some disturbing things."

J.P. nodded, walked around to the driver's side and climbed into the truck. Started the engine.

"Do you need to stop off anywhere before I take you home? The supermarket, maybe?"

Sara shook her head. "No, thanks. I'm good. People have been dropping off casseroles since Eric was hurt, in case you've forgotten. And then there are the groceries you've brought. There's no more room in the fridge."

J.P. smiled as he drove toward the parking-lot exit.

Sara bit her lower lip as they rolled along the highway, then burst out with, "Did you mean what you said today? About loving me?"

"I did," J.P. said. "Did you?"

"Yes," Sara replied.

He must have heard something in the tone of that single word. "Then why do I get the feeling you've changed your mind?"

She reached over, rested her left hand on his muscular blue-jeaned thigh. "I haven't changed my mind, J.P., I promise you."

"Then what's bothering you?"

She heaved out a sigh. "There are a lot of things we haven't worked out," she answered.

"Such as?"

"Such as where we want to go from *I love you*," Sara said. "You and I are both grown-ups, J.P. We know that love, wonderful as it is, won't be enough for the long haul." She paused, working up her nerve. "And I'm not interested in anything *less* than the long haul."

"Okay," J.P. replied in a leading tone that

said, *Go on.*

She wished he would have said that he felt the same way she did.

As good as sex between them was, she wanted *more* than sex. More even than standard-issue romantic love.

She wanted commitment, absolute fidelity.

True partnership.

"I have two children," she stated rhetorically. "I love them more than life. But one of them is chronically difficult and the other, I'm embarrassed to say I've just realized, needs a lot more attention than I've been giving her. I have a publishing contract to fulfill, and even after Eric is released from the hospital, he's going to be a semi-invalid."

J.P. didn't answer. He just waited for her to go on.

"All of that means I'm going to be so busy I'll meet myself coming and going," she continued. "And that isn't going to leave a lot of time for *us,* J.P. It wouldn't be fair to you. Plus —" She paused, bit her lower lip, unsure how to go on.

"Plus?" he prompted gently.

"We need some time to think. About my kids, for one example. Hayley would love a stepfather, I'm sure, but Eric . . . Well, Eric might make things difficult for both of us

— but especially for you. And I want us both to be happy, J.P."

"Is this a breakup?" J.P. asked, his voice measured, as he turned onto Sara's street. If any particular emotions had been stirred by Sara's speech, he gave no outward indication of that.

"Do you want it to be?"

Her house was just ahead, and he signaled to turn into the driveway. "No fair, Sara. You don't get to ask another question instead of answering mine."

She drew a deep tremulous breath.

"It's not a breakup," she said after a long moment. "It's a time-out."

"Okay," J.P. said quietly.

Sara's eyes stung. "Can you trust me a little, here?" she asked. "I love you. I want to spend my life with you. But I need to be sure you feel the same way, J.P. I need to be sure you'll still love me if we don't have children together, whether it's because I choose not to or because I can't."

"Sara —"

She pressed an index finger to his lips. "Don't," she whispered. "Let's think about this separately. We need to get it right."

J.P. turned off the truck's engine, but he made no move to get out from behind the wheel. "Get it right?" he asked. "Or get it perfect? Because that's never going to happen, Sara. Successful marriages require compromise, and plenty of it." A pause followed, during which he gazed into the distance. "I love you. I've always wanted kids of my own, but if there's one thing I've learned in this life, it's that nobody gets everything they want. If you decide Eric and Hayley are enough, or we just don't conceive, I'll be disappointed. But I'll deal with it, I promise you. It won't be a deal-breaker."

Sara felt her eyes widen. "You said it *would* be, though."

"I changed my mind," he said. "Men are permitted to do that, right? Or is it *women only*?"

"You mean that?"

J.P. sighed. "I never say anything I don't mean," he told her.

"All those women you've dated over the past decade or so — you've never promised a single one of them a white picket fence?"

"I live in a ranch house, Sara," he replied. "A white picket fence would be highly impractical, though I *have* thought seriously about putting in a swimming pool. And, no, I never promised any of them anything, beyond dinner, passably good manners and a nice time."

"That raises another question," Sara mused, somewhat feverishly. "If we lived together, *where* would we live? Your ranch or my house?"

"The ranch," J.P. said. "That land is part of me, Sara. It's the best part of who I am."

That, she knew, was true. She'd seen J.P. McCall interact with the land he lived on, not just recently, but when they were kids, younger than Eric and Hayley were now.

She wondered if something hadn't been growing between them, even back then, and only come to fruition recently when, it seemed, fate had risen up and given them both a push toward the other.

"Okay," Sara conceded. "I could live on the ranch." She paused, blushed. "If we decide to move in together, that is."

"We'd have to be married first," J.P. decided, frowning a little.

"Well, *that's* pretty old-fashioned," Sara remarked.

"You have children," he reminded her. As if she needed reminding. "Sure, they're almost grown up, but that doesn't mean it's okay for us to shack up under the same roof."

She'd been right. His attitude toward living together without the benefit of marriage *was* old-fashioned, though she was sure he didn't disapprove of the choice when others made it.

And she was glad he felt that way.

Sara moved to open the passenger's-side door of the truck, ready to step down onto her driveway. For the first time in the very short interval since she and J.P. had gotten involved, he made no move to come around and help her down.

Evidently, he didn't plan to walk her to the front door, either.

She exited the vehicle somewhat gracelessly and reached inside for her laptop and purse, which had rested on the floorboard in front of her seat.

"Eric is on the mend," she heard herself say. It was as if she'd drifted off to somewhere near her body but not inside it. "I'll take it from here."

He merely nodded.

"Thank you, J.P.," she said, in a near whisper, still at a little distance from herself. "For everything."

"You know where to find me," J.P. said quietly.

"Yes," Sara answered, almost in tears.

Asking for time to get some perspective *was* the right thing to do — she was still sure of that.

But for all her certainty, Sara was nervous.

Building a life with another person was complicated.

Her life would change drastically, and so would J.P.'s.

Eric and Hayley would have to make adjustments, too, and Eric might not even be willing to give his mom's new husband a chance. Hayley might want to object — though Sara seriously doubted that — then decide she couldn't, and keep her misgivings to herself.

She was getting a headache.

She stiffened, standing on the front step, punching in the code to open the door, as J.P. pulled out of the driveway.

Again, Sara wanted to cry.

Again, she didn't.

She stepped into the cool quiet entryway. Dropped her purse and laptop on the long narrow table beside the door.

"Hayley?" she called.

Her daughter appeared in the archway leading to the bedrooms, holding a small package.

"It's not even from Amazon," the girl chimed. "I'm intrigued."

Sara crossed the room, took the package from Hayley's hands and pressed it against her middle. "I don't do *all* my shopping on Amazon," she said, somewhat defensively.

After the conversation she'd just had with J.P., Sara's emotions were tied in knots, and the prospect of Hayley opening the plain brown-paper package containing the one and only impulse purchase her mother had made in nearly two decades was more than she could stand.

Sara took the parcel into her bedroom, tossed it onto the bed to be opened later, in complete privacy, and then returned to the living room, where Hayley was parked on the couch, remote in hand, flipping through various channels on the TV.

"Wanna watch some Netflix?" the girl asked.

Her feet were bare, and there was a tiny tattoo of a rose at the base of her left big toe.

"Not now," Sara replied, eyeing the inky flower. "That's temporary, right?"

Hayley rolled her eyes. "*Yes,* Mother," she gibed. "I'm the obedient kid, remember? Eric is the rebel."

Sara took the remote from her daughter's hand, switched off the power and sat up as straight as possible, given her deep fatigue and the fact that she might just have thrown away her one chance at lasting happiness of the man-and-woman kind.

"We need to talk. About you being the

obedient kid and Eric being the rebel."

Hayley huffed out a major sigh. "We don't have to do this, Mom," she said, sounding both reasonable and annoyed. "I know you love me as much as you love Eric. I was just being bitchy. I had cramps when we talked on the phone earlier."

"You don't have them now?"

"No," Hayley replied. "I took some ibuprofen and lay down with a heating pad on my belly. When they come back, I'll do both those things again."

"Sometimes it sucks to be a woman," Sara observed wryly.

"From the looks of you, being a woman is sucking more than usual at the moment. What happened, Mom? Did you and J.P. have a fight?"

Sara shook her head and decided it was time to find out how much her daughter actually knew about what amounted to an affair between her mother and J.P. McCall.

The idea that what she had with J.P. might never be anything *more* than an affair, a fling, made Sara ache all over, inside and out.

"Not a fight," she answered. "A discussion."

"What kind of discussion?"

"It's complicated," Sara confessed. "What

he wants, what I want, what's best for you and Eric."

"Never mind Eric and me," Hayley said, sounding almost angry. "You've given up enough for us as it is, Mom. It's time you got to live for yourself, at least *some* of the time."

Sara's eyes filled. "Thank you for that," she said. "But I'm *always* going to love you and your brother to the nth degree."

"We'll be out of the house and on our own pretty soon," Hayley pointed out, leaning to pluck a handful of tissues from the box resting on the coffee table and handing them to Sara. "You need a *life,* Mom."

Sara dried her eyes, sniffled a couple of times, blew her nose.

"Gross," Hayley decreed, without rancor.

Sara laughed. It was a shaky, wobbly sound. "Thanks a lot," she said, nudging her daughter lightly in the ribs.

"Are you okay, Mom? I mean, *really* okay?"

"I am," Sara confirmed. "Don't worry about me."

Hayley eyed her thoughtfully, heels planted on the edge of the couch cushions, arms wrapped around her drawn-up knees. "Do you love J.P., Mom?"

"Yes," Sara said. She wasn't about to go

into detail, of course, but Hayley deserved the truth — as much of it as she could handle, that was. "I do. And he says he loves me."

"So what's the problem?" Hayley asked.

Sara thought that over for a few moments, then replied, "I'm not entirely sure."

"I think you're scared," Hayley said with conviction. "Because the sperm donor hurt you so badly." She raised blond eyebrows, twisted her ponytail into a bun on top of her head and then let it unwind in a flurry of gold. "Don't let that ruin things for you, Mom. And don't let *Eric* ruin things, either."

Sara didn't respond, but she didn't look away from Hayley's earnest young face, either.

"Take a risk, Mom," Hayley urged softly, giving her mother a one-armed hug. "Give this thing with J.P. a fighting chance, will you? Let yourself be happy."

Chapter Sixteen

It was a good thing J.P. could have found his way back to the ranch blindfolded, because for all the attention he paid, he might as well have been wandering somewhere on the astral plane as he covered the distance between Sara's place and his.

For all practical intents and purposes, he'd been absent from his body the whole time, his mind exploring a grim potential future — one without Sara.

It wasn't, as the old saying went, a pretty picture.

He returned to the present moment with a jolt as he pulled up in front of the ranch house and Trooper came bounding toward the truck, in a literal cloud of dust, barking in frenzied welcome.

The sight of that goofy old dog twisted J.P.'s heart.

They'd been apart a lot since Eric Worth's accident, and he'd missed Trooper sorely, which was something of a dichotomy, given that J.P. had never been happier than he was in Sara's company, whatever the circumstances.

Yep. He definitely loved her.

And the situation was downright crazy.

Maybe even too good to be true.

He got out of the truck, and before he could shut the door behind him, Trooper literally leaped into J.P.'s arms, licking his face with happy urgency.

J.P. laughed, holding the dog firmly, and turned his head to one side. "Whoa," he said. "I'm glad to see you, too."

He set Trooper down gently, patted his head.

The door leading into the ranch house kitchen opened — the front door, oddly enough, was on the other side of the structure — and Becky and Robyn spilled out.

His nieces resembled Josie, their mother, with their blond hair and denim-blue eyes. Becky, the eldest at fourteen, was already making the transition from child to young woman, but Robyn, who'd just turned twelve, was still gawky, all knees, elbows and eyeballs.

As he watched them approach, he wished he could freeze time. Today, Becky and Robyn were innocent, perfectly and purely themselves, safe in the circle of their extended family.

Soon enough, *too* soon, the outside world would teach them to question everything they thought they knew — about themselves, about life and love. It would teach them all about men and women, joy and sorrow, laughter and tears.

All of that was inevitable, of course. Natural and right.

But knowing it squeezed his throat shut for a few moments.

"Are you going to stick around this time, Uncle J.P.?" Robyn chimed. "Gram says she's seen Dickens's Christmas ghosts more often than she's seen you lately."

J.P. laughed, pulled the girl against his side with one arm, held her there for a long moment, then let her go.

"I've been a little busy," he said. "But, yeah, I'm planning to stay close to home for a while."

"Gramps wants to clear away some brush, over at the cabin," Becky put in. She was the more circumspect of the two, quiet and reserved, unlike her outgoing mother. "Gram keeps telling him to drop it, that it'll keep, but he won't. She says he has a bee in his bonnet when it comes to that project."

J.P. felt a pang of chagrin. He'd been the

one to suggest that he and his dad clean up the small burial plot behind the homestead cabin; he hadn't followed through with the plan and now the man he loved and respected most in the world had been disappointed.

Frustrated, too, no doubt.

"I think Gramps would look really funny in a bonnet," Robyn remarked, squinching up her freckled nose.

"It's just an old-people saying, ding-dong," Becky scoffed. "A figure of speech. There *is* no bonnet, and no bee."

"Be nice," J.P. told his elder niece, but he was grinning, too.

The image of his father in a pioneer woman's broad-brimmed bonnet *was* funny, bee or no bee. The old man, with his weathered visage and gray hair, definitely wouldn't be able to carry off the look.

"We're having fried chicken for supper," Robyn informed her uncle as the three of them headed for the house in a sort of moving huddle, Trooper trotting happily alongside. "Gram makes the *best* fried chicken."

"True that," J.P. agreed, going for urban cool and, going by the expression on Becky's upturned face, missing by the proverbial country mile.

When they entered the house, they found

the old man at the sink, peeling potatoes, while his busy wife dissected a plump chicken carcass, one of three, at the butcher block nearby. Her special mixture of flour, seasonings and bread crumbs sat on the end of the nearest counter, waiting.

Sylvia McCall liked to say she used more than eleven herbs and spices, and she meant to be just as secretive about the recipe as the Colonel himself.

"Well," she cried, beaming even as she tried to scowl, "look what the cat dragged in."

J.P. noticed Robyn pulling out her smart-phone and keying something into the Notes app.

"I'm writing down every weird thing Gram and Gramps say," she announced, "for future prosperity."

"Posterity," Becky corrected loftily and with a sniff. "Dingbat."

"Rebecca," Sylvia warned, though mildly. "We do not call each other names in this house. Never have, never will."

J.P. recalled some of the things he'd called his sisters, back in the day, when one or both of them had been roped into babysitting little brother. They hadn't been any worse than *dingbat,* actually, but they'd sure gotten under Clare's and Josie's skins.

For almost a year, he could rile Clare into a typical teenage frenzy of angry diatribes just by whispering *stink* as he passed her.

Of course, because he kept his voice just above a whisper when he tormented his eldest sister, *she'd* been the one to get in trouble.

He sighed. Next time he spoke with Clare, he'd apologize for being such a little shit back then.

"How long till supper?" he asked. "I'll feed the horses and grab a shower —"

"Start with the shower," his dad said. "I've already fed the horses."

"I was thinking we could head over to the cabin tomorrow morning, now that it's relatively safe to wade through tall grass, and clear away some brush," J.P. said by way of a reply. "You up for that, old man?"

John McCall was trying not to look pleased, but he didn't quite manage it.

J.P. felt another tug in his heart.

One day, his dad wouldn't be here to josh around with. It was time to stop taking him for granted, as if he'd live forever. Start spending real time, having real conversations.

The same went for his mom. His sisters, his nieces, his friends.

And especially, Sara.

"I guess I could fit that into my schedule," J.P.'s dad said. "What time are we leaving for the homestead?"

"Right after we feed the horses," J.P. answered. "Say, six thirty?"

"Hell," his dad retorted with mock sternness, "that's the middle of the damned day. I don't know what to make of your generation."

J.P.'s mom smiled and rolled her eyes. "Hush up, John McCall," she told her husband. "I remember when *your* father used to fuss about you sleeping in till noon while he rolled out no later than four a.m. to do all the chores. And kindly don't swear in front of the girls."

"What about my generation, Gramps?" Robyn asked earnestly. "What do you make of us?"

The old man grinned, wiped his hands on a dish towel, and turned away from the sink to tug at one of his younger granddaughter's blond pigtails and give Becky a one-armed hug. "Your generation, my little cowgirls, will save the environment, feed the hungry *and* find a cure for every illness known to man."

Robyn looked thrilled. "You think so, Gramps?"

"I think so," he said gently.

"It's a tall order," Becky remarked thoughtfully. "But we'll try."

"You'll succeed for sure," their grandfather replied, and he sounded as though he believed every word he'd said.

J.P.'s eyes were smarting a little, all of a sudden, so he went off to shower and change clothes. He figured the burning sensation was a delayed reaction to the dust that had roiled up around the truck when he drove in.

When he'd showered, dried himself off and put on clean jeans and a T-shirt, he returned to the kitchen.

Only his mom was there.

"Where is everybody?" J.P. asked, opening the refrigerator and helping himself to a beer.

Sylvia chuckled. "They're outside, bathing poor old Trooper in the yard. He was getting pretty dusty." A pause. "You really ought to have that driveway paved, J.P."

J.P. took a swig of beer, savored it. For now, he had plenty to think about, his mother's suggestion included, but when supper was over and the rest of the evening had gone by, he knew thoughts of Sara would close in on him and pound him into a lonely pulp.

"Trooper loves a good hosing down," he

said. "And I'll think about the driveway."

"How are Sara and her kids?" his mother asked.

So, no blessed period of distraction, after all.

Damn.

"They're doing pretty well, considering what they've been through lately."

"Is there anything you need to tell your old gray-haired mother, J.P.?" Sylvia asked with a twinkle. "About a wedding, maybe?"

Mothers, J.P. decided, possessed an uncanny ability to jump to conclusions, especially in cases like his and Sara's.

"Mom," he drawled, stretching the word a little.

She sighed. "All right, all right. I'll leave it alone."

"A likely story," J.P. said.

"Just tell me everything is okay between the two of you."

"I can't," he admitted with a sigh of resignation. His mom had obviously guessed that he loved Sara, so he'd give her just enough information to appease her curiosity — he hoped. "We're taking a time-out — as she put it."

"I'm not surprised," Sylvia said. She'd put the potatoes on to boil, and now she was breading the chicken, getting ready to drop it into the bacon fat sizzling in the huge cast-iron skillet that had been in the Mc-Call family since covered-wagon days. "Sara's probably got all she can handle, with her boy hurt so badly and that rat fink of an ex-husband back in town."

For Sylvia McCall, *rat fink* was the mother of all insults.

It made J.P. smile a little, even though he wasn't sure how he was going to get through the days — and especially the nights — ahead.

"He's met his match in Sara," he said. "Evidently, his plan was to get himself appointed to administrate the trust funds his father put in place for Eric and Hayley. It seems Zachary's wallet is a little thin these days, and he's looking for ways to fatten it up."

"That's terrible!" his mother said, adjusting the gas in the burner under the big skillet, lowering the blue flame. "What kind of man steals from his own children? From anybody, really, but *his own children*?"

"Zachary Worth," J.P. answered after willing his back molars to stop grinding together. "Sara's tough, and she can handle this, but there's another problem."

"What?" Sylvia looked sincerely worried.

"Worth has been trying to turn Eric

385

against her, and he's using me to do it."

"Using you? How?"

"A word here, a word there. You know the drill. I'm going to be the evil stepfather. Once she and I start living under the same roof, Sara won't have time for her kids anymore. That kind of drivel."

"Some women do that," Sylvia said sadly. "Get a new husband and pretty much forget all about their kids."

"Not Sara," J.P. replied with certainty. "If she had to choose between me and her children, she'd choose her children. And that's one of the reasons I love her so much. Her character is rock-solid."

He must have looked sad, because his mother went to the sink, washed her hands and came over to hug J.P.

Looking up at him, she said, "So are you, J.P. McCall. You've sown more than your share of wild oats, and there were times when your dad and I fretted because you couldn't — or wouldn't — settle down, but you've turned out to be as fine a man as your father, and that's saying something."

She stepped back from J.P., eyed the beer can in his hand and frowned. "Just watch your alcohol intake, son. A few generations back, on my side of the family, by the way, we had a drunkard in our midst."

J.P. sucked in a breath, pretending to be horrified. "Say it ain't so!" he teased. "Was this miscreant a blood relative, or did he marry into the family?"

Sylvia laughed and swatted at him, washed and dried her hands again, and went back to dredging chicken parts through her eleven-plus herbs and spices. *"She,"* his mother corrected. "And, yes, she did marry into the family, but she was still an ancestor."

"Life was hard in those days," J.P. remarked charitably. "Nothing but work from sunup to sundown. Chopping wood, carrying water, weeding and hoeing the vegetable patch. Having to wear corsets and long heavy dresses and pinchy shoes all the time. Maybe she needed a nip or two to keep from going out of her everlovin' mind."

Sylvia made a mildly indignant face. "It wasn't like that for Mabel," she said. "She was a real princess, from someplace back East. Her father owned a factory. Never lifted a finger from the day she married into the family."

J.P. frowned. "How do you know all this?"

"Diaries," she said. "We have a pile of them, your father and me. It's all there. Practically the whole history of my kinfolks and his."

"Seriously?" J.P. was fascinated, and he thought Sara might be, too, in her capacity as a writer. "How is it that you've never mentioned these diaries?"

"You wouldn't have been interested," Sylvia answered with a little tilt of her chin. "Now, get some of my old towels out of the laundry room, go outside and help dry off your dog. He's not coming in here sopping wet. It's all I can do to keep these floors clean as it is!"

J.P. raised the beer can in a salute, finished off its contents, tossed it into the recycling and headed for the laundry room.

He slept in his own room that night, for the first time in several days, and of course the very walls seemed to exude memories of himself and Sara, talking, making love or simply lying in each other's arms, content to be together.

Restless, he tossed and turned.

He wanted Sara, and not just sexually. Without her beside him, he felt diminished somehow, less himself than usual.

He rolled over, punched his pillow into shape — or tried to, anyhow — and then lay staring up at the ceiling for a long time.

When he finally slept, the first of several nightmares was there to greet him.

It was a reconnaissance mission, and he

was riding in the back of a truck, the third vehicle in a long caravan. He saw dust and palm trees — nothing unusual about that.

The soldier seated across from him, on the greasy truck bed, was scrolling through pictures on his phone, smiling now and then.

J.P. had seen those pictures a thousand times, but he never got tired of them. His buddy had a beautiful family. He was due to muster out in two weeks, and much as J.P. liked the guy, he envied him a little, too — because he had a wife and kids, because he was going home.

J.P. thought about home, about the ranch and his mom and dad, and his friends Eli and Cord. He imagined saddling up a horse, in the cool of a summer morning, riding out through oceans of grass, listening to the bawling of cattle and the song of the creek, the mountains forming a half circle around him, like a protective arm.

And then it happened.

The very air vibrated, like silent thunder.

Then the world split itself like a walnut, and fire rained down all around the trucks.

There were screams.

Volleys of gunfire.

And J.P.'s pal, the one with the family and the ticket home, turned to crimson vapor before his very eyes.

That was the last thing J.P. remembered about the attack, until weeks afterward.

He woke himself deliberately, a skill he'd acquired through long and careful practice, and bolted upright in bed.

Trooper, curled up on the rug nearby, whimpered quizzically.

J.P., sweating and sick to his stomach, shoved a hand through his moist hair. "I'm okay," he said for his own benefit as well as the dog's. "I'm okay."

This, he thought, *is what I have to offer Sara. My nightmares.*

In that moment, he came as close to weeping as he ever had.

He read after that, knowing he wouldn't be able to go back to sleep.

Knowing he didn't dare.

He knew he looked like five miles of bad road when he joined his dad in the kitchen about an hour before sunrise.

Without speaking, the two men left the house, stepping out into the cool stillness of the predawn hour. Trooper followed as always.

Father and son tended to the horses in companionable silence, their work choreographed by years of practice.

J.P. had been helping out with ranch

chores since kindergarten, and before that he'd fed chickens and gathered eggs, among other simple tasks.

It was comforting to work with his dad again. J.P. made a point of staying in the moment, feeling the play of his arm and shoulder muscles as he hauled bales of hay down from the stacks in the back of the barn, the give of the shavings under the soles of his boots as he entered and left the stalls, checking on the water supply.

Later, they led all the horses through the pasture gate, four at a time, each of them leading two.

Light, the color of pale apricots, rimmed the foothills to the east, and the sky gradually turned periwinkle blue.

J.P. breathed it all in.

Assimilated everything.

His dad stepped up beside him, slapped him lightly on the back. "I'll throw together some breakfast and we'll head over to the homestead in my truck. Get some work done."

"I'm making breakfast," J.P. replied with a grin. "I'm a better cook than you are."

The old man laughed. "Yep," he conceded. "You take after your mother that way. I was just trying to get you talking."

J.P. frowned as they returned toward the house.

Dust rose from beneath their boots, and he made a mental note to look into getting a brick or concrete driveway put in.

"I don't talk enough to suit you?" he asked his dad.

"You talk about the cattle, the price of beef, the state of the stock market, and what Cord Hollister and Eli Garrett are up to at any given time," his father allowed. "But I haven't heard much about Sara."

They'd reached the kitchen door, and J.P. pushed the door open, letting Trooper and his dad go ahead of him.

"When I have something to say, Dad, I'll tell you about Sara and me."

"Is there some big secret?"

They were inside now.

"Not really," J.P. answered with a sigh. "Things are in a state of flux, that's all."

"Sounds serious."

His dad went to the sink to wash up, and J.P. followed suit when he was done.

"I need time," J.P. said.

And that was the end of that line of discussion.

After a simple breakfast, they tossed some tools into the back of John McCall's ancient pickup truck, along with a couple of jugs of water, and headed overland, toward the homestead, Trooper perched between them on the tattered bench seat.

There was no road, just a series of cattle trails, so the journey practically rattled J.P.'s teeth. His dad, who drove that old rust bucket of a truck all over the ranch, in all kinds of weather, didn't seem bothered.

When they reached the cabin, J.P. insisted on doing a cursory search of the immediate area, just in case the feds had missed one of the Becker gang's bear traps.

Fortunately, nothing turned up, so they let Trooper out of the truck, rolled up their shirtsleeves, grabbed scythes from the back and set to work.

They'd been working in silence for the better part of an hour when J.P.'s phone buzzed in his jeans pocket. Evidently, they were in a cellular hot spot.

It might be Sara.

He pulled it out, saw Eli's personal number on the screen, thumbed the answer button.

"McCall," he said, worried. "Everything okay with Sara and Eric?"

"They're fine," Eli answered. "I'm calling about something else."

"What?" J.P. asked, a little impatient.

"I need you to come to my office, J.P.,"

Eli said. "Right now."

"What's this about?" He'd accidentally thumbed the speaker button, so his dad was privy to everything that was said.

"It's not an emergency," Eli relented. "But it *is* important. Important enough that I don't want to discuss it over the phone. Just get here, okay?"

"I'm on my way," J.P. said.

"You rob a bank or something?" his dad asked when J.P. had ended the call.

"Or something," J.P. muttered, gathering tools and whistling for the dog, who'd been down by the creek, splashing around in the cold water. "Do you want to come along?"

"I don't see any other way for you to get there," came the gruff reply. "Leave the tools. We can come back for them later, after I've paid your bail."

"Very funny," J.P. responded.

They all got back into the truck, Trooper included, and J.P.'s dad drove over rough ground, then across a shallow place in the creek, making for the dirt road that would lead to the highway.

Stressed, and unwilling to let it show, J.P. clamped his teeth together to keep from biting his tongue when the pickup hit another bump in the landscape.

"You don't have *any idea* what's going on

here?" his father asked when they reached the highway and things smoothed out a little.

"Not a clue," J.P. answered. He was racking his brain — had been since he'd spoken to Eli — but nothing came to him.

At least nothing had happened to Sara or either of her children.

That gave him solid ground to stand on.

When they reached the sheriff's department, about twenty minutes after leaving the cabin, Eli came out to meet them.

"What the hell?" J.P. half growled.

"Just come in," Eli ordered grimly. He acknowledged J.P.'s dad with a nod. "You, too, John. This is a family thing."

J.P.'s dad hesitated, went pale. "My daughters? Is this about my daughters?"

"No," Eli said, holding the glass door open for both of them. "It's nothing like that. I think it'll come as a pretty big surprise, though."

They passed through the reception area, where the dispatcher and several deputies watched them solemnly.

J.P. caught Eli's eye and frowned. His stomach was doing backflips.

Eli went ahead of them, pushed open his office door, held it.

J.P. entered first, and stopped so suddenly

that his father bumped into him from behind.

Mary Collins, a local social worker and good friend of J.P.'s mother's, sat in a chair near Eli's desk, holding a toddler in her arms.

The little boy looked up at J.P. with eyes so like his own that he was stunned.

"Do you want to explain, Mary?" Eli asked quietly, after closing the door and offering J.P.'s dad a chair, which he took, looking mystified.

J.P. had never seen the child before, but he knew instantly who he was.

He might have been looking at a much younger version of himself.

Mary, a stylish woman in her late fifties, with neatly coiffed silver-gray hair and warm brown eyes, smiled at J.P. "Relax," she said. "I'm pretty sure this is a good thing."

J.P.'s knees buckled, and it was a good thing Eli had had the foresight to shove a chair up behind him, because he might have landed on his ass on the floor otherwise.

He rested his elbows on his knees, trying to settle back into himself.

"Hey, there," he said to the boy, very gently. Very quietly. "What's your name, buddy?"

The child regarded him with solemn McCall eyes, one small finger hooked behind his lower lip. His hair was the same pale shade of blond as Becky and Robyn's — the same color J.P.'s had been until he'd hit adolescence.

"This is Tyler," Mary said. "He's three."

As if to verify the woman's statement, Tyler took his fingers out of his mouth and held up three of them.

J.P. lifted his gaze to Mary's face. After managing those few words of greeting, he'd been stricken to silence again.

"A woman named Ellie Parks brought Tyler to the fire station about a couple of hours ago and, of course, the chief called Eli, who called me," Mary said. "And here we are."

Ellie Parks.

The name was familiar, but barely so. He'd dated Ms. Parks briefly, about four years back, and they'd agreed, after a few weeks, that the relationship was going nowhere.

"Where is she now?" J.P. asked.

Mary glanced at J.P.'s father, who took the hint quickly and got up to hoist the boy into his strong rancher's arms. His smile was gentle, full of surprise and pleasure and concern.

"Give us a few minutes, John?" Mary asked. "Please."

Tyler, clad in miniature jeans, scuffed boots and a tiny faded T-shirt with a cartoon character on the front, offered no protest as J.P.'s dad carried him out of Eli's office.

Eli closed the door quietly behind them.

"He's mine," J.P. said. It wasn't a question.

"No judge would ask for a DNA test," Eli confirmed.

"Where's Ellie? Why did she leave him at the fire station?"

Mary held up one manicured hand. "Slow down, J.P.," she said. "I'll tell you everything I know."

J.P. waited respectfully, though a part of him wanted to grab this woman by the shoulders and shake the information out of her.

Not that he'd ever do anything like that, of course.

He'd never laid a hand on a woman in anger or frustration in his life.

Mary smoothed her linen skirt, crumpled from holding Tyler. "It seems Ellie is overwhelmed with the responsibilities of motherhood," she began. "She told Chief Martin that she couldn't cope and that she was in some trouble, back home, in Oregon. She wouldn't say what, and she was gone by the time Eli drove over there to talk to her."

J.P. nodded, gathering the fragments of what he remembered about Ellie Parks and trying to corral them into a concept that made sense.

Mary went on. "She left Tyler's birth certificate, a few of his clothes and a toy horse behind. We only have her word that you are the boy's father, since your name doesn't appear on the birth certificate, but Ellie swore up and down that you'd know Tyler belongs to you as soon as you laid eyes on him."

Ellie had been right. He'd known instantly.

"Why didn't Ellie ever contact me?" J.P. asked. "Tyler is my *son*. I would have helped raise him, paid child support, made sure both of them had whatever they needed."

Mary's eyes were sympathetic. "According to the chief, she was afraid you would take Tyler away from her."

J.P. shoved both hands through his hair and swore. "And yet she's willing to hand him over now? Just turn around and walk away from her own child?"

"I don't think it's as simple as that," Mary said in a soothing voice. Clearly, she had a lot of experience pouring oil onto troubled waters. "Ms. Parks is in some kind of trouble, like I said. She wants to grant you permanent custody of the child — on one condition."

A mixture of hope and fury flared within J.P. What had been happening to his son all this time?

"*What* condition?"

"That you pay her three years' child support in one lump sum."

"Done," J.P. said, slapping his palms down on his thighs.

"Don't you want to know how much she's asking for?" Mary inquired. She'd pulled out her phone now, and commenced to scrolling through the notes she must have made while hearing the story from Chief Martin.

"I don't *care* how much she's asking for," J.P. replied tersely. "Can I take Tyler home with me? Right now, today?"

"I'm sorry," Mary said, "but no. There are procedures, J.P. Ellie has to surrender the child to you legally, and that means an investigation will have to be carried out. Your lawyer will need to contact hers — if she has one — and an agreement will have to be reached. *Then* there will be a hearing."

J.P. stood up so suddenly that Mary

jumped, and Eli, who'd been leaning against a credenza with his arms folded, instantly straightened.

When he didn't explode, they calmed visibly.

"You didn't know that Ellie Parks was carrying your child?" Eli asked, in sheriff-mode now. No doubt he already had some feelers out, learning what he could about Ellie and her situation. "You're sure she never tried to contact you?"

J.P. stopped, glared at one of the two men he'd called his best friend since he could walk under a horse's belly without ducking. "Yeah, Eli, I'm *sure,*" he bit out. "If I'd known about Tyler, I'd have gone after a fifty-fifty custody agreement — at the very least. And either way, I *sure as hell* would have provided for him!"

"Take it easy," Eli counseled with a conciliatory smile. "It's part of my job to ask these questions. You know that."

J.P. sighed again, heavily. "What's it been like for Tyler?" he asked. "Did Ellie take good care of him?"

"Physically, he's healthy," Mary assured him. "No signs of abuse or neglect. He's well nourished and seems to be comfortable around other people. Eli and I took him to the ER for a checkup before we brought

401

him here."

"Has he asked for his mother?"

It killed J.P. to think of that little kid calling in vain for the one person who should never *ever* have left him.

The social worker and the sheriff exchanged glances.

"What?" J.P. demanded.

"He doesn't speak," Mary admitted. "At least, he hasn't said anything so far."

"Maybe he's scared," Eli suggested. "He's pretty little, and there's a lot to take in."

A pause. "Will I be able to see him?" J.P. asked.

"Yes," Mary said. "Until things are settled, Tyler will be staying with one of our best foster families — the Sanfords, Bob and Rayleen. You probably know them."

J.P. *did* know the couple. They were good people, the kind others referred to as pillars of the community, and they'd been providing intermittent foster care to younger children for years.

When babies or toddlers had to be removed from their homes, or simply didn't *have* a home, due to abandonment or the death, incarceration or medical problems of their parents, they went to stay with Bob and Rayleen.

J.P. collapsed back into his chair, dizzied

by conflicting emotions.

He was shocked.

He was pissed off at Ellie Parks and, at the same time, sad that, for whatever reason, she was willing to give up her child.

Why hadn't she contacted him? Asked for help?

He would have handled this reasonably.

But then, Ellie hadn't known that, had she?

They'd been virtual strangers to each other.

She'd been afraid to tangle with him, legally or otherwise, as Mary had already stated, because he was wealthy, an established member of one of the Creek's pioneer families, while she was . . . ?

He tried to remember but came up dry.

All he could have said for sure was that she was blonde.

Probably.

Until Sara, he'd had a thing for blondes.

What a selfish, shallow bastard he'd been.

He was overwhelmed by regret for the things he'd done, and the things he hadn't.

And then there was the flood of emotions that came with the totally out-of-the-blue discovery that he was a father, at least in name.

If he got the chance, he'd be the real deal,
or die trying.

Chapter Seventeen

Sara knew the decision to step back from her relationship with J.P., at least until they could each get some perspective, had been the right one.

Like two people standing briefly on either side of a blazing fire and then meeting in the heart of the flames, they'd gotten too close, too fast.

For her part, Sara figured she'd been so blinded by the sheer power of their mutual sexual attraction that she couldn't think straight. In the throes of J.P.'s lovemaking, she lost her everyday practical self, the self she knew and understood, and became someone entirely different.

Someone fierce and primitive, without a name, without a fixed identity.

A naked essence of a person, set ablaze, all-consuming and destined to cave in upon herself, like a dying star shooting its last and brightest brilliance in all directions, piercing the darkness of space with streaks of glorious light.

It was wonderful.

It was also damn scary.

She was thinking these thoughts as she and Hayley sat in Eric's new hospital room, waiting for him to return from another round of X-rays.

The text from J.P. jolted her, made her heart skip over a few beats.

I know we agreed on low-to-no contact, Sara, but there's something I really need to tell you, and it won't fit into a text or even a phone call. Could we meet up sometime today?

Semi-alarmed, Sara glanced toward Hayley, who was playing a farm-animal game on her tablet on the other side of the room. "Can you hold down the fort for a while, sweetheart?" she asked. "I need to go out."

Hayley looked up. "Sure," she said, sweetly distracted, part of her mind clearly still on the game. "What's up?"

"Nothing drastic," Sara replied lightly.

You hope.

"How long will you be?" Hayley asked reasonably. She had plans for the afternoon, a barbecue at her friend Susan's house.

"Not sure," Sara replied. "Probably not long."

She was already texting J.P. back.

I can meet you now. Where and when?

His response was immediate.

I'll pick you up in ten minutes, if that's okay. You're at the hospital, right?

Sara's answer was Yes. Main entrance?

It's a plan, J.P. responded.

Minutes later, J.P.'s truck drew up in front of the hospital, and he leaned across to push open the passenger's-side door.

Sara scrambled in, a little breathless.

And worried.

They hadn't set a time limit on their sabbatical from each other, but now, as she studied J.P.'s profile, noting the tightness in his jawline, she wondered if he'd decided he'd had long enough to work things through from his side and come to the conclusion that they'd be better off going their separate ways.

"You're scaring me," she said when she finally found her voice.

By which time they were out of the hospital lot and driving along one of the Creek's many side streets.

"Don't be," J.P. replied, glancing at her once before turning his attention back to the road.

He seemed sad and, conversely, quietly elated.

They drove into a semirural neighborhood, where most of the homes were well-kept trailers, fancy double- and triple-wides. Sara knew a lot of the people who lived in the area, including several of Hayley's friends from school, and a few of Eric's, too.

She'd been here often herself, attending book clubs, bridal and baby showers, fund-raising meetings for locals who'd fallen on hard times or had a family member who'd succumbed to accident or illness.

J.P. brought the truck to a stop in front of Bob and Rayleen Sanford's place, a gleaming structure encircled by a wooden deck and surrounded by green lawn, recently mown, judging by the scent wafting through the truck's open windows.

There were flower beds everywhere, along with a few scattered toys, and an elderly golden retriever lay comfortably in the shade of a towering cherry tree.

A standard white picket fence embraced the property.

Sara was confused — why had J.P. brought her here? — but she smiled, thinking what good people the Sanfords were. Childless themselves, they took in foster children, usually babies or toddlers, and the whole community admired them for their kindness and dedication.

"Where are all the children?" she asked, musing. On other occasions, when she'd driven past on some errand, she'd seen Rayleen and one of her teenage helpers in the yard, riding herd on three or four active toddlers or rocking babies on the shady deck.

"Inside," J.P. answered. "Rayleen gives them snacks right about now. Brings them back outside for a while in the afternoon, when the temperature starts to go down."

Sara turned to J.P. then, struck by his familiarity with Rayleen's routine.

"So," she began, "what's going on, J.P.? Why are we here?"

He told her then.

About Ellie Parks, about his son.

Sara was surprised, but not horrified. J.P. had a reputation for dating a lot of women, and while he'd probably taken precautions, there was never a guarantee that pregnancy wouldn't happen.

"Did you love her?" she asked when he'd finished a fairly detailed account of receiv-

409

ing a call from Eli, heading into town with his dad, meeting with Mary Collins, finding his three-year-old son.

J.P. sighed, shook his head. "No," he said. "I can't say I regret fathering Tyler, though. He's a gift I never dared hope for. But I *do* regret being so careless. Ellie and I barely knew each other. I couldn't even tell you where she's from or what she does for a living — not without doing some research. We didn't make plans or promises. It was all up-front — let's have fun, then you go your way and I'll go mine."

She had no idea how she felt about this latest development in the saga of Sara and J.P., but she understood what this child must mean to him. He'd made it clear how much he wanted a family and now he was about to have one.

Not necessarily including Sara.

The thought made her feel as if the ground had fallen away beneath her, leaving her suspended over a deep abyss.

"What happens now?" she asked. "Are you going to marry Ellie Parks?"

J.P. blew out a breath and his eyes widened in what looked like genuine surprise.

"No," he said, sounding just emphatic enough to calm some of the doubts whispering at the ravaged edges of Sara's heart. "I

love *you,* Sara. And *only* you."

"Okay," Sara said, because nothing else came to her in the moment.

Some writer she was. Once again, her usual extensive vocabulary had deserted her.

"There are some things that have to happen before I can bring Tyler home to the ranch — legal things, mostly — but Ellie basically agreed to sign custody over to me, full stop. Eli has deputies out looking for her now — we're not sure what kind of mental state she's in, and she said she was in trouble, back home in Oregon."

"Sounds like she's in a tough place financially," Sara observed.

"Yeah," J.P. agreed with another sigh. "I want to be fair to Ellie. If she can't afford legal representation, I'll hire an attorney for her."

"That's kind," Sara said. "Some men would be furious." She thought of Zachary. "And some would deny any involvement at all. Walk away."

"Not gonna happen," J.P. said without hesitation.

Just then, Rayleen's front door opened, and she stepped out onto the deck, a small boy perched on her right hip.

A plump woman in her midforties, with chin-length auburn hair and a winning

411

smile, Rayleen beckoned with her free hand and called out, "Come on in, you two, and have some lemonade. I just made a batch, and it's ice-cold."

"I could wait here," Sara volunteered, feeling a little like an intruder.

"Come with me," J.P. urged. "Please."

They both got out of the truck.

J.P. opened the gate in the picket fence and held it for Sara.

The dog remained in his shadow-dappled spot, thumping the ground with his tail.

Rayleen met them in the middle of the stone walkway.

Tyler was already leaning toward J.P., reaching out for him with both arms.

"Da," he said.

J.P.'s eyes glistened as he took the child from Rayleen.

"See there?" Rayleen said with a note of triumph. "I *told* Mary he'd start talking when things settled down a bit. He's a smart little fella."

The little boy clung to J.P.'s neck.

"Hello, there," Sara said, speaking quietly to the child.

He regarded her solemnly for a long moment, then turned shy and buried his face in J.P.'s shoulder. "Da," he repeated.

Automatically, Sara rested a hand on J.P.'s

lower back.

They all went inside then, led by a chattering Rayleen, who was one of the most sociable people Sara had ever known, and sat at her pristine kitchen table, Tyler still clinging to J.P.

They drank two rounds of Rayleen's delicious lemonade, and Rayleen shared what she knew about the situation, which, as it turned out, was nothing more than J.P. knew already.

When it was time to leave — Sara needed to get back to the hospital, and J.P. had a meeting with his attorney — Tyler cried and clung, wailing, "Da! Da!"

Gently, Rayleen peeled the distraught child away from J.P. and mouthed the words *don't worry* before rocking the boy in her arms and telling him softly that his *Da* would be back to see him again soon. Very soon.

In the truck, J.P. sat still as stone behind the wheel, and Sara reached over, laid a hand on his shoulder.

"Everything is going to be all right," she said. "You'll see."

"Will it?" he asked, his voice gruff.

Sara loved this man — that was a fact. But the seismic shift that happened as she watched him, separated once again from the

413

child he hadn't known he had, deepened that love by fathoms.

"Yes," she told him with conviction. "It will be difficult, and it will take time, but, yes, at some point, you and Tyler will be together, for good."

"He spoke, Sara. He called me *Da*. How could he possibly know who I am?"

"Maybe Ellie has videos of you, on her phone, perhaps. She might have wanted him to know he had a father."

"Maybe," J.P. agreed, starting the truck.

"He's unreasonably cute, you know," Sara observed, smiling.

"I agree," J.P. replied. "No doubt, he'll be a handful, though."

"Does that bother you?"

J.P. shook his head. Smiled. "No," he replied. "I figure we'll get along just fine, the boy and I. Does it bother you?"

"No," said Sara without hesitation. "I believe I fell in love with that child at first sight."

J.P. was silent, but the smile lingered on his lips.

"Where do we go from here, J.P.?" Sara asked minutes later when they had almost reached the hospital and he still hadn't spoken. "You and me, I mean?"

"I don't know, Sara. Where do you *want*

us to go?"

"I don't know, either," Sara said, feeling defeated.

And more in love with J.P. McCall than ever.

"Then I guess we have to decide not to decide, for now," J.P. replied.

And no more was said.

That afternoon, while Eric was sleeping off a hectic morning of tests, X-rays and examinations, and Hayley had gone to her friend's house for the barbecue and a swim in the pool, Sara found a quiet corner in another part of the hospital and called Brynne.

"Did Eli tell you?" she asked before Brynne could say more than *hi, there.*

"Tell me what?" Brynne asked, sounding honestly puzzled.

Sara sighed. "Sorry. I keep forgetting that my brother is about as talkative as any of the carved heads on Mount Rushmore."

Brynne laughed, her voice hushed. "That's my husband," she affirmed. "What does he know — what do *you* know — that neither one of you told me?"

Sara opened her mouth to answer, hesitated, then decided she was going to burst if she didn't tell *someone* what she'd just learned.

J.P. hadn't asked her to keep the news of his son's existence to herself, and while she certainly wasn't planning to blab it all over Painted Pony Creek, she was reasonably sure telling Brynne wouldn't do any harm.

Besides, Eli would share the information sooner or later, given that Brynne was, after all, his wife. And once he was sure all his many scruples wouldn't be breached.

"J.P. has a three-year-old son," she said.

Brynne was suitably surprised. "Are you serious?"

"Oh, yes," Sara replied. She told Brynne what she knew, as succinctly as possible, and then she started to cry.

She didn't know why.

She wasn't sad, and she wasn't happy, either.

She *was* ridiculously tired and over-whelmed in general. Nothing new there.

Too many things were coming at her from too many directions.

"Oh, Sara," Brynne said. "Is J.P. still involved with this woman?"

"No, I'm sure he isn't," Sara responded, sniffling and wiping at her tears with the back of one hand. "He wouldn't hide something like that."

A passing orderly, pushing a supply cart,

paused and looked at her with curious concern.

She waved him onward with a sheepish smile, body language for *I'm fine. No worries here.*

"You're right," Brynne said. "J.P. has one hell of a reputation, but I don't think he's done much dating, if any, since Carly showed up. *That* was a wake-up call for all three of them — Eli, Cord *and* J.P. Brought them up short for sure, and made them take a good look at how they were living their lives."

What Brynne said was true.

Carly's arrival had changed those men profoundly.

"Would you be willing to raise another woman's child, Sara?" Brynne pressed.

"I hadn't really thought that far ahead," Sara confessed. "Tell you a secret?" She paused, and when Brynne didn't speak, she continued, "I love my kids more than my life, but when I think about starting over as a mom, I get scared. *Really* scared."

Brynne was quiet for a few moments. Then she spoke again, very gently. "Having babies, raising them, would be different with J.P. — very different. You do realize that, don't you? J.P. isn't a kid in a man-suit, like Zachary. He's an *adult,* and he'll *be there,* for you, for this little boy and for any children the two of you may decide to have."

"But what about Eric and Hayley?"

"What about them, Sara?"

"What if they don't — adapt?"

Brynne sighed. "You know Hayley would be delighted to be a big sister. She's marvelous with the twins. As for Eric, well, he's more of a challenge, I admit, and now he needs more care and attention than ever, but he'll be eighteen years old in a few months, Sara. It's time he grew up, isn't it?"

"Yes," Sara said with a sigh of her own. "That's true enough, but he's badly injured, Brynne. Who knows what such a terrible experience does to a person's psyche? He'll probably have PTSD to deal with, on top of having more surgery, and months of physical therapy —"

"And we'll see that he makes it through just fine — all of us, not just you. We're his family."

Tears welled in Sara's eyes. Eli had always been a good brother to her, but Brynne added a whole new element to the Garrett tribe.

She was both a dear friend and the sister Sara had always wanted.

"Thank you," Sara said.

418

Abruptly, Brynne took the conversation in a whole new direction. "You're at the hospital, aren't you?"

"Yes." The word was tremulous.

"Go home, then," Brynne counseled. "Kick off your shoes and lie down for a while. Pamper yourself a little. You're worn to a frazzle."

Home seemed a lonely place, now that J.P. was keeping his distance. Eric, of course, was confined to the hospital, and Hayley was off doing her own thing a lot of the time, which was undeniably a good thing.

Still, she'd be at loose ends, especially since she'd finished making the necessary changes to her latest novel the day before.

"Sara?" Brynne prompted when she didn't get an answer.

"I'm here," Sara said. "Just thinking."

"You're *over*thinking, I'll bet. Considering this scenario and that, trying to prepare yourself for every conceivable problem or situation."

It was true.

Sara was a storyteller, and while that trait served her well as an author, it was less beneficial when she pondered the possibilities — good and not so good.

Okay, bad.

"You're right, Brynne. So how do I stop?"

"You go home. You lie down on the couch with a cool cloth on your forehead and you binge-watch something on Netflix or Amazon Prime. It's almost as effective as meditation."

Sara laughed, picturing herself stretched out in her living room, focused on the adventures of characters whose lives bore no resemblance to her own.

"Okay," she said. "I'll go home. But I can't guarantee that I'll switch on the TV. I'm not in the mood for clanking swords or lumbering zombies or well-coiffed women in Regency gowns."

This time, Brynne laughed.

"Call me again if you need to talk," she said.

They bade each other temporary farewells and ended the call.

When Sara got back to Eric's room, expecting her son to be sleeping peacefully, trying to convince herself that she ought to take Brynne's advice, she got her second shock of the day.

Zachary's father, the legendary Richard Worth himself, was there, seated in a wheelchair.

He looked ancient and crumpled in his tiny suit.

A cannula pumped oxygen into his nostrils, fueled by a small box under his seat, and his skin was a greenish-gray.

Behind him stood a much younger man; Zachary's brother, Sara intuited. He too wore a suit, but his was immaculately tailored and very, *very* expensive.

He was handsome, a better, undebauched version of Zachary. She couldn't recall his name, if she'd ever heard it in the first place.

"Hello, Sara," he said.

Sara answered with a crisp nod, glanced Eric's way — he was wide-awake — and then turned her gaze on the old man in the wheelchair.

"What are you doing here, Mr. Worth?"

The shrunken, weathered man sat up a little straighter and somehow managed to look down his nose at Sara, even though she was standing and he was sitting.

"I've come to see my grandson," he said.

Sara pretended to consult the wristwatch she wasn't wearing, then glared at him. "You must have been held up somewhere along the way," she said tersely. "For almost eighteen years, by my count."

Worth the elder sniffed disdainfully. "Spare me the drama," he said. "If you recall, you made it quite clear you wanted nothing whatsoever to do with me. You refused the help I offered and I was forced

421

to conclude that I was to have no part in my grandchildren's lives."

He was right — she had written him off.

And she wasn't sorry.

"I think your anger is displaced," he went on when Sara was too scrambled inside to reply, "at least partially. My son behaved abominably, and you were right to kick him to the curb." He paused and took a few laborious breaths. Went on. "He's been hanging around here again, as I understand it."

"Do you even live in Painted Pony Creek?" Eric asked, without rancor. Under the circumstances, the question seemed to come from left field.

Sara moved closer to her son.

The old man sighed. "I've been living in Seattle for years," he told his grandson. "It's Wyatt here who's kept the international side of the business going, despite our long — er — estrangement."

The younger man stepped out from behind his father's wheelchair and extended a hand to Sara. "Wyatt Courtland," he said. "I don't think we've met."

Sara recalled what Eric had told her, before the accident, about the uncle he'd never encountered. That he'd taken his stepfather's last name after his parents were divorced.

No wonder father and son were estranged, as the old man had pointed out.

And yet here they were. Together.

Was this really just a visit, or did they have an agenda?

Sara was betting on the latter.

"What do you want?" she asked bluntly.

Cadaverous old Mr. Worth smiled. It was sort of scary.

"I told you. I'm here to see my grandson. And where, pray tell, is my grand*daughter*?"

"Hayley is with friends," Sara said stiffly. "Not that her whereabouts are any of your concern."

"Mom," Eric pleaded with shaky dignity. *"Chill."*

Sara felt a pang of pure chagrin. Whether she liked it or not, these men shared her children's DNA. And both Eric and Hayley were old enough to decide if they wanted to associate with them or cut them off completely.

Worth turned, straining to look up at his tall son. "Wyatt, can you take over here? I seem to be getting nowhere."

Wyatt rested a hand on his father's slight shoulder.

Just by being in the man's presence, Sara could tell that Wyatt Courtland was nothing

423

like his brother, and that was a small comfort.

With Zachary and his father's track record, it was only sensible to be suspicious.

"We *did* come here hoping to speak with you, Mrs. Worth —"

"Don't *ever* call me that," Sara interrupted evenly.

"Sara, then?"

"Sara will be fine," she relented, albeit grudgingly.

"Mom," Eric half groaned.

Wyatt went on, "When my father heard that Eric had been hurt, he insisted on coming here — despite his doctor's orders — because there are things that need to be explained."

Sara waited. So did Eric.

"First, we know Zachary has been messing around behind our backs — he does that a lot — and trying to gain control of the trust funds my father has set up for his only grandchildren, Eric and Hayley. Essentially, we're here to assure you that the management of said funds is in my hands, not my brother's, and will be until your son and daughter are of the age we decided upon."

Sara sat down in a chair near Eric's bed, as winded as if she'd just run a marathon under a blazing sun.

"It's very generous of you, Mr. Worth," she told her former father-in-law calmly, "to establish trust funds for Eric and his sister. Thank you."

The old man simply inclined his head in acknowledgment of her words.

It was Wyatt who had the floor now, and he continued, "There is more to our visit, however. We wanted to meet you, Eric, and see how you were faring, of course. But we also have some news that may be difficult to hear."

Sara's stomach clenched, but she kept her spine straight and her chin up. And she reached over to clasp Eric's hand.

"Go on," she said, sure that Mr. Courtland was about to say that his father was teetering on the verge of death. He certainly looked as though he were.

She'd never liked the man, but she wouldn't have wished him, or anyone else, dead.

"While Zachary was unsuccessful in his attempts to get his hands on the money set aside for you and your sister," he continued, focusing on Eric now, "I'm afraid we've discovered that he's been running sophisticated cons for a long time, mostly in the Los Angeles area, but in other parts of the country, too. He's been arrested."

425

Eric squeezed Sara's hand so tightly that she nearly cried out in pain. "*Arrested? My dad has been* arrested?"

"I'm sorry," Wyatt told his nephew, "but, yes, he has."

"If he stole from you, he was probably desperate," Eric argued, sounding desperate himself.

Wyatt spoke solemnly. "He's cheated at least a dozen women over the years, and now they're coming forward, pressing charges. This is a serious situation."

"*No,*" Eric protested, but it was a whisper. A ragged one. "He wouldn't do that!"

Sara wanted to hug him, but she knew he'd balk at that, so she refrained.

"The prosecutors have proof, Eric," Wyatt said, not without sympathy.

Eric squeezed his eyes shut, shook his head.

Sara's heart caved in on itself.

"If he's stolen a dime from Worth Enterprises," his grandfather put in, "I'll have him thrown in the slammer myself."

"Shut up," Wyatt told his father. Yep, the two of them were definitely on the outs with each other. "This is difficult enough for the boy without you blustering on about Zachary's failings."

Sara felt a flash of respect for this stranger.

426

And gratitude.

"The whole world will know soon enough," the old man huffed, sucking in so much air that he choked on an inhalation and began to cough. "It'll be — all over — the news!"

"I'm sorry," Wyatt said, still watching Eric, who was in the early stages of a genuine panic attack. "About everything."

"I think you should leave now," Sara told the visitors.

Wyatt nodded, took the wheelchair by the handles and steered it — and his protesting father — out of the room.

Sara cupped her hands on either side of Eric's face.

"Breathe," she instructed sternly. "*Breathe,* Eric. Everything will be all right. We can handle this, together."

Miraculously, Eric began to settle down. He finally sank back onto his pillows, still practically hyperventilating, but making an obvious effort to regain control.

"I'm here," Sara reminded him.

He opened his beautiful eyes, and Sara caught just the briefest glimpse of his sweet, troubled young soul. She saw the little boy he had been, and the man she'd always believed he would one day become.

"He's a *criminal,*" he murmured. "My

father *is a criminal*"

"Yes," Sara agreed gently. She wasn't surprised by this development in the least, but she meant to keep that to herself.

"What if I'm like him?" Eric fretted. "What if I'm a thief and a con artist and a cheater and I end up going to prison? I got into all that trouble before, with Freddie Lansing and the others —"

"You're nothing like Zachary," Sara said, and she knew she spoke the truth. "If you take after anyone, it's your uncle Eli."

Eric blinked, as though he'd never made the connection before. Until Zachary had come along, and upset the proverbial apple cart, Eli had been Eric's hero.

"I'll bet Uncle Eli didn't get himself caught up in a shitstorm, like I did," he protested hopefully. "He's *always* been strong, and he's always done the right thing."

"Oh, he had his moments," Sara said, remembering. "I'm not going to talk out of school, so to speak, but if you ask your uncle if he was the perfect kid, right from the cradle, he'll tell you otherwise, and back it up with facts."

"Like what?" Eric asked, intrigued and a little eager.

"It's not my story to tell," Sara said firmly.

A nurse hurried into the room, probably concerned about Eric's vital signs, which, of course, she could access from various monitors in the nurses' station.

"What's happened?" she fussed.

Sara stepped aside to let the woman check Eric out and examine the various machines and monitors to which he was connected.

"I just got a little excited, that's all," Eric told her. A weary grin played around his mouth but didn't quite come in for a landing.

"You *must* rest," the nurse said, wrapping a blood-pressure cuff around his upper arm. "And too much excitement is bad for you."

This last was directed at Sara, along with an expression of impatient reprimand.

"Go home, Mom," Eric said, not unkindly, wincing as the nurse pumped the cuff tighter and tighter with the little bulb in her hand. "Nurse Ratched is right. Both of us have had enough drama for one day."

The nurse chuckled at the reference, amused rather than offended, apparently.

Like everybody else, she'd seen the movie.

"All right," Sara said. "I'm going."

She waited until the nurse was finished taking Eric's blood-pressure reading and had moved aside, then leaned over to kiss her son's forehead.

Both of us have had enough drama for one day, Eric had said.

"Oh, son," Sara muttered, under her breath, as she left the room. "If only you knew."

CHAPTER EIGHTEEN

J.P. visited Tyler the next day, and the day after that.

Swabs were taken for a DNA analysis, but that was only a formality; J.P. knew the results would prove he was the boy's father.

And he was right.

The report came two weeks later, on the day Becky and Robyn left for home, tanned and healthy and eager to see their parents and friends again. Tyler was indeed his flesh and blood.

That part was pretty straightforward.

Dealing with the legalities was not, however.

Ellie Parks returned to the Creek, ending up in one of the conference rooms of the sheriff's department, accompanied by a lawyer she had chosen and J.P. had paid for, to sign papers. She didn't want to see Tyler at all, she claimed; she was too ashamed, and it would be too painful. She'd just gotten her third DUI, her court date was coming up soon and, in all likelihood, she would be going to jail for a period of six to twelve months.

J.P. didn't judge her. He was just glad that she'd acted in their son's best interests, bringing the child back to Painted Pony Creek and telling the truth.

She could just as easily have kept the boy a secret, and J.P. would probably never have known he was a father.

Small and blonde and earnest, Ellie had not been the woman J.P. had imagined her to be, during their brief association. She looked fragile, as though she'd snap in two in the first high wind, and the pain in her eyes told a story all its own.

J.P. had asked her if she'd gotten pregnant deliberately.

Ellie had shaken her head no, biting her lower lip.

He'd believed her.

Mary Collins, the social worker, had asked many more questions than J.P. did, and Rayleen and Bob Sanford, sitting in on the session, presented a few concerns of their own.

The gist of the story was that Ellie had never wanted Tyler, never bonded with him, probably because her life had been collapsing around her ears.

She'd met a guy, fallen for him, partied with him.

Tyler, meanwhile, had been shuffled back and forth between various friends of Ellie's, none of whom were able to give him a permanent home.

He needed a family, a home.

A place to belong.

As far as J.P. was concerned, that place was Painted Pony Creek, and he was the loving, attentive parent.

Mary Collins was in favor of granting permanent custody to J.P., with supervised visitation for Ellie, when and if she got a handle on things and proved herself a responsible person.

Privately, J.P. thought Ellie might well get it together, eventually, and make a decent life for herself.

Unfortunately, there probably wouldn't be any room in that life for Tyler. She wasn't cut out to be a mother and that wasn't likely to change, no matter what other strides she might make.

Through his attorney, J.P. had offered to pay for rehab, before or after she went to jail.

Ellie had accepted the offer.

And she'd said, straight-out, in front of all those witnesses — J.P. himself; his mother and father; Mary Collins, the social worker; Bob and Rayleen Sanford, Tyler's foster parents; two lawyers; a child psychologist and Sheriff Eli Garrett — that she *just couldn't cope with small children.*

All she wanted was to straighten out her legal problems, get clean and sober, and be free.

After the meeting, she and her lawyer left for Oregon.

That, J.P. thought at the time, was the end of it.

Except, it wasn't.

J.P. had to undergo numerous interviews and answer all sorts of questions.

All good — he had nothing to hide.

And so much to give.

Ellie turned herself in, on the advice of her attorney, once she got back to Oregon, and the judge sentenced her to six months in the county jail, following thirty days in rehab.

A little over a month had passed by the time another judge, a local named Seth Dunnett, granted J.P. sole custody of his son.

And now it was time to drive to the Sanfords' place, newly purchased top-of-the-line car seat in the back seat of his truck, and take Tyler home.

Back at the ranch, there was a welcome-supper scheduled, though it was low-key, because nobody wanted to overwhelm the child with too much fuss. J.P.'s mom and dad would be there, and Trooper, and that was it.

The room that had belonged to J.P.'s sisters had been transformed, with Clare and Josie's delighted approval, into little-boy central.

The bed was shaped like a racing car, and one of the two bureaus resembled an old-fashioned gas pump. The wallpaper and curtains continued the theme, and the closet was full of tiny jeans and T-shirts — selected by J.P.'s mother.

Then there were the toys.

It looked as though Santa's sleigh had come in for a rough landing, spilling presents everywhere, though in an oddly neat way.

Tyler had seen the room. He'd been permitted occasional overnight visits, thanks to Mary Collins.

The first thing he'd done each of those times was to climb up onto the race-car bed and jump, trampoline-style, laughing and swinging his little arms in wide loops.

When it came time to settle down for the night, J.P. would read to him — both new books and remnants of his own childhood — and the child would listen solemnly, as though it were vitally important to absorb every word.

Tyler had seemed content, but by the time J.P. turned in, he'd get restless. Invariably, J.P. would hear small bare feet pounding down the hallway toward his room, and Tyler would scramble in beside him.

"Stay, Da," he would insist, making himself comfortable. "Stay, Da!"

J.P. didn't have the heart to turn the kid away, but he hadn't wanted to set any problematic precedents, either. He'd wait, reading or just thinking about Sara and missing her, and once he knew Tyler was well and truly asleep, he'd get up, carry the boy back to his own room and tuck him in.

Tyler rarely stirred during these intervals, except to murmur, "Da?"

And J.P. would whisper back, "I'm here, son."

Now the big day had come and, as eager as J.P. was to begin his life as a full-time father to the child he already loved from the depths of his being, he hesitated.

On impulse, he took a detour and drove to Sara's place.

He was there, parked in her driveway, when he realized he should have called. It was probably rude, or at least socially incorrect, but, he concluded, with a tiny *yee-haw* sounding in the center of his heart, it was too late now.

A text was the best he could do, but before he'd managed to thumb the message into his phone, the front door opened, and Sara stepped out onto the small porch, shading her eyes from the bright July sun.

She looked downright delectable, standing there in a wispy yellow sundress and sandals. J.P. noticed her welcoming smile next and her haircut after that.

The long braid she'd always worn was gone, replaced by a breezy, shoulder-length cut, layered and highlighted with faint streaks of copper.

In short, she was more beautiful than ever.

And he loved her so much.

He rolled down his window and took her in in one long visual draft. "Hey," he called.

"Hey," she called back, approaching the truck. "Why are you sitting there? Come inside."

"Can't," J.P. said. He wanted to get out of that truck, gather her into his arms and kiss her senseless, in front of the whole damn neighborhood, but he didn't. "Tyler's waiting for me, over at the Sanfords'. Today's the day he comes home for good."

Her face lit up. "J.P., that's *wonderful!*"

You're wonderful, he thought. For the past couple of weeks, he'd only caught an occasional glance at Sara, always from a distance.

"I don't suppose you'd like to go along for the ride," he ventured, feeling young and shy and very, very awkward all of a sudden.

Her lovely face lit up. "I'd *love* that!" she said.

"Good," he said, himself again. And full of joy.

He got out of the truck, planted a noisy kiss on Sara's forehead and rounded the front of the vehicle to open the passenger's-side door for her. "Get in."

"Wait," she said. "I need to get my phone."

J.P. grinned. These days, smartphones were practically part of everybody's anatomy. "I'll be right here."

She went back inside the house, leaving the door open, and soon reappeared, phone in one hand, small purse in the other. She juggled both to lock up behind herself.

When they were standing face-to-face, J.P. smiled at her. "I like the haircut," he said.

"Thank you," she replied pertly. "Now, let's get going. Like you said, Tyler's waiting."

Minutes later, they were at the Sanfords'

front door.

Rayleen answered their knock, her eyes full of happy tears, toting the child on one generous hip. "It's hard to let them go," she whispered. "I never seem to get the hang of that part."

Sara touched the other woman's arm. "I don't think I could, either," she said sympathetically.

"Anytime you want to see Tyler," J.P. put in, addressing Rayleen, "just call or shoot me a text. I'll bring him here, or you and Bob can stop by the ranch. You'll always be welcome."

Rayleen blinked rapidly, and one tear spilled over and trickled down her cheek. "Thank you, J.P.," she said. She'd joined them on the porch by then, and he noticed the small suitcase waiting beside the mat. "You're a good man, and you'll make a wonderful father."

"I agree," Sara said, with another smile.

For his part, J.P. was too choked up to say anything at all. He reached out, ruffled Tyler's thick crop of fair hair and then picked up the suitcase.

"I'm Sara," said the love of his life, opening her arms to the child.

"Sa!" Tyler crowed, leaning toward her.

She laughed, though her eyes were full of

tears now, too, and took the boy from Rayleen, simultaneously planting a kiss on top of his head.

J.P. was downright stricken by the sight of them together, Sara and his son.

She met his gaze, and something sweet passed between them.

They said their goodbyes and see-you-soons to Rayleen, and returned to the truck.

Tyler studied Sara's hair and stroked her cheek once.

"Sa," he repeated.

Practically the moment Tyler was securely strapped into his space-age car seat, he fell asleep. His cheeks had plumped up some, in the last month, and they were pink with good health.

Silently, J.P. blessed Bob and Rayleen Sanford and everybody like them.

In the wider world, there were many foster-care horror stories, but here, in Painted Pony Creek, Montana, there were only happy ones.

Thank God.

"I've missed you," J.P. told Sara once they were settled and rolling back toward the main highway.

"No more than I've missed you," Sara countered. "I love you to distraction, J.P. McCall, and if you don't propose marriage to me in the next five seconds, *I'm* going to propose to you!"

He laughed quietly, not wanting to wake up the little wrangler snoozing in the back seat. "I come with baggage," he said. "I have a son now. You'd be signing on for more than just a husband."

She smiled. "Tyler isn't baggage," she said. "He's a sweet child who needs a mother as well as a father."

J.P. looked at her. "Are you saying . . . ?"

"That I want to help raise Tyler? Yes."

"It won't be easy."

"Tell me something I don't know, J.P. Mc-Call," Sara replied. "I'm no greenhorn when it comes to being a mother, remember?" She paused, tilted her head to one side. "So are we getting married or not?"

"I'd like nothing better." He paused. "Well, there's *one* thing I'd like better, right about now, but there's a child present."

"That isn't a proposal."

"All right, all right," J.P. conceded. "Sara Garrett Worth, will you marry me? Immediately, if not sooner?"

"Yes," Sara said, beaming, her eyes glistening again.

"You're sure. I still get flashbacks sometimes and —"

"You've already told me that, J.P.," Sara

interrupted gently. "And it's okay. It's part of who you are, and I love *all* of you — mind, soul and body."

"If it weren't for a certain sleeping kid, I'd roll down my window and let out a whoop of celebration the whole county would hear."

Sara leaned across, straining against her seat belt to do so, kissed his cheek, then took a mischievous little nip at his earlobe.

Heat rocketed through him, and he hardened instantly.

She rested a hand on his upper thigh. Teased him a little.

He groaned. "Stop it, Sara," he said, wanting her to do anything *but* stop.

"No," she replied, her voice soft and sultry. "I've been wearing this weird underwear for *days,* hoping you'd stop by."

"*What* weird underwear?" J.P. asked.

"The kind we talked about," Sara purred.

"I don't remember that," he lied.

"Fine," Sara said. "As soon as we're alone, I'll show you."

J.P. groaned. "You, Sara Garrett-soon-to-be-McCall, are driving me crazy."

She giggled. "That's the idea, cowboy," she said. "That is definitely the idea."

ABOUT THE AUTHOR

The daughter of a town marshal, **Linda Lael Miller** is the author of more than 100 historical and contemporary novels. Now living in Spokane, Washington, the "First Lady of the West" hit a career high when all three of her 2011 Creed Cowboy books debuted at #1 on the New York Times list. In 2007, the Romance Writers of America presented her their Lifetime Achievement Award. She personally funds her Linda Lael Miller Scholarships for Women. Visit her at www.lindalaelmiller.com.

The employees of Thorndike Press hope you have enjoyed this Large Print book. All our Thorndike, Wheeler, and Kennebec Large Print titles are designed for easy reading, and all our books are made to last. Other Thorndike Press Large Print books are available at your library, through selected bookstores, or directly from us.

For information about titles, please call:
  (800) 223-1244

or visit our website at:
  gale.com/thorndike

To share your comments, please write:
  Publisher
  Thorndike Press
  10 Water St., Suite 310
  Waterville, ME 04901